Also by Davis MacDonald

The Hill (set in Palos Verdes), Book 1 in the Judge Series

The Island (set in Avalon, Catalina Island), Book 2 in the Judge Series

Silicon Beach (set in Santa Monica and the LA West Side), Book 3 in the Judge Series

The Bay (set in Newport Beach), Book 4 in the Judge Series

Cabo (set in Cabo San Lucas), Book 5 in the Judge Series

The Strand (set in Manhattan Beach, Hermosa Beach and Redondo Beach), Book 6 in the Judge Series – Due out in the Fall, 2018

Recipes and Philosophy from A Los Angeles Semi-Serious Epicurean and Bon Vivant.
(Recipes from Certain Memorable Dinners Prepared by Amazing California Chefs and Cooks)

I hope you enjoy Cabo, and if you do, please drop a brief positive review on Amazon for me.   Your review will be greatly appreciated.

Watch for announcements for future books on my Website:
http://www.websta.me/n/davis.macdonald

Davis MacDonald

CABO

**A MYSTERY NOVEL
SET IN
CABO SAN LUCAS,
MEXICO**

**"All animals are equal,
but some animals are more equal than others."**

Old Major's ideals, "refined", as read off the wall by
Old Benjamin
Animal Farm
George Orwell
(1945)

Davis MacDonald

CHAPTER 1

"You what?" The Judge's voice went up an octave. He was tired, he was hot, he was sticky. He wasn't in the mood for this horseshit.

"Don't snap at me, Judge," Katy shot back. "You heard me the first time. I signed us up with the nice young man outside by the taxis for a timeshare presentation. He's going to give us two free tickets to go snorkeling on a boat, and a twenty percent off coupon for his grandfather's taco truck."

"Katy, Katy, Katy. I don't snorkel, I don't like tacos, and if I did, the last place I'd be eating them is off some rat-trap taco truck on a Cabo backstreet."

"But Judge…."

"And, and, and… I don't ever, under any circumstances… there's not enough money in this world to pay me to ever, ever, do a timeshare presentation."

The Judge folded his arms across his chest, trying to signify the issue was settled, discussion ended, wishing he could shove his head in a refrigerator somewhere and cool off.

People in the fancy hotel lobby were glancing at them, sensing juicy domestic strife, making him even more irritable. This would be their hotel. That was if they ever got to the head of the check-in line, clogged with a gaggle of middle-aged Southern ladies on some tour, as broad as they were tall.

His Tommy Bahama shirt was clinging to his back like a wet rag, beads of perspiration were forming under his USC baseball cap, and he was damn hot. He wanted to stomp his foot he was so agitated, but the other guests and staff were waiting to see what he'd do next. He'd be damned if he'd give them the satisfaction.

"Where is this young man you talked to?"

"He's there, by the ticket stand for the valet, but Judge can we talk about this?"

The Judge harrumphed. "Hold our place in line, Katy."

The Judge marched out of the non-air-conditioned lobby and into the non-air-conditioned portal and looked about, then headed for the back of a young Mexican, who turned, sensing he might be under attack. He looked early twenties, soft brown eyes, a quick, boyish smile showing ivory teeth, sending out waves of charm at the Judge as though it were his primary means of defense. To say he was buff would be an understatement. One may as well say the aircraft carrier USS Abraham Lincoln was a boat.

Beautiful tan skin and muscle rippled under a fish net tank-top out of date in L.A., but still fashionable in Cabo San Lucas. The fringy bottom was tucked into white pants too snug for the Judge's taste, showing tight buns before he turned, and a pouch of plumbing the size of a grapefruit in front, further agitating the Judge. He could see the young man was preparing to charm his way out of whatever was the problem.

The Judge had almost reached him, considering what it would feel like to wrap his hands around the kid's neck, when his sleeve was plucked from behind by Katy's small hand, sans engagement ring because she'd left it at home. She was quite determined to hang on and deflect the raging bull. Her voice hissed in his ear, "Judge, stop behaving like a bully and come over here and talk to me. Right now!"

He sighed. He could rarely resist her. He loved her too much.

In horror, he saw she'd abandoned their hard-sweated place in the line for the check-in desk, and now marched him across the lobby like a small boy to a settee next to a standing fan, waving her hand across the lobby to order drinks.

A complimentary white creamy concoction was thrust into his hand, all coconut, sugar and rum. He hated coconut. At least it was cold. He pressed the glass to his temple and tried to ignore the smell.

"Now Judge, you just sit here for a minute next to the fan and cool down. This is a vacation, remember."

"I'm hot and I'm tired."

"It's no surprise. You were up until three last night working. Of course, you're tired."

"It's the way it works, Katy. If you're a solo practicing lawyer, you play hell trying to set things up so you can go on a vacation. Then you play hell trying to catch up when you get back."

"Yes dear. Well we're here now. So now you can relax."

"You really want to go on a... a... a timeshare?" He could hardly get the word out it so boggled his mind.

"What's the first timeshare presentation you ever went on, Judge?"

"I don't remember. It was years ago."

"But you went once?"

"Well of course, once."

"And it was all new. You'd never been before?"

"I suppose."

"Well I'm young, Judge, twenty years younger than you to be precise, and I've never been to a timeshare presentation. So, I wanted to go once, just like you did so many years ago, to see what it was all about."

"But, but, but it's like being locked in a room for several hours with six ravenous used car salesmen. They take turns chasing you around and around a single desk in the room, wearing you down. And they won't let you leave. You're like a mouse in a maze, pursued by snarling dogs."

"I understand the psychology of it, Judge. I'm a high school guidance counselor, remember. But I'd like to see it, experience it, understand what it's about, just like you were curious to do once."

The Judge sighed. Katy had somehow picked up his legally trained way to think, argue and persuade, almost by osmosis or something. Now she used it at will against him with impunity when it suited her. She was really a better advocate than he. In the end, he'd do anything to make her happy, and she knew it.

"All right," he sighed. Resigned. "When do we go?"

"Great, Judge. Three p.m. today. He'll pick us up out in front. We'll be back in plenty of time for an early dinner."

They wouldn't be back for their early dinner.... In the end, it turned into the first step of a journey from which they almost didn't return. They'd look back at the Judge's knee-jerk reaction to avoid the timeshare presentation and wish they'd heeded his protestations. But that was later, much later.

Cabo

The Judge would muse how little we understand the consequences of small decisions like a time-share excursion; taking for granted life among our herd of mammals in our so-called civilization, surrounded by fellow Homo sapiens, a species of walking brains with opposable thumbs and a proclivity for violence.

CHAPTER 2

They waltzed out of the hotel lobby at two p.m. sharp into a blinding heat reflected off the sterile concrete retaining walls that held back the mountain into which the resort was carved. It overhung the blue Pacific, a wide sandy beach, and some of the most dangerous surf in the world. The Judge was hotter than Hades on a griddle, damp all over as soon as he'd stepped out of their air-conditioned room.

The Judge was a tall man. Broad shouldered and big boned. With just a bit of a paunch around the middle, hinting at an appetite for fine wines and fine food. He had the ruddy and rugged chiseled features of Welsh ancestors, a rather too big nose, large ears, and bushy eyebrows. With his big hands and feet and short dark hair, he might have passed for a dock worker in another locale. In many ways, he was unremarkable. Except that he had large piercing blue eyes, intelligent and restless. Except that his eyes swept the space around him continually and missed nothing. Except that he thought like a judge.

He had a given name, but after he ascended to the bench people began calling him just Judge. Even old friends he'd known for years affectionately adopted the nickname. Back then it had seemed to fit. And somehow it had stuck, even though he was no longer a judge. Now just another L.A. lawyer scrambling for business in an over-crowded profession, the victim of a nasty re-election campaign where he'd been blindsided by unscrupulous opponents bent on stacking the judge pool. Unceremoniously voted off the bench.

Katy wore a turquoise halter-and-shorts affair that matched her eyes and allowed her breasts to swing provocatively as she moved. Breasts considerably larger now that little Ralphie had arrived, eight months old and dumped with Granddad Ralph and Granddame Florence. Her abdomen stretched the shorts tight, a reminder of the stress child-bearing inflicted on a woman's body and the difficulty of working one's weight back down. She was still beautiful, all long blond hair and bright blue eyes set against pale white skin, a few new crinkle lines around her eyes. A testimony to increasing maturity, the rigors of being a mom, and perhaps the stress inherent in living with the Judge and his erratic lifestyle.

The Judge on the other hand looked ridiculous. And he knew it. Decked out in a florid yellow and green Tommy Bahama shirt, untucked, hanging over a pair of extra-extra-large shorts, puke green, that only emphasized his ever-expanding paunch and his skinny, knobby legs. He looked like a seasick kiwi.

The young man with the sculpted body was outside to meet them. He'd changed into a white linen shirt, freshly pressed, unbuttoned one too many for the Judge's liking. He never seemed to sweat. Katy rushed over, gushing a hello, turning to make an introduction to the Judge.

"Judge, this is Juan, our guide for this afternoon. He's going to show us some sights, take us to see an exciting timeshare opportunity, introduce us to his grandfather's taco trunk, and give us some free snorkeling tickets and other goodies. Did I get that all correct, Juan?"

"Si señorita. A pleasure to meet you, señor." Juan stuck out a paw to shake, tanned, soft, manicured, and spotless. The Judge resisted an urge to try to pulverize it in his gnarled grip.

Juan escorted them to his car, freshly washed, smelling of pine, a bright tensile crucifix dangling from the mirror. They were immediately immersed in the kaleidoscope of sights, sounds, and smells of Cabo, the 'Americanized' Mexican colony at the tip of Baja California.

Small bungalows, dilapidated shacks, old dusty stores, smart new American franchise outposts, open-air clubs and tired restaurants shimmered in the heat, competing for space with block after block of sparkling new hotel resorts along the beach. And everywhere, in a glimpse down a side street, or in a suddenly opening panorama at a turn of a corner, stretched the vast blue Pacific to the south. This was Land's End.

After thirty minutes of careening around the city, bouncing over potholes, around children and tourists, over partially-dirt tracks with deep ruts, and briefly along the new Coast Highway which spanned to San Jose Del Cabo, Juan pulled the car up into the turn-around of a new hotel skyscraper, perched on the sand overlooking Bahia de Cabo San Lucas, the beach and the bay.

CHAPTER 3

Juan handed Katy and the Judge off to a friendly young lady waiting in the hotel portico to meet them. She introduced herself as Mary Whittaker. Mary looked about Katy's age, late twenties, blond, blue-eyed, with an engaging smile set in a face that had seen too much sun for her white complexion. She wore a white sundress with lace around the edges, and heels which made her wobble a little when she walked. She welcomed them in a Southern drawl that disarmed Katy immediately, giving Katy a hug and telling her how well she looked in the heat. The Judge got a firm handshake, accompanied by a direct look in the eye, seeking to bond.

The Judge had warned Katy the sales person would immediately ask personal and leading questions, trying to get information, trying to buddy-up close, trying to establish a personal rapport that would make selling them a timeshare easier. He'd told Katy to give the sales person no personal information whatsoever.

But they'd barely walked into the vast lobby, not yet across to the elevators, and Katy was already blabbing away to her new friend, telling Mary of their new son, her new husband, what the Judge did, where they lived, how there were here in Cabo for R and R because the Judge was a workaholic.

She was even talking about child-care expense and their household budget, responding to Mary's questions.

Son of a bitch!

The Judge clamped his teeth shut, resisting the rebuke he so wanted to make. Katy had lapsed into uncontrollable chatterbox mode. Meanwhile Mary pumped away for all she was worth, filing away tidbits and emotional soft spots for later fashioning a sales pitch, paving the way to her close.

They were whisked to the 19th floor Timeshare Sales Suite and out to the balcony for scrumptious hors d'oeuvres, wine, and an over-the-top cheese tray. They looked out over the pool below, the other resort's two towers to either side, and the vast Cabo Bay. The bay was anchored to the right by The Arch, Cabo's signature sea-eroded stone landmark, nestled into the cliff at the very tip of the bay, and to the left by a cruise ship looking much like a toy boat from this height, perfectly positioned to hold the left flank. The Judge had to admit it was a spectacular view.

They watched a four-minute video of enchanting couples swearing how wonderful their timeshare 'investment' had been, then back to the lobby and a Mr. Toad's ride in a golf cart touring the facilities and the beach.

Mary was now Katy's best friend. When Mary brought up pets and Katy spoke of the pesky golden retriever the Judge had at home, it turned out that was Mary's childhood dog too, allowing them to share anecdotes and bond further.

Mary launched into her personal story, telling how she used to be a ski bum in Colorado in the winter and sell timeshares part time in the summer, but now she had a child to support by herself, and so she was selling timeshares full time in Cabo. Relying on sales income to support the two. It was all very sad and brave. Katy gave Mary another hug, just on general principle.

Finally, they were taken back to the main tower lobby and Mary pushed the button for the 20th floor, the penthouse floor, which turned out to be mostly a communal area for residents. There was a rec-room, a small gym, a sauna, a jacuzzi, and a small library and lounge, all done up in 18th century English motif.

There was a swank looking boardroom, long and narrow, across from the hall containing the two elevators and an exit door to stairs, viewed through a floor-to-ceiling wall of glass, punctuated by a glass door in the left corner. Looking through the glass reminded the Judge of a fish bowl; you looked through the room and out an opposite wall of floor-to-ceiling glass framing the extraordinary view of Cabo Bay, The Arch, and the vast Pacific spread to the south. The bay was still sparkly but a deeper blue now the afternoon was receding, small boats darting here and there, one large sailboat, a square rigger, underway near the Arch.

The boardroom sported a long marble conference table in purples, greys and a hint of tans, under three magnificent chandlers, French antique, rewired, and updated with small powerful spotlights in their middles. The right wall was dark mahogany stripped from some rainforest, with a built-in bar in the interior corner loaded with rare tequilas, legendary Scotch, bourbons, and fancy new brands of vodka and gin.

An empty bottle of Giacomo Conterno Barolo Monfortino Riserva 2006, $700 on the hoof, sat on the counter, no doubt pulled from the under-bar wine cabinet, which ran for some twelve feet with glass doors, backlit for display. Further along was a built-in cooktop and separate grill, with under-the-counter refrigerator, ice maker, dishwasher, and cabinets, no doubt for china.

The Judge decided he was ready to move in, air-conditioning and all. But the room was already occupied, and a small plaque on the glass door read: Private. ASAM Board Members Only.

There were eight people in the room. An older woman and a younger man stood in front of their dark leather high-back chairs, the power chairs at each end of the table, facing each other across its length. Anchoring the right side of the table were another older woman, a rumpled middle-aged man with the look of an attorney, and a young attractive woman, all looking slightly bored, as though they'd heard the same dialogue several times before.

On the left side of the table sat a young man at the Judge's end, a very old man at the other end, and a middle-aged guy about the Judge's age in the middle. A door built into the left paneled wall of the room, closer to the view corner, opened, and another middle-aged man, short, muscular, bearded, stepped out of the executive washroom, leaving the door ajar, sliding into his seat next to the younger man on the right side of the table. He looked vaguely familiar, but the Judge couldn't place him.

The two people standing at opposing ends of the conference table were trying to out-shout each other. The older woman with her back to the view end had iron grey hair, snapping pale brown eyes, and looked to be sixty. She wore an expensive looking floral dress of fuchsias, purples and pinks, cut full and flouncy, clearly designer. She had her voice raised and looked angry.

The younger man standing at the hallway end of the conference table had his back to the Judge. But he turned briefly to look out at the Judge and Katy, perhaps feeling their eyes on his back. He was about thirty. A lean face with small dark eyes, angry now.

He turned back to continue his harangue against the older woman, pointing an accusing finger, yelling over her in a loud voice, the sound bouncing off the separating glass and carrying through.

As the Judge, Katy and Mary watched, entranced by the drama, the grey-haired woman glanced at a cell phone in her hand, then turned her back on the finger-pointer in mid-spiel, grabbed a pack of cigarettes and a lighter out of a purse on the table, and marched the length of the room, past her young antagonist and out the glass door in front of the Judge, back stiff, head held high. She briskly stepped around the three, Katy and Mary big-eyed, opened the exit door across from the elevators, and slammed it closed behind her. They heard the click-click of her heels marching upstairs.

"Well," said Mary, "someone's having a bad-hair day."

Mary pushed the button for the 21st floor. This proved to be the roof. It had a large patio, partially covered with a trellis, from which the entire complex and bay could be viewed in a 180-degree panorama. At the far corner of the patio the grey-haired lady sat on the low parapet, face toward the bay, playing with her lighter.

When Mary saw the lady, she tried to hustle them back to the elevator. Apologetic. Whispering the woman was the CEO of the company that owned the project. But the Judge wouldn't be herded.

"Go ahead ladies, I want a picture of this view. I'll be right behind you."

Mary saw the opportunity to work on Katy alone and acquiesced, taking Katy back to the elevator and disappearing with her inside. The Judge brought his cell phone out and moved to the roof parapet to take his shot, leaving a discreet distance between himself and the grey-haired lady. She turned to watch him, waved a hand in a friendly, old fashioned way, then returned to her cigarette, drawing in deep puffs the way some smokers do, staring out at the bay and the boats.

CHAPTER 4

The Judge ambled back to the elevators and returned to the 19th floor to find Katy, glass of wine in hand, engaged in girl talk with Mary.

As the Judge settled into their little table on the balcony, Mary turned to the Judge and formally launched her pitch.

"So, let me show you how it works, Judge. This is not really a timeshare you know."

"Oh," said the Judge, doubtful.

"Seriously, it's not. This is just an old fashioned great deal. For ninety-eight thousand dollars, you are investing in something where you become a part owner!"

"And that gets me what?" asked the Judge.

"Two weeks," Mary said. "Two weeks of paradise."

"That sounds like a lot of money."

"Oh, but it's not, Judge. This is your forever dream vacation! And it's not really ninety-eight thousand because we have financing. For you, for today, for here and now, all you put down is ninety-eight hundred. You'd normally spend more than that over... what? Perhaps two years of vacations. This is a great deal."

The Judge just looked at her, deadpan, letting the silence build.

"How much are you spending on this trip, Katy?" Mary turned to address the weakest link.

"About $4,000 per week," blurted Katy, before the Judge could kick her under the table.

Mary produced a small calculator from somewhere, much like a magician produces a rabbit, and drew boxes, arrows and numbers on a white pad of paper, explaining quickly how much the Judge and Katy would spend on vacations over their joint lives if they used their trip as an average.

"Two weeks a year, thirty years, you could easily spend a hundred and fifty thousand," Mary declared with triumph, turning the pad so the Judge could see a bunch of meaningless squiggles, boxes, arrows and numbers.

Suddenly a salesman got up from another table on the balcony, a sheaf of papers under one arm, leaving a young couple who looked recently married gazing out at the view. He marched over to an antique-looking Chinese gong standing beside the water cooler, picked up its mallet, and gave it a healthy blow.

Bonnnnng.

"Whoops," said Mary. "There goes another unit. These are selling fast, Katy. We should look at the floor plans while I can still guarantee a choice."

Katy bit her lip, looking to the Judge for direction.

"We don't vacation that much," said the Judge.

"You can rent the unit out under our hotel plan when you're not using it."

"We wouldn't want to always come back to Cabo."

"You can trade your time through our swap time program with some forty hotels around the world. Perhaps you'd like to go to Paris one year, Rome the next, and then Tahiti. This opportunity is going to cost you only about four hundred and seventy-three dollars per month. Come on Judge, this is a great deal. Is there anything else preventing you from buying right now?"

"It's too much for us," said the Judge, trying to put some finality into his voice.

"Oh. Well hold on a second. Let me call over my manager."

The manager was introduced as George, a nice enough looking guy, except for the crocodile eyes hidden behind his dark rimmed glasses.

"Hi Mary, what's going on?"

"The Judge says that four seventy-three is too much."

"Too much! Did you explain everything? The accommodations? The benefits? The fact that you can travel anywhere? You can sell the weeks you don't use?"

"Yes. Yes. Yes. He said.... He said that they can't afford it right now." Mary looked very disappointed.

"Hmmmm.... Hold on a minute, Judge. Let me check back in my office. There was a memo from an owner who wanted to sell. Just sent me this morning."

George darted away before the Judge could protest, returning three minutes later.

"Okay guys. How does three fifty-four a month sound?"

George pushed another white paper with unintelligible boxes, arrows and numbers across the table at the Judge with a flourish. Mary's countenance turned to hopeful.

"We don't have that sort of excess cash in our budget right now," said the Judge.

George looked like he'd taken a blow to the stomach, all gaping mouth and gasping. "But it's a wonderful price."

Mary and George talked it over, classic good guy bad guy, George arguing they'd never see a deal like this again, Mary pleading for more adjustment, so it could be squeezed into their budget. Katy and the Judge watched like spectators at a ping pong match, back and forth, back and forth, the Judge unable to get a word in edgewise. It was as though they didn't exist.

A third person stopped by the table in the middle of one of Mary's serves, asking Katy what was holding them back.

"We can't afford it," muttered the Judge at him.

The Judge peeked at Katy. She caught him looking at her and gave him a mischievous smile. She was enjoying this, watching with fascination as the salespeople circled their prey, looking for an opening that might clinch a sale. And she enjoyed watching the Judge, batting them away each time they darted in for the kill. Then he felt Katy's shoe gently rubbing his foot under the table. Did this mean he could end the game, go back to the cool hotel, maybe get lucky with his new wife in their fancy digs? He wanted that. It was going to be a smashing vacation.

Finally, Mary and George were done, Mary putting an arm on Katy's sleeve to say, "Okay, we have another option. A fifteen-year vacation plan for two thirty-six a month. Some of the perks are not included, but I'm sure it will fit your budget. The rooms aren't quite as nice, but they're still very good. It's only one week per year but you can always upgrade to our regular plan."

"No," said the Judge.

"Pardon me?"

"I said no. We are not buying a timeshare."

There was a stunned silence as Mary and George looked at each other. Then George snatched his papers back, got up, and muttered under his breath, "I'll send Jeff over to do the exit survey, Mary. You'd best get back out and find a more serious buyer."

Mary's face collapsed. She looked like she might cry. Katy put her hand on top of Mary's arm to console. But the Judge couldn't take any more of the theater. He was hot, and he was tired. Again. These people had had the 90 minutes Katy had committed. He was damn well ready to go back to his air-conditioned room at their hotel, have a serious drink, and some good sex.

He ignored Mary's histrionics, turning in his chair, taking one last look across the balcony to the view, all water and sky to the horizon. Blue on blue.

As he did so, an apparition floated across his view, just off the balcony's bannister, almost in slow motion. A grey head, upside down, parallel to the balcony, looking up, face contorted, eyes squeezed shut, mouth in a silent scream. The body jack-knifed in its fall. Fuchsias, purples and pinks of fabric twisted in the wind around scrawny legs in support stockings stretched skyward, the last to disappear.

Jesus, someone just fell off the roof!

CHAPTER 5

Mary screamed. Standing by the watercooler, George spilled coffee over the front of his pants, muttering, "son-of-a-bitch."   Jeff, the exit man on his way over to subject them to one last ditch sales harangue, dropped his papers and rushed to the rail beside the Judge, who had leaped from his chair. Katy looked around puzzled. She'd had her back to the view.

The female half of the young married couple started to wail, pointing toward the balcony, their salesman and her husband mystified. The gong-ringer stopped in mid-stroke of another bong, having glimpsed fuchsias, purples and pinks out of the corner of his eye in a place that should have been all blue.

The Judge peered over the rail, 19 stories down, at the crumpled lump on the concrete below, partially covered by a flowered dress. Not moving. Then he dashed for the elevator, shouting, "Call nine-one-one!"

The Judge was first on the scene, quickly followed by a gardener who'd been working on the grounds, and Jeff the exit man, who'd grabbed the elevator behind him.

It wasn't a pretty sight.

It was the older lady who'd left the boardroom meeting to smoke on the roof patio. She'd landed on her back and her head, exposing grey matter across the back of her skull, blending with the iron-grey hair, soaked now with red. Blood pooled under her with other liquids of death as her muscles let go.

Her arms and legs sprawled away at odd angles, like some stick-picture gone wrong. The fuchsia, purple and pink dress twisted around her core like a Gordian knot. One red pump was still on her foot, the other several feet away. Her pale brown eyes were open to the sun, but didn't blink. He checked for a pulse at her neck. There was none.

Her forearms had fine cuts, as did the palms of her hands. Curious, since she'd obviously landed on her back. Maybe she'd scraped them along the side of the building as she fell. As he bent closer he caught a whiff of something. What was it? Vaguely familiar. But he couldn't place it.

"Is she alive, señor?" the gardener asked. The Judge shook his head. The gardener trotted over to his lawn cart and retrieved a dusty tarp which he brought back and gently spread over her body.

More people were spilling out of the building behind them now. Including a knot of people who looked to be the participants in the board meeting on the 20th floor. Shock and horror were etched across faces. Even the young man who'd been yelling at her in the boardroom looked appalled, color drained from his face.

The Judge stood up and stepped back into the crowd, looking for Katy. He saw her and edged his way toward her, suddenly coming to a stop against a short rotund Mexican moving forward, inquisitive dark eyes staring up at him above a pug nose and manicured Hitler-style mustache. The faint smell of garlic wafted between them as the man stood his ground, refusing to move so the Judge could pass.

"Where do you think you're going, señor?" It was more command than question.

"To join my wife. Who are you?"

"Policía. I think it's better if you retrace your steps to where you were, bending over the body."

The Judge sighed, threw his hands up in a classic helpless gesture to Katy, turned and threaded his way back toward the body.

The Policía guy followed, his short legs moving double time to keep up with the Judge, giving the Judge a bit of mean satisfaction. He was very short, and very rotund, mid-forties, dressed in a tight-fitting dark suit with vertical stripes, emphasizing what little height he had, augmented by long black hair, piled in a pompadour across the top of his head, and a long narrow tie with vertical purple stripes on a dark field. His dark dress shoes looked to have an extra half inch in the heel, buttressing him further, and he walked formally and very erect. The Judge supposed if you were truly a short man, and particularly a policeman, you'd do whatever you had to do.

What had been the grey-haired lady looked no better. Someone had removed the tarp. Eyes stared at the sky again without luster. The ever-expanding puddle under the body spread further the scent of death.

The Policía guy now turned back to the crowd, holding his hands high, speaking first in Spanish and then in English with a slight accent.

"Nobody leaves. Everybody goes back to the sales office on the nineteenth floor, and I mean everybody. We're going to sort this all out." He was silent for ten seconds, as though counting them out. Then he snarled in English, "Now!"

The Judge could see three uniformed police officers and another suit herding the crowd, including the gardener, back toward the entry to the tower with the sales office, like sheepdogs herding their flock. Katy was in the middle, caught up in the flow, carried along into the tower lobby.

As the Judge turned and started to follow, Señor Policía thrust an arm out, blocking his path. "Not you, señor."

The Judge's head snapped up. Jesus. He was hot, he was sticky, and he was tired. This was the final straw.

"Look amigo, I'm a U.S. citizen, a retired judge, and an active member of the California Bar. I'd like to see your badge and your card. I want to understand your rank, and I'd like to know how you just happened to be here so Johnny-on-the-spot when this occurred. And where the Hell is the paramedic team?"

The rotund Mexican just looked at the Judge, his jaw thrust out. Since he was short he had to look up, giving the Judge a certain primitive satisfaction. But it didn't seem to bother the policeman. He didn't budge. They stared at each other like that for perhaps ten seconds, each letting the silence drag.

One of the uniforms started to stride over, unsnapping his holster. Señor Policía held up one hand, stopping him. He slowly reached into his pocket and withdrew a small leather case, flipping it open to display a badge on the bottom and a credentials card on the top. He held it out. The Judge leaned over to take a careful look, each playing out their part in the pantomime in slow motion. The Judge nodded. The other man snapped it shut and returned it to his inside pocket. He was Chief Inspector Alejandro Garcia of the Cabo San Lucas Police Department. A big name and a big title for a short guy, mused the Judge.

The Judge slowly reached into his puke green shorts and produced his wallet, extracted a card from it labeled 'Rent a Judge', and handed it over to the Chief Inspector, who took a similarly long time examining it, then a further time looking up at the Judge, mouthing the words 'Rent a Judge' with a smirk, before placing it in his pocket. Jesus, the Judge didn't like this guy.

"So why are you singling me out, Mr. Chief Inspector Garcia? Out from everybody else?"

"Simple," he said, Mr.… ehh.".

"They call me 'Judge', and exactly what's so simple?"

"You're the person kneeling over her body when the others arrived. And from some inquiries reported by my lieutenant, you're the last person to see the deceased alive."

"Me?"

"Yes. Do you know who she was?"

"The CEO of the company that owns this project?"

"Oh no, señor. Yes, but oh no. More, much more than that. Señora María Cervantes was one of the richest women in Mexico!"

CHAPTER 6

Chief Inspector Garcia escorted the Judge back to the center building, through the lobby, and onto the elevator, staying close. The Chief Inspector pushed the button for the 19th floor, the sales office. They didn't speak. The Judge silently wished someone would give the Chief Inspector some gum or something to calm the garlic, which permeated the closed elevator space they shared like an invisible cloud. The man seemed blissfully unaware, contentedly sucking a toothpick from his recent lunch.

The 19th floor, relatively empty before, was now crowded with the boardroom group, the sales staff, the lone gardener, the newlyweds, Katy, three uniformed police, and now the Judge and the Chief Inspector. The sales staff and the boardroom group had collected at separate ends, with the rest slumped on chairs and couches in the middle.

The Judge headed for the sales office group. These included Mary Whittaker, George the sales manager with the crocodile eyes, and Jeff, the exit survey guy qua final closer. They were huddled in the far corner of the room, as was Katy, looking relieved to see the Judge. This group also included other sales people the Judge had seen on the floor, and the young couple, still looking into each other's eyes, oblivious to their surroundings.

Infatuation was grand he supposed, if only it could last. It never did. The human animal was built with a bias for change; anything that lingered too long became old, staid and less interesting, hardly competition for new baubles and sparkles that beckoned. We sprang from a line of clever mountain monkeys, down from the rocks, hard-wired to follow our innate curiosity and leave the commonplace behind.

The Chief Inspector pointed his finger at Mary Whittaker, and crooked it, then pointed to a separate office that said Sales Manager on the door. Mary reluctantly walked across the room and into the office, followed by Garcia. He slammed the door behind them. Ten minutes later the door opened, and Garcia stepped out with a flourish, allowing Whittaker to slip out behind him and move quickly to the cover of their little knot of people, ploughing her way into its center like some startled quail. She looked smaller for her ordeal, shrunken, red faced; perhaps she'd been crying. The Judge felt sorry for her. Garcia was obviously a bully.

The Chief Inspector looked at the Judge, raised his hand again, and crooked his finger to beckon the Judge, nodding at the office. The Judge, already antagonized by their initial meeting, was steaming now. He was hot, he was sticky, and he was fuming. He strode out of the group, parting its members with his hands like Moses parting the waters, and marched, head held high, into the office, leaving Katy with a distressed look on her face. He settled his bulk into the chair behind its small desk, the place he was sure the Chief Inspector was intending to sit. It was a small victory, but they all count.

Garcia frowned as he closed the door, discovering his seat taken. He flashed daggers at the

Judge, then perched on the corner of the desk, deciding it was okay, towering now a tad over the Judge.

"Alright, señor. Shall we, how do you say it… cut the crap?"

"Fine by me, Chief Inspector."

"It is confirmed you were the last person we know of to see Señora Cervantes alive, Mr. Judge."

"So, she jumped off the roof after she saw me. I have that effect on women."

"Don't be flippant, Judge. This is very serious. The woman had no reason to jump. She was very wealthy and in good health."

"I thought the drug lords were the richest people in Mexico," said the Judge, watching with satisfaction as Garcia's face clouded. Garcia took a deep breath, controlling his anger.

"Look señor, if you want to be provocative, do it on your own time. I've Googled you. Something of a debutante detective in Los Angeles apparently. Often making embarrassing trouble for your police."

"Me?'

"Yes, quite. The Palos Verdes Police Chief was quoted as saying you destroyed the chain of evidence and such in his case. The Santa Monica Police Chief seemed equally disenchanted; withholding material evidence necessary to his investigation into a Silicon Beach murder; and your FBI. Well, they seemed quite livid about the way their investigation into the death of one of their own in Newport Beach was smeared as a result of your comments."

"Politics has never been my strong suit, Inspector."

"No. I guess not. So, what do you suppose happened here to Señora Cervantes?"

"You're asking me?"

"Yes. Why not. Perhaps you can show this humble Mexican policeman how to do his job as well."

"I don't know."

"Well now, good. Finally, we have some common ground." When the Judge made no response, Garcia said, "There's only one stairwell to the roof, Señor Judge. There's video cameras in the stairwell and the elevators, but not on the roof. The only people shown as remaining on the roof after your wife and Mary Whittaker came down, were Señora Cervantes and you. You left, no one else came up, and as you leave, the Señora jumps, or falls, or is pushed…."

"I was downstairs in the sales office. Then she fell."

"Yes, so you say. I think we'll go to the roof now Judge. You will retrace your steps up and onto the roof terrace, and back down. You will tell me all you saw and all you heard, and what you felt." Garcia's voice was cold, hard. Almost daring the Judge to object so he could call his deputy in for assistance.

The Judge sighed. He'd thought an hour ago they were leaving; leaving the timeshare hard sell, leaving the sales office, leaving the building, leaving for the comfort of the cold air in their hotel room. Now it wouldn't happen for a while. Damn Katy and her female logic to go see a timeshare as if it was a cultural experience. Damn, damn, damn.

"Fine," he muttered.

Garcia opened the door and allowed him out first, staying uncomfortably close with his garlic breath.

The knot of people stared at him as he and Garcia passed through the sales office and out to the elevators. He felt like a small boy again, hauled by the ear to the principal's office for punishment. It had been a frequent occurrence in his youth. Some things never change.

They boarded the elevator and the Judge pushed 20.

"I said the roof, señor."

"I first saw Señora Cervantes on the twentieth floor. If you want the full story, we need to start there."

"Okay."

They got off on 20th floor, and the Judge described the scene in the conference room, Señora María Cervantes and the younger man at opposite ends of the long table, locked in argument. Then how Señora Cervantes stormed out and into the stairwell.

"The man is now on the sales office floor?"

"I think so."

"Okay, let's go to the roof. The place where you say you last saw her alive and well."

They stepped out onto the roof terrace. The Judge retraced his steps to the edge of the parapet, pointing across to where Cervantes had been sitting on the wall.

"And what did she say to you?"

"She didn't say anything."

"Don't be cute, señor, what did she tell you?"

"She didn't tell me anything."

"You were twenty feet from her. You two just stood there, staring at each other, with not a sound." Garcia's hands went to his hips.

"She wasn't standing, she was sitting on the edge of the parapet. And yes."

"Yes, she told you something?"

"No, she told me nothing. She nodded an acknowledgement in my direction, and then continued to work her cigarette. Then she brought out her cell phone."

"She talked on her cell phone?"

"No, just played with it. Texting or something."

"I find that inherently unbelievable."

"You can find it any way you want, Garcia. But that's the way it was."

"Did she look distressed?"

"No."

"Scared?"

"No."

"Angry?"

"No. She looked relaxed."

"Relaxed people don't jump off roofs."

"I know."

"Let's go back to the nineteenth, and you can identify the man she had the argument with in the conference room."

CHAPTER 7

They took the stairs down, dark, poor lighting, traversing the path Cervantes must have taken from the 20th floor to the roof, and then down again, to the 19th floor. There was nothing and no one in the stairwell.

Katy slumped with relief as they re-entered the sales office.

Garcia's cell phone went off. He glanced at the number, surprise on his face, then turned away, stepping to an empty corner of the balcony, taking the call, talking softly. The Judge heard a 'Yes, sir' several times. The other end of the call was doing all the talking. Garcia slapped his cell shut, jammed it back in his coat, and marched to the center of the room.

"Okay," he snapped, "I want everyone who was in the board meeting, and Judge, you too, and your wife, in the corner over there. Now."

There was a shuffling of feet and a muttering of disquiet as the better dressed crowd from the conference room stood up, or un-lounged from a wall they were leaning on, and drifted into the designated corner, the Judge and Katy falling in behind.

Chief Inspector Garcia marched into the middle of the cluster like a band conductor, the group parting and circling around him. He obviously loved the attention. It was the way of short people, mused the Judge.

"Alright, Judge, which man was arguing with Señora Cervantes?" Garcia asked, turning the Judge into an accuser. The Judge nodded at the slight-faced man with short hair who turned pale as all eyes turned on him.

"All right, gentlemen and ladies, I want to tell us who you are, what you were doing in the boardroom, what the argument was about, and who was on which side of the dispute. Let's start with you, señor Cervantes." Garcia turned to the man fingered by the Judge, slightly differential now in his manner. "State your name, Luis."

"Luis Cervantes."

"Your relationship to the deceased?"

"She was my second cousin."

Luis looked to be thirty. Designer slacks, maroon golf shirt, worn under an expensive looking blazer, tailored to a T. He looked… well… posh was the word that came to mind. He looked like he'd just stepped out of a fancy club.

"And why were you yelling at her, Luis?"

"It was a small disagreement… of no importance."

"About what?"

"He wanted to take the company into illegal activities!" This came from an angry female voice, thrown shrill and sharp like a dart from behind Luis Cervantes. All heads turned to see a woman step forward, mid-fifties, lean and leathery from too much sun, decked out in a silk business suit of olive, punctuated by a squash- colored blouse, also silk. "And you are?" asked Garcia, eyes narrowing, sure he was finally getting somewhere.

"Ana Cervantes. María was my older sister."

There was suddenly a babble of voices, rising in octave and volume, as recriminations were lobbed back and forth between what appeared to be two branches of the Cervantes family.

"Silence… Silence!" Garcia's voice roared like a lion, deep for such a small man, as he waved his short arms over his head for attention. The corner group immediately clamped their jaws shut, as though they were synchronized snapping turtles. "Now that the Judge and I have met Luis and Ana, the rest of you introduce yourselves, please."

"Juan Moreno, lawyer for the company." Juan was particularly shifty looking, even for a lawyer. Sharp beady eyes looked out from behind thick panes of eyeglass, punctuated by an aquiline nose over a thin-lipped mouth, framed by mean nasolabial lines. He was tall and skinny, his suit a size too big and cut to a fashion popular several years before. His hair was a comb-over across his bald pate, mostly grey but oddly speckled with black flakes, as if someone had slipped with the dye-bottle. He looked to be late-fifties.

"You can't hold us here like this detective. We've done nothing wrong."

"This is an interrogation, señor. We can conduct it here and now, or over several days downtown at the police station. It's your and your clients' choice." Moreno visibly slumped. Garcia surveyed the rest, looking for other resistance. There was none, except for the Judge, who glowered at him as he imagined the ruins of his extended-stay vacation spreading out in front of him like an ugly French film noir.

There was a commotion at the back of the little group, and a shorter man, rotund and swarthy, pushed his way forward between the group's taller members. The Judge had noticed him in the conference room and thought him vaguely familiar.

The man had powerful arms and shoulders, encased in a beautifully cut sport jacket the color of... of... pink. There was no other way to describe it. Grey slacks offset a starched white dress shirt with French cuffs, open at the collar, several buttons undone, exposing the beginning of a forest on his chest. His dark hair was tightly cropped in military fashion, slightly receding, and a beard ran down the sides of his jaw, ending in a modest goatee. His swarthy complexion and features suggested Southern Italian descent. As he burst through to the center and saw the Judge his face broke into a big smile, his dark eyes softening with warmth and affection.

By God, the Judge knew him. From Silicon Beach, and an S&M club the man frequented. What was his name? Alex, no, Alan.... Alan... Carter... no. Clark, Alan Clark. That was it. Damn, it was Alan Clark.

"It's my old friend the Judge," announced Clark, stepping forward and offering his hand to the Judge.

"One of the greatest sleuths in the country."

Garcia didn't take this well. He felt upstaged. He no doubt considered himself the greatest sleuth in Mexico.

"Who are you?" Garcia asked. "What were you doing here? And how do you know this man?" Tossing his thumb toward the Judge dismissively.

"Name's Alan Clark. An old friend of the Judge's from Silicon Beach."

"What are you doing here, Alan?" asked the Judge.

"Luis Cervantes hired me as a consultant to advise him on the company's plans for a possible new agricultural business."

"You were in the boardroom meeting, weren't you?"

"Yes."

Garcia said, "So, you saw the argument between Señora Cervantes and Luis Cervantes?"

"Oh yes. They were angry each other for sure. She started it. Started yelling at Luis. Luis stood up, yelled back, pointed his finger at her. Really pissed her off. She got so mad she started to hiss, like a snake. It was all very... dramatic."

"Then what happened?" asked Garcia.

"She stormed out, marched over to the stairwell door near the elevator, and disappeared into the stairwell. We all watched her go. I was in shock that she'd just walk out."

"Maybe you were, Mr. Clark," said Ana, "But no one else was. We all knew where she was going. To the roof for her smoke. She only lasts an hour in these meeting before she must get her fix."

"Alright. Good," said Garcia. "Who else do we have here?"

"Pablo Cervantes." An old man, in his eighties, waved his hand.

"Rosa Cervantes," said the young woman at the back.

"And Roberto Cervantes, her brother," said the man standing next to her.

"Miguel Cervantes. María was my sister."

"Okay, that seems to be everybody. As you are likely aware, I'm Chief Inspector Garcia of the Cabo San

Lucas Police Department, and I'm here to get to the bottom of what happened."

CHAPTER 8

The group broke out into a babble of voices again, Alan Clark moving to stand next to his new-found friend the Judge, perhaps for protection, introducing himself to Katy with a formal bow and dancing eyes. The Judge recalled Alan liked beautiful young women.

"Alright, ladies and gentlemen, quiet." When this did not produce results, Garcia bellowed, "Quiet!"

Everyone stopped and turned again to look at the Chief Inspector.

"This little group is going to go back to the conference room on the twentieth floor, and we're going to recreate what happened. I want to see how this all played out. Those of you who brought your purses or briefcases with you will have them searched outside the boardroom, and they will be left outside. Those of you who left purses, briefcases, files or personal belongings inside the boardroom will have then searched as well, and they'll be deposited outside the boardroom. Nothing else comes into or leaves the boardroom except you, my people, and the Judge here. Mrs. Judge, I'll ask you to stay here with the sales staff."

Garcia directed them to the elevator, following behind, talking softly to one of his patrolman, a tubby slow-looking man with the name Gonzalez emblazed on the name-plate on his chest. They squeezed into the two elevators, rode one floor up to the 20th, and then walked out and into the conference room.

"Okay," said Garcia, "I want everyone to take the same seats they had earlier during the meeting. Judge, you stand outside and press your nose to the glass, showing us where you stood when you saw the argument. Señora Cervantes, is it Ana? I'd like you to play the role of your sister, María. Pretend to be angry with your fellow board member, Luis, shake your finger at him, just like it happened an hour ago. Then you storm out, walk over to the stairwell, and take the stairs to the roof. Officer Gonzales here will accompany you. Come on people, let's do it, just as it happened."

The Judge turned to the Chief Inspector, speaking quietly. "I don't think this is a good idea, Garcia."

Garcia's chin went up, his dark eyes narrowing as he looked up at the Judge. "This isn't for bon vivant detectives, señor. This is a real fatality investigation, and I'm going to determine if it was suicide, or something else. Now be quiet and play your role."

The Judge shrugged.

Juan Moreno, the corporate attorney, settled into a chair on the left side of the conference table, followed by Rosa Cervantes and Alan Clark. Pablo Cervantes, Miguel Cervantes, and Roberto Cervantes took chairs on the right side of the table.

Ana and Luis Cervantes took positions standing at opposite ends of the conference table and started arguing with each other. The exchange started slow but quickly became heated, Luis labeling Ana and her fellow board members obstructionists, standing in the way of the company's future.

Ana responded, standing a little straighter, leaning forward, that Luis hadn't worked a full day in his life and didn't know what it was to build a company from scratch, a step at a time. She called him a ne'er-do-well, happy to spend other people's hard accumulated money, but with no ability to make his own.

It was clear there was no play-acting here, just mutual dislike. But the rest of the board seemed blasé about it all, as though they were watching a rerun they'd witnessed twenty times before. Juan Moreno opened his portable computer and started working on a brief, Rosa got her nail polish out for a touch up, Luis Cervantes was on his cell, talking quietly. Miguel Cervantes was texting on his. Old Pablo looked almost asleep. Roberto Cervantes was paging through a Robb Report he'd pulled from his briefcase.

The Judge took his position in the corridor outside the glass and watched Ana storm out past him and disappear into the stairwell, officer Gonzales in slow tow behind.

Chief Inspector Garcia prodded the Judge to the elevator and they rode up to the roof, where the Judge stepped out and showed Ana where María had been sitting and what she'd been doing. The Judge went back by the elevator doors, and then stepped forward, going through the same motions as before. Walking to the parapet to look at the view, turning to study Ana sitting on the edge twenty feet away near the corner. She nodded at the Judge, then scowled at Garcia.

The Judge and Garcia marched to the elevator, rode back to the 20th floor, and stood in the hall observing through the glass.

Luis, seated now at the elevator end of the conference table, looked bored. Roberto Cervantes was pacing up and down the length of the boardroom.

Miguel Cervantes stepped out of the washroom and stretched. Pablo Cervantes was standing, leaning against the back of his chair for support, looking tired and frail. Rosa Cervantes was seated, still playing with her nails. Juan Moreno was still busily typing, his computer carefully angled against the wall, so no one could see its screen. Alan Clark was at the bar on the left, pouring Scotch over ice from a bottle that looked old and expensive. The whole lot looked like high school truants detained after school.

Garcia entered the room, dragging the Judge with him. "Okay, ladies and gentlemen, I want you to remember where you were when María jumped off the roof."

"We were all here, Inspector," said Luis.

Beyond the end of the conference table, through the glass, the stairwell door opened, and Officer Gonzales stepped out into the hall. All heads turned to watch him as he stood uncertainly, looking for direction.

Garcia marched to the glass and gestured angrily at the hapless Gonzales and then up, toward the roof, pantomiming that Gonzales was supposed to be on the roof with Ana. Gonzales looked confused, spread his hands in a silent 'but...', then slowly turned and stepped back into the stairwell, moving like his feet hurt.

It was then a screech from Rosa at the conference table brought the Judge's head around, just in time to glimpse Ana, plummeting in a panicky ball of olive and squash silk past the window, disappearing beneath the glass sill, her face a mask of terror, eyes narrowed to slits, her scream whipped away by the wind and canceled by the separating glass.

CHAPTER 9

"Oh my God," muttered the Judge.

There was a stampede to the window, heads looking down. Rosa went hysterical, sobbing, "Ana, Ana, Ana," folding her arms across her chest and rocking. Miguel turned, shock written across his face. The old man, Pablo, rose from his seat, hands on the table, looking wobbly. Roberto turned away, looking sick. Alan Clark had his mouth open and his jaws working, much like a large fish feeding, but no sound came. Luis stood from his seat at his end of the table facing the window, his face contorted in a mixture of emotions hard to interpret.

The Judge looked at Garcia. Garcia's face was sliding from startled disbelief to horror, realization seeping in. This play had been Garcia's idea; a half-baked Hercule Poirot sort of grandstand resulting in another death of a prominent board member. The result was on his head. The Judge wondered a little maliciously how he'd explain the result to his superiors.

The Judge shook himself and turned, making another dash for the elevators. Garcia clumsily moved to follow, stunned, still trying to comprehend the consequences of his little pantomime. Yelling back at his officer, "Take them back to the nineteenth-floor sales office now, Hernandez. Then find Gonzales. And search that roof."

When the elevator hit the lobby, the Judge bounded outdoors to the cement walk where Ana lay. Garcia followed, still in shock, moving stiffly.

She'd landed on her buttocks, her feet and legs jackknifed in the air, the impact collapsing her torso into her hips, smashing them together like an insane jigsaw puzzle that could never be put right, spine shattered, legs and arms flung out at odd angles. The smell of puddling blood and fluids, warming in the hot sun, made the Judge suspect he might be sick. It was so God damn hot.

Garcia and the Judge squatted to either side of her. Garcia, his face drained of color now, automatically checked for a pulse. It was clear to the Judge there'd be none.

The Judge lifted one of her forearms and then the other, noting fine cuts on her palms and the undersides of her forearms. Just like María. Had she hit the same bit of outstretched plaster that María had hit, scraping her way down the side of the building? The Judge looked up at the sheer wall towering above them, Garcia following his gaze. There were blocks of plastered beams jutting out periodically along the floor line of the roof, hacienda style. Decorative additions seeming to serve no structural purpose. Perhaps window washers attached lines there and lowered themselves down the face to clean. Is that what she had hit? Both women had similar marks.

The Judge leaned over Ana's face and sniffed. There was that same whiff of something he'd sensed on María Cervantes. Vaguely familiar. Pungent. He still couldn't quite identify it.

"Madre de Dios," muttered Garcia, looking around at his minions swarming from all directions toward the body. Then he yelled.

"Keep the building sealed, all exits. Take four men and search the roof, and I mean SEARCH! Search everything. No one gets in or out. Someone is hiding up there. Confirm with Gonzales when he was in the stairwell climbing to the roof that no one came up or down. Seal off that stairwell at the roof level. Check the window washer's equipment, for lines down the building. Did someone rappel down the building face? Did someone take off from the roof in a glider or a parachute or something? I want answers. And I want them now!"

Garcia turned back to the Judge. "How, Judge? How? There's nowhere to hide on the roof. No one came up or down the elevator. The elevators didn't move. No one came up or down the stairwell, except Gonzales against orders, but he blocked the only stairwell. There can't be two suicides in the space of an hour. It has to be murder. But how? How could it happen?"

"See these small cuts?" said the Judge, raising Ana's arm again, pointing to her palm and the underside of her forearm. "Both arms."

"The fall, the parapet," said Garcia.

"I don't think so. They're the same as on María Cervantes. I think they both fended someone off with their hands, then in desperation covered their faces with their forearms."

"It's possible."

"And the smell."

Garcia leaned over the body to sniff, the Judge doubting the man could smell much over his garlic breath.

Garcia looked up. "Pepper spray," he whispered.

Of course, thought the Judge. And something else too. Some other chemical. Something he couldn't identify.

The Judge said, "She backed away, fending off with her hands, panicked, then threw her arms up to protect her face. Blind, eyes stinging, disoriented, driven off backwards over the low roof wall by her attacker."

"But who? Where'd the attacker go?"

"I don't know, Garcia."

"Ay, Dios mío, he didn't disappear into thin air."

"You should check the other towers," whispered the Judge. "The roofs. See what you find. Maybe someone is on one of the other roofs."

Garcia nodded. He turned and barked more orders, sending officers scattering toward entrances to the two other towers in the project. "Seal off the other two buildings. Seal off the whole damn complex. No one leaves. Search everywhere."

The Judge got off his knee, stiff now, tired, hot, depressed. Death was always depressing. It reminded him of his own mortality.

Just a short time earlier he'd been shaking the hand of this charming older woman, all done up in olive and squash silk, vibrant, opinionated, engaged in protecting her company from, what did she call it... 'illegal activity'. And now there was just this sorry pile of bone, flesh and liquid, squashed on the pavement, as though stepped on by some giant foot. Lifeless. Gone. Existence terminated. 'Joss'.

He slowly trudged away, back to the shelter of the lobby, up to the sales office, seeking Katy.

CHAPTER 10

The elevator doors opened on the 19th floor to hysteria. Mary Whittaker was holding her hands over her eyes, head down, small tear streaks etching her face. George, the sales manager, was babbling incoherently, too in shock to make sense of it all. Jeff, the exit closer, was taking large drafts on a Mexican cigarette, staring off into space. The recently married couple were drinking from a large bottle of vodka. The board members were collected again in one corner of the room, looking despondent, avoiding each other's eyes.

Katy spotted the Judge immediately, rushing forward, throwing her arms around his neck, holding tight, limpet-like, gasping, "Thank God you're okay."

"I'm okay, Katy. But this doesn't seem to be the safest spot to be, particularly not the roof."

Alan Clark came rushing over, flushed, almost hyperventilating.

"Get us out of here, Judge. They're going to pick us off, one by one."

"Who?"

"Whoever. The one who's pushing ASAM's directors off the roof. I don't know. You're the detective. But the police won't let us go. Talk to them. Make them open the doors."

"I don't have any sway with the police, Alan. In fact, Inspector Garcia and I are barely on speaking terms. But I can try, as long as you answer some questions first."

"Like what?"

"What was the board meeting about?"

"Luis Cervantes and his faction want to go into growing medical and recreational marijuana for the California market. Grow it in Mexico. Ship it across for US consumption."

"Why? Don't they and the others have enough money already?"

"It was a generational thing. The older shareholders, technically his second cousins, but everyone calls them the aunts, María and Ana, Miguel, and his great uncle, old Pablo, hold the controlling bloc in ASAM. They pay themselves large salaries and a bonus. Apparently, they pay the younger generation, Luis, Rosa and Roberto, pretty much squat. Luis wanted more. He wanted the corporation to fund a partially owned subsidiary in which he would have the controlling interest. A subsidiary with which he said would coin cash by growing and distributing to the states a very top grade of Mary Jane, providing a lush flow of cash to the company, and of course to Luis."

"But Luis didn't have the votes?"

"No. But he does now. With María and Ana Cervantes gone, Luis Cervantes' faction controls the board."

"And how are you involved, Alan?"

"Luis Cervantes brought me down to consult on the shipping, customs and marketing end, and the dispensary networks in California and elsewhere in the U.S."

"But it's illegal."

"It's legal in several states, illegal under a Federal law, but the Justice Department has decided not to enforce. And most think the Federal law will be rolled back soon."

"Even with our new Attorney General?"

"Yes. There's too much political pressure not to see it happen. Besides, I'm a consultant. They pay me either way."

Alan produced a large smile.

The Judge asked, "How'd you meet Luis?"

"A mutual friend brought him to our special club near the airport. You know, Judge, the one in Silicon Beach where we first met." Alan winked, triggering Katy to instinctively moved closer so she could eavesdrop.

"Luis is something of a celebrity in Cabo. Part of the founding families of the town. Belongs to all the best clubs, spends lavishly for goods and services, maintains an elegant lifestyle, is on several charity boards, often on the social page of the Cabo San Lucas Daily News, always donating large sums and his time to charitable causes. Well-liked and well respected here."

"Tell me about the company."

"ASAM? Originally formed by three brothers, José Cervantes, Antonio Cervantes, and a then-young Pablo Cervantes, in the nineteen-fifties, to explore for oil in Mexico. They were very successful. Became the biggest privately-owned oil company in Mexico, vertically integrating with a string of refineries, a trucking fleet for distribution, and a network of service stations. The brothers sold out to PEMEX in the seventies, keeping the trucking company, and used the proceeds to buy up a ton of the best farm land in Mexico, establishing an empire in agriculture, then moved into product distribution, manufacturing, and real estate development."

"And today?"

"Today ASAM S.A.B., or just ASAM, is one of the larger privately-owned companies in Mexico. In addition to their agriculture and household supply businesses, subsidiaries produce auto components, aeronautical parts, missile parts, drones, petrochemicals, and oil and natural gas. They also provide IT and telecommunication services, and undertake real estate development, like this project."

"And the current board of directors are descendants of the original three brothers?"

"Yes and no. José Cervantes, the original founding brother, died in 1995, and his two daughters, María, and Ana, and his son by a later marriage, Miguel Cervantes, came onto the board, taking an active hand in management, transitioning the company into high-tech manufacturing. Antonio Cervantes, the second brother, and his son, Jorge, died when their private twin-engine slammed into a swamp on a trip south for duck hunting. That was in 2000. Brother Antonio's grandchildren, Luis Cervantes, Roberto Cervantes and Rosa Cervantes, all took positions on the board when they turned twenty-five. Pablo Cervantes, the old man, is the third brother, the only surviving founder."

"Are Luis, Roberto and Rosa all Jorge's children?"

"Yes. This morning, the board consisted of María, Ana, and Miguel, all children of José Cervantes, the original brother. Also, old Pablo Cervantes, the remaining surviving brother of the original three. They're the Senior Bloc. Also on the board are the three grandchildren of Antonio Cervantes, the second

49

founding brother who crashed in the swamp: Rosa, Roberto and Luis, the oldest. The Millennial Bloc."

"A classic seven-man board," said the Judge, "with a four-to-three split."

"That's about it, Judge. But two are now gone from the Senior Bloc, leaving the Millennial Bloc in control with a three-to-two majority."

Katy piped up. "Can you give me the Who's Who, Alan?"

"Sure." Alan pointed to the slight-faced man who'd been arguing with María in the boardroom earlier. "Luis Cervantes leads the Millennial Bloc." Luis was leaning against a wall, his arms folded in front of his chest, looking aristocratic. But the Judge noted he was watching the other board members carefully. He missed nothing.

"And Roberto Cervantes is over there."

Alan pointed to a young man, perhaps 28, walking out to the balcony. He had the long narrow head and pointed nose of a Spaniard, and white skin, almost alabaster. He wore designer jeans, and a Nautica sport shirt, his dark hair piled on the top of his head in a man bun, a small man's purse slung over his shoulder.

Feeling the attention, Roberto turned to look at the Judge, dark eyes regarding the Judge with intensity and a certain animosity the Judge suspected was characteristic of his personal relationships.

"Roberto's sister, Rosa Cervantes, is over on the sofa."

Rosa was in her mid-twenties, her expensive ivy blouse pulled tight across small breasts, her black silk skirt hiked up high, exposing spindly legs encased in pale stockings, the tip of a tattoo showing above one stocking.

"Miguel Cervantes, the son of José, the original founder, but from a later marriage, is the one in the Tommy Bahama shirt. Quite a sportsman I understand, fast boats, fast planes, fast cars, fast women."

Miguel's Bahama shirt was bright blue with large white flowers. His shirt had no pocket, so a pair of expensive aviator glasses hung from a top button like a badge of derring-do. He wore expensive silk pants, cream, matching the shirt flowers. Mid-fifties, he sported an expensive looking diamond ring on one hand and a Rolex Submariner on the other. His hair was long and combed back at the sides and on top, displaying a generous widow's peak. Perhaps hiding a bald spot toward the back, the Judge speculated a little jealously, since his own hair hid an evolving open patch only tall people could see. Sometimes, if he was feeling self-conscious, he would take that into account when deciding when to sit, and where, and what direction to face.

Alan said, "The old man is Pablo Cervantes."

Pablo was slumped on a sofa, staring glumly out at the view. Early eighties, a large stomach defining his silhouette, his round face marked by age spots from a life well lived, squinty eyes set deep in wrinkled folds astride a hawk-like nose, swollen hands, perhaps arthritic, cuddling a whisky glass. He didn't look well.

"María was the CEO, Ana was Secretary/Treasurer, and Old Pablo mostly just showed up to vote as María told him, as did her brother, Miguel."

The Judge said, "Isn't it unusual for women to be running a big company in Mexico, Alan?"

"It is Judge, although it's slowly changing. But these were strong women, and they had the votes."

"And now?"

"And now who knows. The Millennial Bloc has control of the board, at least until estates are settled and we see where María and Ana's shares land. I suspect Luis will move quickly to consolidate his power, appoint himself CEO, appoint Roberto Secretary/Treasurer, and approve our new medical marijuana project. The path has been cleared."

"That's good for you, Alan."

"Yes. Luis brought me down here. Has relied on my knowledge and my contacts. It looked earlier like my trip was a waste of time, but not now. I believe I'm going to be in the money, Judge." Alan looked like he might dance a jig.

"Can you introduce me to the board, Alan?"

"Yes, but only if you keep your word and get me out of here. Bully that little Mexican inspector or something. Keeping us penned up here is unconscionable."

"Let's meet Pablo."

Alan walked the Judge over to the old man, collapsed in the corner of a couch, looking small and tired.

"Pablo, meet a friend of mine. This is the Judge. We call him that because he was one."

Pablo didn't get up, but reached a tired hand up to clasp the Judge's with a soft shake. The old hawk nose pointed skyward, and Pablo's small beady eyes examined the Judge with interest. Not unfriendly, just cautious.

"I'm sorry about your loss, Pablo."

"Loss? You mean disaster. Both my nieces gone. Gone because of the incompetence of this Inspector Garcia fellow. Putting Ana up on that roof alone after what happened was the worst of poor judgment. Señor Garcia isn't going to be the Chief Inspector very long if I have my way... and I usually do." Pablo ground what was left of his teeth.

"I understand there was some disagreement in the board meeting earlier on the direction the company should take."

"We built this company by hand, Judge, my brothers and me. We didn't take any short cuts. We didn't sell poisonous drugs. We made honest products. We manufactured items with integrity. We produced things people wanted and needed. And we stood behind everything we made. Not like this younger generation. Their only interest is to swan around and spend money.

They think I'm too old. That I don't understand. But I understand fine. There are no short cuts. We wade into this marijuana trade, we throw away sixty years of what our company's about. We become no better than the scum that run drugs now. Running marijuana that we know is Federally illegal in the United States. And for what? So, our erstwhile next generation can get a little more money out, a little earlier, that they haven't earned."

Pablo settled back into his chair, exhausted, bitter, angry.

Miguel Cervantes came over then, settling in on the sofa next to his uncle. His face was rigid, hiding swirling emotions difficult to read.

"I'm so sorry, Pablo. How could this happen? I just don't know what to think."

Pablo nodded, a small tear escaping down one cheek, brushed aside with a swollen, age-spotted hand.

Miguel looked up at the Judge. There was anger in his eyes now.

Alan pulled the Judge away and walked him across the room to meet Rosa Cervantes, sprawled in the corner of another sofa, her long stockinged legs tucked under her now, her hiked skirt barely covering her bottom. She seemed to have recovered her composure and now was idly playing with her nails.

She watched them approach, disinterested, but uncurled herself, displaying a flash of aqua panties, and stood, extending a small hand as an introduction was made.

"I had nothing to do with this," she blurted, not asked. "I didn't get along too well with my aunts. They were foolish out of date old women, but they meant well, treated me well. I had no hand in this... this awful mess. Jesus, when are they going to let us go?"

She plopped back onto the sofa.

"Do you think they were both suicides, Rosa?" asked the Judge.

Rosa looked up into the Judge's eyes.

"I'm not stupid, Judge. Two women, both jumping off the same building, an hour apart, leaving no note, no indication they were depressed. Aunt María was a tough old bat, no way she'd take her own life. And Aunt Ana was the same. This was something else and everyone knows it."

The Judge nodded. Alan look worried again.

"Do you think someone will come after you next, Rosa, or even perhaps company advisers?" whispered Alan.

Rosa and the Judge just looked at him. Then Rosa studied her nails some more. They were detailed with small sparkly bits, colored an aqua that didn't go with her tan skin but matched the underwear.

"Nobody wants Rosa dead, Alan," she said. "Everybody likes Rosa. But you. You might be next, flouncing around this company like Luis's pet toad, pontificating about this and that like you know something. Collecting a handsome consulting fee, I'll bet. Yes. I think perhaps you should be worried."

Alan paled.

"Is that a threat?" asked the Judge.

Rosa's eyes flashed at the Judge, seething anger there, well beyond that warranted by the Judge's provocation. Then she fell back further into her sofa, laughing, relaxed again, like a disturbed cat plucked back down.

"Luis said you're a fancy Yankee lawyer. Very good, Señor Judge, very provocative, for an old guy. You might have a little fun left in you."

Alan pulled the Judge away, still pale, guiding him onto the balcony to meet Rosa's brother, Roberto. Roberto was leaning on the balcony, staring out at the view, motionless. As they approached he turned, a small hand-wrapped cigarette hanging from his mouth. The Judge smelt marijuana.

He looked at the Judge, his dark narrow eyes sizing up the Judge immediately.

"You going to solve this case for Chief Inspector Garcia? Good luck on that." He gave the Judge a tight smile.

"It looks like the position of you and the younger generation has suddenly improved," said the Judge.

Roberto smiled again.

"The king is dead, long live the king."

Roberto's voice was loud, perhaps because of the weed, carrying inside and across the room. Heads turned.

Luis Cervantes swung around, focusing on the tableau of the three on the balcony, shaking his head at Roberto, making a cutting motion with his hand.

"Bossy over there doesn't want me to talk. But as far as I'm concerned, fuck him. He's a dominating asshole. We should be having a party here. A wake. Celebrating the release of this company to its new generation. The old generation had rusted out. No cojones anymore. Actually, my aunts never had cojones in the first place."

Roberto swung back to look at the view, dismissing the Judge and Alan with his back, nothing else to say.

The Judge led the way over to Luis Cervantes, who was inside leaning again against the wall, hands in his pockets now.

"This is the Judge, Luis. A retired California judge, an old friend of mine, and something of an amateur detective around L.A. He's a real gentleman."

"Nice to meet you. Do I call you the Judge?" Luis, smiling, gave a small nod with his head as he shook hands, as one might do when introduced to a senior. Christ, mused the Judge, he wasn't that old. Luis looked about Katy's age.

"I'm sorry for your loss, Luis. Call me Judge if you wish."

"This is tragic. Both my aunts, well technically my cousins. And it's hard to believe this was a double suicide. They weren't depressed. They were of sound mind. They were solid adversaries on this board."

The Judge turned to find the company attorney, Juan Moreno, at his elbow, business card in hand as though produced from a card changer on his belt. He smiled through thin lips and crooked teeth. The light reflecting off his thick glasses made it difficult to read his eyes.

"You can refer all questions of board members to me first, Judge. I'm their legal counsel."

"I'll keep that in mind," said the Judge, taking the card and turning away.

Garcia strode in, two gendarmes as his attendants, and motioned the Judge over.

"Nothing, Judge. No one on the roof, no one in the stairwell. No one came up to the roof or down again through either the stairwell or the elevator while Ana was on that roof. No window washer apparatus, no rappel down the side of the building, no helicopter off the roof, no place to land and we would have heard it. Nobody on the other tower roofs, no suspicious or even unknown people around the project."

"Yet Ana fell over the edge, practically in the same spot as her sister."

"Yes. It has to be homicide, but how? How?"

"Do you trust all your men? Could one be complicit in murder?"

"Impossible. I know my men, their families. None of them would do this."

"Was Ana so overwrought, that she had to join her sister?"

"Hardly, señor, you saw her as I did. If anything, she was combative."

"Yes. She certainly was that."

From across the room, Alan waved his hand to get the Judge's attention, and then dramatically pointed to his watch.

The Judge said, "Chief Inspector Garcia, can't we let everyone go now?"

Garcia looked up, pleased to hear the formality of his title again.

Luis stepped around Alan, marching over, taking the Chief Inspector by the arm and directing him out to the hall for a side-bar. The Judge saw a wad of paper money discreetly leaving Luis' hand, Garcia's hand folding around it with a caress. Garcia nodded, marched back in, barked an order at his men, then made an announcement to the room.

"Everyone can now leave. We have your names and contact information. The entire floor and the roof is being sealed off and will be unavailable, so take your belongings. Be sure it has been searched first, and tagged, like this." He held up Katy's purse. "I'll be around tomorrow or the next day to talk separately to each of you."

There was a herd movement for the door, Alan cutting his away across the flow to the Judge.

"Thank you, Judge. I'll just make my appointment. Where are you having dinner tonight?

"We were thinking the hotel."

"Oh no. The buffet at the hotel will be so… so… tired. And the desserts, forty-five diverse ways to disguise flan. Ugh. Come join me for dinner. We'll go to Edith's, and then do a little clubbing, perhaps look in on Cabo Wabo. I'll be pleased to show you around. Why don't I pick you up, say, at eight p.m.?"

Cabo

A gracious decline was still forming in the Judge's mind when Katy's voice popped past his ear and into the conversation, her arm snaking in to entwine with his.

"We'd love to, Mr. Clark."

Damn! The Judge was hoping for a light dinner and an early night. He was tired. He probably had heat exhaustion. But his young wife was determined to extract every ounce of nightlife and excitement out of their trip. And out of him. She would probably expect him to dance. Good God!

Katy and the Judge headed for the door behind the crowd, only to come up short, blocked by Chief Inspector Garcia.

"Leaving so soon Mr. Judge? Surely a famous amateur detective like you would want to stick around and see how we conduct our investigation in Mexico."

"He's leaving with me, Mr. Inspector," said Katy, standing straighter, her chin thrust out, ready for trouble. "This is our vacation. He's not going to squander it on some stupid case."

"Oh, come now Señorita, I'm asking for just a bit of help, as a professional courtesy from your learned husband. Perhaps he could just sit in as I interrogate each of the board members tomorrow. It won't take long. After all, he was the last one to see María Cervantes alive, and the first one to see her dead. Quite a coincidence, don't you think?"

Katy was getting mad. She was tapping her foot, a clear sign.

"It's okay, Katy," the Judge said, reaching over to put his arm around her small shoulders, smoothing her feathers. It'll be just a couple of hours. We can send you off to the spa, and when you come back to the room we'll start our vacation."

Katy signed. "We're starting our vacation tonight, Judge. You're taking me to dinner and then to Cabo Wabo with Alan Clark. I'm going to dance the joint into the ground." She tucked her arm in his again and marched him around the Chief Inspector and down the hall to the elevator.

CHAPTER 11

They headed down to the lobby a little before eight and had drinks. Katy dressed in a powder blue summer dress that displayed her ivory shoulders and neck, with espadrilles on her feet, her hair worn up. She was excited. Alan showed up promptly at eight in a rented SUV with a driver, ready to whisk them off to dinner. Edith's proved to be a patio set under an expanded grass hut, popular with tourists and locals alike. Katy was in a festive mood, taking Alan's arm and swinging into the restaurant, leaving her curmudgeon Judge to grudgingly follow behind. Where he belonged, he supposed. He wasn't near as dapper as Alan, nor as young.

Edith's entrance was flanked by a large tank of lobsters, crawling around actively, but looking despondent. The Judge supposed he'd look despondent too if he were in their predicament. There was something primitive about staring at the watery insects you were about to eat, while they stared back at you with mean white pin eyes. Were their situations reversed, he was sure they'd eat him.

The evening moved along with great spirit, helped by lots of the liquid kind, multiple waiters swarming around them like bees. A large platter of porterhouse, lobster tails, and fresh fish of the day covered in saranwrap was shoved under their collective nose at one point, while 64 ways to order more food than one could eat in a week were rattled off at various extravagant prices, Gatling gun style.

Four mariachis appeared from nowhere and surrounded the table, singing Amapola, La Cucaracha, and then, at the Judge's request, an amazing performance of Granada, high notes, flourishes and all… or so it seemed from his vantage point on the empty side of three double blended margaritas.

They settled in for flaming Mexican coffee afterward, created by a young waiter who must have been a fire thrower in his former life, the liquid ablaze and streaming in a fiery four-foot drop into their cups from a pan held high above. The preparation was a wonderful performance.

Katy asked how the Judge had met Alan, and together the three compared notes about their escapades on Silicon Beach the year before, and the series of murders that had interrupted the Judge's life. This naturally led to a discussion of the disastrous afternoon and the two deaths which may have been sequential suicides, or maybe something more.

"So, Judge, what do you think?"

"About what, Alan?"

"About today, the board meeting, the deaths?"

"I wasn't at the board meeting."

"But you think it was murder, Judge?" asked Katy.

"Indeed, I do. Two in a row. Same spot, practically the same time. No note, no indication of depression, what else could it be?"

"Who did it?" Alan asked.

"Well, Alan, I don't know. What do you think?"

"No one on the board could have killed them, Judge, since we were all in the same room when bodies were dropping off the roof."

"Maybe you were all in collusion."

"Judge!"

"The more interesting question for me, Alan, is how? No one on the roof, no one escaping from the roof, nowhere to hide on the roof."

"It is a puzzle."

"Tell me Alan, do you have any qualms about helping the company go into this marijuana business?"

"Why no. It's legal now in California. There's tremendous money in it. It will take organized crime out of it. It's a perfect business, and there's a land rush now across our country to stake out ground in the new industry."

"What do you think about smoking tobacco, Alan?"

"A good analogy Judge. A legalized habit and very profitable."

"But from a society point of view, look at the enormous cost in health care, and the premature destruction of life from cigarettes. And consider all the families who've lost love ones from lung cancer because of tobacco."

"Well, they use it at their own risk. Everyone knows it's harmful."

"But that doesn't stop the use, does it? Young people try it for a variety of reasons, and some proportion make it a habit, and then can't quit. But like you say, there's tremendous money in it."

"Surely, you're not comparing weed to tobacco, Judge?"

"No. Marijuana is worse, Alan."

"How so?"

"Joints are smoked. The same or similar carcinogens go into your lungs. And for many it's addictive. Once addicted to marijuana, they just check out, don't they? It's a way to escape life with all its pressures and responsibilities, sort of a permanent la la land where there's no pain."

"Isn't that a good thing?"

"Is it? I think it's the saddest sort of escape from having a real life."

"You're wrong about marijuana being worse, Judge. Marijuana doesn't make the top ten list of the most addictive drugs. Besides, the average tobacco smoker smokes ten to twenty cigarettes a day, and the average marijuana user smokes two or three times a month. A recent UCLA med school study found that moderate marijuana use did not increase the risk for lung cancer."

"I've read that, Alan. But suppose people smoke marijuana a lot more if it's fully legalized? Are we adding another harmful and addictive drug that's going to ruin our health if we legalize marijuana?"

"I think legalization is a good thing, Judge, and will provide certain classes of people with a lot of relief. But I respect your position. Its good friends like us who can agree to disagree."

"You mean money relief." Huffed the Judge as he settled into an after-dinner port. "Let me ask you something else, Alan." Shifting subjects now. "Did you see Luis slip the good Inspector a wad of money? What was with that, Alan? We might still be there if Luis hadn't paid the Chief Inspector off."

Oh, you mean the mordidas," said Katy.

"The What?"

"Translated as 'small bites', Judge. I traveled a lot in Mexico with my dad when I was growing up. He's done petroleum engineering here and there along the gulf. It's the way the system works in Mexico. Small bribes everywhere."

"But that's corruption."

"You're not in the United States now, my dear. There is a different sense of what is right and proper here."

"But... but... he's the police."

"She's right, Judge. It's their custom. It's the way business is done in Mexico." Said Alan.

"But... But..."

Katy said, "Look at it this way, Judge. In colonial times, the Spanish conquerors assigned offices of power to certain favored individuals in Mexico. They were expected to collect revenues, maintain order, and maintain the government and civic authority in their region, but Spain didn't give them money to accomplish those tasks, or even to sustain themselves. They were expected to live off the land."

"Okay, but this is the twenty-first century, Katy."

"It was more complicated than that, Judge. Church corruption was widespread back then. People of money or connections could outright purchase important positions inside the church to gain social status and power, and then they were allowed to usurp land and wealth from the local populace. Local people were in the middle, caught between the politicians and the church, so they learned to play the regional political leaders and local religious leaders against one another.

They would hold fiestas in honor of church officials, currying favor. But at the same time, they'd seek support and protection from the political officials, primarily through bribes, to prevent encroachments onto their land or into their businesses by the church."

"It's true," said Alan. "After independence, the system of bribes and favors became a primary way of advancement for many. Even at the lower levels of society, poorly paid bureaucrats found they could supplement their income and raise their wealth and standing in society by collecting small payments on the side for their services, favors and attention."

"And today, Alan?"

"Much the same. Local officials boost their social standing and influence in the community by delivering favors to some and not others. They supplement their low incomes by accepting small payments for carrying out their duties, cutting red tape to produce quick results. Bribery is still widespread in both the country's judiciary and police, and in the municipal functions involving permits, licenses and so on."

"Does this happen on a larger scale with more prominent politicians?" asked the Judge.

"Oh yes," said Katy. "Look at Carlos Hank Gonzalez, the Mayor of Mexico City, formerly a Governor of Mexico State, also Agriculture Secretary, and a power in the Institutional Revolutionary Party. He was asked to explain how he'd managed to amass a very large fortune while being solely a public servant. What do you think he was alleged to have said?"

"What?"

"A poor politician is a poor politician...."

CHAPTER 12

They got into the SUV outside Edith's and went tearing off down one-way streets loaded with parked cars to either side, pedestrians meandering across here and there, all sharp colors and contrast, garish. Finally, as the street gave up its lights to a more pedestrian, commercial district, the driver cut suddenly left, and left again, back on another one-way street in the opposite direction, back to the garret of harsh shadow and neon.

They were unceremoniously dumped in front of a small sloping plaza area, the logo Cabo Wabo emblazoned on the brick patio floor from a laser mounted above. They wandered downhill, into a crowded bar, mostly guys, and then through an archway, also neon embroidered with Cabo Wabo, into a much larger space.

A stage was set up at the far end, a five-piece band going at it. Two of the five were drummers. A raised runway ran across the center of the space, hung with attractive young men and women, dancing wildly, displaying with their bodies all the sexual motions they knew.

The noise was deafening. There was no way to talk over the blast from the multi-speakers mounted in the ceiling and around the side walls. People were crowed at the tables and in the aisles, milling about, as though part of some single larger organism.

Katy lit up, all energy and excitement, pointing at the tiny dance floor at the base of the stage, jammed with bodies gyrating about, packed like passengers on a Tokyo train. The Judge thought he would be sick. He wasn't much of a dancer, and trying to do the modern hopping around the floor solo with your partner to music that had no rhythm, particularly on a crowded miniscule floor of gyrating bodies, was his worst nightmare. He'd look like a dancing bear he was sure.

Alan Clark, more perceptive than the Judge thought, interceded, extending his hand to Katy as he turned to the Judge. "May I?"

The Judge gestured with open hands to have at it, relief in his eyes.

The evening wore on, the loud music assaulting the Judge's ears, the flashing lasers accosting his eyes, the sweaty bodies on the dance floor perfuming the odor of stale beer permeating the venue, and the rum and Cokes coming and going in a progression over which the Judge lost count. Somewhere along the way he was persuaded to switch to margaritas, assured they wouldn't give him a headache the next morning. Their salty rims made him even more thirsty, requiring a top off or replacement periodically.

Katy was having the time of her life, spinning and twisting, kicking out legs and arms in a frenzy, trying to keep up with Alan, who turned out to be an expert dancer, saying he'd paid his way through school by giving dance lessons.

After a while they settled again at the table to recuperate, temporarily danced out, Katy taking the Judge's hand with a thank-you in her eyes, flushed and sparkly. They watched the dancers for a while, Alan and

Katy catching up on drinks, the Judge drifting, still dazed from the onslaught of music, lights, cheap booze, and of course the heat.

Katy departed to powder her nose, and Alan leaned closer to the Judge, conspiratorially now.

"I'd like to hire you to be my lawyer, Judge."

"What?" muttered the Judge, finding it difficult to bring his head around to a professional perspective.

"I'd like you to be my lawyer. Help me negotiate the terms of my contract with ASAM, and document it so they can't screw me over. We are discussing things tomorrow afternoon, at their emergency board meeting."

"I'm supposed to be on vacation, Alan. And I'm only here for a short time. And as I said, I'm not in favor of the legalization of marijuana."

"This won't take much time, Judge. And it's a new contract, retaining me to provide general financial consulting services to the corporation. Nothing to do with the pot venture that ASAM wants to pursue. The board meeting is tomorrow afternoon. The follow up to actually draft the contract can done in your L.A. office."

"I suppose I can do that," said the Judge. "As long as Katy doesn't mind. This is her vacation too."

"Personally, I wouldn't tell her, but it's your call."

The night chugged on and suddenly it was two in the morning, Katy finally saying she was ready to go, having danced herself into a frenzy, and then more or less collapsed. They wandered unsteadily out of Cabo Wabo and up the sloped plaza, Katy leaning on the Judge's shoulder and complaining of sore feet, the Judge's head buzzing from too many margaritas. Alan, walking on the other side of Katy, also looked wobbly.

"We'll do Squid Roe tomorrow, people," said Alan. "It's another popular place in Cabo. Katy will enjoy that too."

Katy looked up, excitement in her face. "Great, Alan. Let's."

As they walked, a willowy young lady stepped out from the shadows suddenly, dark eyes, brown skin, mismatched blond hair, and loose full breasts framed by a low-cut silk blouse. She threw her arms around Alan's neck, pressing her chest to his, and whispered something in his ear. Alan smiled politely, uncoupling her arms and gently pushing her away, shaking his head. He turned to the Judge, covering his embarrassment by muttering, "If you've got it, you flaunt it, I guess." They laughed as they piled into the waiting SUV.

As they pulled up to the Judge and Katy's resort, the Judge got his wallet out, suggesting he at least pay for the SUV and driver for the evening.

"No. No, Judge," said Alan. "This evening is entirely on me. I insist."

Alan reached for his wallet, then stopped, a puzzled look spreading across his face.

"Son of a bitch. My wallet's gone. Damn, Damn, Damn! That blonde outside Wabo pinched my wallet."

The Judge quickly paid the SUV driver for the evening, covering Clark's distress, and slipped Alan two one-hundred-dollar bills to see him home, despite protest. Then Katy and the Judge got out, turning to watch and wave as Alan departed, still shaking his head in disbelief.

CHAPTER 13

The phone in the room rang at precisely nine a.m. the next morning, shattering the Judge's sound sleep and provoking a serious headache well earned from the frolics of the night before. The Judge fumbled with the damn thing since it was on his side of the bed, and finally got it to his ear. Next time he'd choose his side of the bed more carefully. Katy lifted her head briefly, groaned, and then rolled over, throwing an arm over her head and settling back to sleep.

"This is Chief Inspector Garcia, Judge. We're going to talk to Rosa Cervantes this morning, you and me. I'll pick you up outside your lobby in about thirty minutes."

"I'm not awake. I'm not dressed. I'm on vacation."

"No excuses, this is a police order." Garcia hung up.

The Judge dragged himself out of the bed and staggered to his open suitcase to retrieve an aspirin bottle, clutching it to his chest like a cross as he wobbled back to the bathroom, and downed three of its pills. They'd better work.

Twenty minutes later Garcia whipped into the turnaround in front of the Sandos Finisterra Los Cabos and momentarily slid to a stop, so the Judge could crawl in.

"Good morning, señor. You don't look so good. Didn't you sleep well? I heard you closed down Cabo Wabo last night. You Americans seem to have an inbuilt need for self-destruction when you're on vacation."

The Judge muttered, "I'm okay," wishing he were back in his hotel bed and that the aspirin would kick in.

"We're meeting Rosa Cervantes at the Starbucks here in town. I think we'll get you coffee there too. We need to buck you up, amigo. You're not going to be sick in my car, are you?"

The Judge could feel himself grinding his teeth. This little Chief Inspector had the personality of a dental drill. "Did your superiors blame you for Ana's death, given your insistence on reenactment of the first murder?" asked the Judge, deliberately needling him. Garcia's brow furled as though it had been reefed. He glared at the Judge for a second, then relaxed, a bland public smile siding up his face.

"We still don't know for sure it was murder. No one was on that roof as far as we can determine. They both may have voluntarily jumped."

"Ana jumping just to make you look bad?" carped the Judge.

Another glare.

"You're not much of a diplomat, are you Judge? This is not California, señor. You don't go out of your way to insult a Chief Inspector here, lest you wish to find yourself 'disappeared' as they say. Our justice system moves at a different pace, but sometimes it can move with lightning speed to remove obnoxious fat Americans."

It was the Judge's turn to glare.

Finally, Garcia silently sent his hand out for a handshake, which the Judge accepted, relaxing some. Like two small boys, endeavoring to make peace and find mutual purpose.

Starbucks turned out to be tucked into a small shop, built in an extended L-shape, with service at the bottom and tables strung up the L, alongside windows mostly shrouded in dark plastic because of the merciless sun beating against the outside wall like an incessant drum. The drum was also in the Judge's head.

Garcia led the way into the semi-air-conditioned store, which smelled of coffee grounds and tea. The Judge spotted Rosa snagging the table at the very top of the L, guaranteeing some privacy. She was a slender girl, much younger than Katy, with small breasts and narrow hips, emphasized this morning by hot pink shorts, cut so high at the back that patches of matching flesh from her bottom squished out on both sides as she bent over the table to clear someone else's cups.

She turned as they approached, displaying her matching pink blouse, unbuttoned one too many buttons, and matching pink nails. The Judge bet her toes shared the color. Her long black hair, swept into a ponytail, swung back and forth across her back like a broom as she turned again to squeeze into the chair next to the rear wall. She was hot. And she knew it.

The Judge collapsed into a chair across from Rosa. Her scent of vanilla and jasmine, plastered on a little heavy for his taste, made him feel queasy again. Garcia fumbled with the chair on the left, scraping it across the floor, making noise like nails on a blackboard, further adding to the Judge's misery.

Rosa's dark snapping eyes in her delicate face appraised the Judge with a mixture of suspicion and curiosity.

"You don't look so good señor."

"The Judge is fine, señorita. He always looks like this," said Garcia. "Pasty."

Garcia and Rosa shared a smile at the expense of the gringo. The Judge tried not to look as cranky as he felt.

"He's helping me on this case." Garcia's loud voice, sharp, rattled through the Judge's skull like a freight train. Jesus!

Rosa and Garcia exchanged further brief pleasantries. Then Garcia jumped into it.

"Tell me about the board, Rosa."

"Ugh. The board... the board. Everybody wants to know about the damn board."

"Yes. So, tell me."

"I've been on the board a year. It's a great lesson in dysfunctional."

"It's a dysfunctional board?"

"It's a dysfunctional family. And that carries over onto the board."

"How so?"

"Ay Dios mío. The stories I could tell. Luis hates María. María dislikes Roberto. Roberto can't get along with Miguel. Pablo dislikes Ana. Ana can't stand me. I don't get along with Miguel. Miguel dislikes María. This family is crazy."

"Why does Luis hate María?" asked the Judge.

"Hah, why do you think? They're both control freaks. Luis chafed under María's dominance and control. And María's cheap. Doesn't pay us younger members a fair share of the corporate profits. She, her siblings and old Pablo, hog most of the profit for themselves. Luis loves his money. And he seems to have lots of it. I'm not sure where he gets it all, but money for him is like… like a security blanket. Anyone who gets between him and his precious money is an immediate threat. He's angry all the time about our treatment in the company."

"You mean the treatment of the younger board members, you and your siblings?"

"Yes. Yesterday's board meeting of yelling and screaming at María was just one of many."

"And how about you, Rosa? Are you angry that the senior board members keep most of the profits?" asked the Judge.

Rosa shrugged. "What the fuck? I don't need so much. My boyfriends' pretty much cover all my expenses and entertainment. One rents my condo for me. Another leases my car. They all give me cash, take me shopping, to parties, the theater, trips, screw my brains out periodically. For a minimum amount of my attention they provide a grand lifestyle."

"Sounds like you keep busy."

Rosa smiled, her eyes twinkling now.

"I like to keep a stable of three: a young athletic one, a medium age one who is well connected and can take me to the best parties and social events, and an older goat with pots of money. I rotate them around, occasionally dump one when I come across a more exciting replacement. Are you in the market for an arrangement, Judge?"

"Which role would I play?" he heard himself asking, not believing he'd done so.

"Oh, sweetie. You'd be a brand-new category for me. One who could bring me to Los Angeles."

Garcia was eyeing the Judge now, wondering if the Judge was serious.

"Sorry, I'm happily married, even a new dad, and fully committed."

"Probably just as well, Judge. Too many men and there's not enough time for yourself." Rosa played with her hair. "You know, I always figured by the time I'm too old to compete, the older directors in this crazy corporation will have died off. But it's happening sooner than I thought. Us millennials are going to be sitting pretty."

"Why didn't Ana like you, Rosa?"

"She thinks, or thought, that I'm uppity, wild, undisciplined. Course she's right. Ana didn't like the way I have fun with men. But then Ana and María were ancient relics. Had no capacity to understand the freedoms of a modern woman. They were stuck in the Dark Ages."

"Why don't you get along with Miguel?"

"Miguel's an asshole. He hit on me when I was thirteen, even tried to force me once. I kicked him in the shin so hard I bet he still has a mark. My own uncle for Christ sakes. He's always chasing young girls. He's a letch."

"Why did María dislike your brother, Rosa?"

"Roberto? Hah. There's a story. María caught him cheating in his accounts last year. Roberto runs the division that brokers the consumable household goods. Paper products, plastic plates, trash bags, all that exciting shit. As I heard it, Roberto embezzled about a hundred grand before he got caught. There was a bank audit of inventory. Then the shit hit the fan, along with the feathers, and just about everything else. María was incensed. Tried to have him removed from the board. But Miguel sided with us during the vote. Said 'boys will be boys', whatever the fuck that means. It was a great board meeting; fun watching María grind her teeth."

"So, the company didn't press charges?"

"Nah. That's one advantage of being family. But Roberto's got to pay it back."

"But you said Roberto doesn't like Miguel. If Miguel voted to keep Roberto on the board and out of jail, wouldn't that make them friends?"

"You'd think so wouldn't you? But no. They barely speak. I suspect Roberto had to pay Miguel off some way for that vote. But I don't know. My brother won't speak of it."

"And Pablo disliked Ana?"

"They've had kind of a running battle over the years. I heard it dates back to when Ana's dad, José, died. Something happened. I'm not sure what, but Ana was apparently in the middle of it."

"And what about Miguel and María? You said Miguel disliked María?"

"That goes back too. Miguel came along late in José's life, when José married some dancer floosy. I never knew her. But I guess after José died the family didn't get along. Ask Miguel."

"But Miguel got stock."

"Yes. It was left in trust for him until he turned twenty-five, like the rest of us."

"When you arrived for the board meeting, who was there ahead of you?"

"Let's see. I was early. Only Moreno, the company's attorney, was there. He usually opens everything up. He was working on his laptop."

"And then who came?"

"Luis, with his consulting friend, Alan Clark, then Roberto, Pablo, Miguel, and then María and Ana came together, the last to arrive."

"Do you think any of your family members were angry enough to kill María or Ana?"

"Hah. They probably all were. I don't really know, Judge. I didn't have anything to do with it. I've got my own life. I just attend these nasty board meetings to keep an eye on my stock interest. The only person I see outside these meetings is Roberto. He certainly didn't kill anyone."

"How can you be sure?"

"He's my brother, for Christ sakes. He's a softy. He made a mistake in his books. Tried to recapture the money he and Luis feel the senior members steal from us. But he's paying that back. It was a wrong approach. We've just need to wait these bastards out. He's not a killer."

Cabo

CHAPTER 14

The three rose together and walked out of
Starbucks, the heat striking the Judge like a blowtorch.
He realized he'd left his sunglasses in his room. Damn.

Rosa headed for her car while Garcia dragged
the Judge across Boulevard Paseo de la Marina, one of
Cabo's main drags, in the hot morning sun, stepping over
pot holes and dodging the traffic now picking up. Garcia
seemed immune to the heat, and to the fumes and noise
from cars whizzing down the dusty street at them.

"What do you think, Garcia?"

"About Rosa?"

"Yes. A candidate for murder?"

"I don't know. Was it Don Quixote who wrote,
'What man can pretend to know the riddle of a woman's
mind?'"

Garcia led them down a block and across Lazaro
Cardenas, Cabo's other main street, to the front of a
small restaurant serving breakfast which proclaimed
itself as Pan di Bacco on a black sign between folding
half-glassed doors closed to the street and its heat.

The Judge pushed his way through into the shade
behind, bolting for an empty table close to an air-
conditioning unit which seemed to work overtime with
negligible effect. Just like the Judge. The place had the
smell of frying chicken and lard, staples for Cabo's
denizens. They settled in, Garcia ordering a plate of fried
eggs and tacos, the Judge politely passing on food,

settling instead for an iced can of 7-Up which he pressed to his temple, ignoring decorum.

The door opened again with a blast of hot air, and Roberto Cervantes walked in, dressed in the same designer jeans of the day before, a little dirtier now, and a fresh Nautica sport shirt, light blue. His long hair was pulled back tightly on the sides of his head and wrapped in his man-bun. It seemed the only thing about his appearance he cared about. His small man-purse was slung over his shoulder.

His dark eyes focused on them with the same intensity and animosity the Judge had noted at the time-share, like a coiled spring, ready to unwind in an aggressive and unpleasant fashion at the least provocation.

"It's the famous Sleuth, the Judge. And his sidekick… is it Robin? Oh no. It's Garcia, Mr. Chief Inspector himself."

He stuck his hand out and gave a limp handshake, no enthusiasm in his face.

"One of these days your mouth's going to get you in trouble," hissed Garcia, his dignity offended.

"But not today, old amigo, not today. Is he sick?" Focusing on the Judge. "He looks bad."

"He closed Cabo Wabo last night. But I think he mostly just looks like that way."

"Oh. Poor bastard." He circled his arm in the air for the waitress and ordered a Dos Equis.

"The Judge is assisting in my investigation of the possible murder of your aunts."

"Murder? They jumped, pure and simple. Couldn't stand living with themselves any longer I suppose. Miserable old bats."

"We suspect murder. We think they were pushed."

"Oh, come on. No one was on the roof and you know it. You sealed it off as soon as María jumped, and your man was in the stairwell when Ana jumped. No place to hide. No place to run. You think the hand of God came down from on high and plucked them off that roof?"

"Something like that," said the Judge. "We're wondering if it might have been your hand."

Roberto's face colored. He wasn't used to being talked to so bluntly.

"I may have chafed a bit under their iron rule, but that's hardly a reason to kill them."

"When you get caught embezzling large sums of money it can be," said the Judge.

"Who told you that?" snapped Roberto, his face turning angry, clutching his Dos Equis as though he might pulverize the bottle.

"I thought it was common knowledge around the board."

"I don't know where you get your information, but it's all lies. There is a personal loan is all, and I'm making payments."

"You mean a theft of money, quickly converted to a loan and covered up, once your crime was discovered?"

"Fuck you, Judge."

"You couldn't have been happy when María discovered your embezzlement, confronted you, and put you in a box to pay it back."

"So what if that's the way it went down? It's all settled now. No one gives a rat's ass."

"What about the reconciliation of inventory accounts for prior years? That work's still going on. How much more will they find was embezzled since you headed the Division?"

The Judge was bluffing. It was a shot in the dark. But embezzlers often syphoned off money for years before they were caught.

Roberto's face twisted into rage.

"Shut your mouth, asshole. You know nothing. Nothing about our company. Nothing about our family. Nothing about the two lying screwed up old wrecks that ran this company as their own private fiefdom, treating everybody like shit. Nothing."

"So, they deserved to die?"

"Of course they deserved to die. But they chose to jump off the roof. No one pushed them. I was downstairs in the boardroom with everybody else, including you and the Chief Inspector. You two buffoons are my alibi."

"That just means you hired someone to do it."

"Sure, an invisible man. If I were going to kill someone, I'd just shoot them."

Garcia said, "Roberto is a crack shot with the long rifle, Judge. A Colonel in the Army Reserve, he's won many contests and keeps his hand in. Right Roberto?"

"Oh, you know about that do you, Garcia? Well, you should tell your partner here to show a little respect. Perhaps even a little fear, hey? The army in Mexico is different than in Norteamérica. We run this country."

"Not everyone thinks that," said Garcia.

"Did you kill your aunts, Roberto?" asked the Judge.

"Go fuck yourself. I'm saying nothing more."

Roberto slammed his beer down, stood up, threw a twenty-dollar bill on the table, turned and stalked out, not looking back. The Judge sipped at his now warm 7-Up and looked at Garcia, wishing his head would clear.

"What do you think, Chief Inspector?"

"He certainly has motive. He was downstairs in the boardroom, but he could have arranged for someone to be up there. Everyone knew María would go up for a smoke. But where did his man hide? How did he remain undiscovered after María was pushed off the roof so he could kill again?"

"Maybe his man was invisible, like he said."

"Sure. The invisible man. Not funny, Judge. And not helpful. You're here because the Chief is breathing down my neck. I need help. I thought you'd have some constructive ideas. And all you can give me is Roberto's Invisible Man."

The Judge spread his hands in sympathy, acknowledging he had no better ideas. But something about the invisible man was appealing to him. What was it?

CHAPTER 15

The Judge was dropped off back at his hotel and made a dedicated run through the lobby, up the elevator and to his room, squeezing himself through the door, trying to keep the door mostly closed and the air-conditioning air in. Katy was there, strewn on the bed, peach bra and panties, reading an Elmore Leonard novel, looking fetchingly sexy. She spread her arms up, reaching for him, and he fell in beside her, burying his head in her breasts, wishing it would help his sore head.

"Oh, poor baby," she whispered, stroking the hair across his patch of bald, as though he were some Great Dane that had collapsed onto her chest. She put one hand on each side of his head and said she was focusing her brainwaves through his skull, putting everything back into parallel order. It seemed to help.

One thing led to another and soon she was astride him and he was buried in her. She slid her torso forward and back across his loins, rocking him to an excitement that evaporated his sore head, ratcheting him ever higher until suddenly he was at the top, then over the edge, sliding down in a spasm of climax that left them both gasping and spent.

He slept then. For a long time. Around five she awoke him, suggesting an early dinner, and reminding him they were going out clubbing again later in the evening with Alan Clark. He groaned at the thought, wishing he could just stay at the hotel, vowing to Katy that no alcohol would pass his lips ever again.

"Yeah, Judge. That'll be the day."

They had a quiet dinner under the big palapa down by the beach, holding hands, sharing dreams, talking about little Ralphie, who was sorely missed, as was Annie the Dog. At ten p.m. they were in the lobby waiting, as Alan Clark pulled up in a limo taxi, dressed all in white.

"White on white on white on white." He said, lifting a trouser leg to display a white leather shoe and white socks.

"You and Katy will match," said the Judge. Katy was all in black cocktail attire, sporting five-inch heels and black fishnet stockings. The Judge never understood how females balanced on high heels, or why they'd want to. He supposed it was inferiority complex revolving around their shorter stature.

The Judge had brought nothing fancy to wear, and besides it was still hot, even at ten at night, so he'd slung on his puke green shorts again and added a blue golf shirt. Jesus, the shorts would walk by themselves by the time he returned to Los Angeles.

He wore his black dress shoes with leather soles and dark blue socks, neither of which he could see because of his damn protruding paunch. Katy gave him a funny look when he walked out of the bathroom dressed and ready to go, but said nothing. So, he guessed he looked reasonably okay, although a few impolite people seemed to stare at him as they'd crossed the lobby, Katy walking ahead, almost as though she weren't attached to him.

Squid Roe had a small footprint along Lazaro Cardenas, the main drag of Cabo, distinguished only by the size of its overhead sign proclaiming its presence. But its narrow front opened into a more cavernous space in the rear, and sailed up two and a half stories, with surrounding balconies and platforms overlooking its main dance floor. The tables had rails rising from table height upward, allowing dancers to climb and dance on tabletop in pairs, trios, and even sixes and eights. Complemented by extraordinarily loud music and a continual and incoherent laser show of light beams, flashes, alternating black lights, and cloud vapor, it reminded the Judge of Dante's vision of Hell.

But Katy and Alan didn't seem to mind, cutting people off to snag a table being vacated by a couple likely deaf from sitting too close to the speakers. Somewhere in the middle of the second round of drinks Katy and Alan were dancing on the table, forcing the Judge on to alert to protect himself and his drink from flying feet. The patrons at the next table, four young men... well... men in their thirties... crap, everybody was young to the Judge... were enjoying Katy's long legs as she and Alan cavorted atop the table like two crazed monkeys, moving to some sort of rhythm only they could make out amidst the din.

Two drinks in, the Judge could feel his headache coming back, mostly from the onslaught of the random noise considered music, at decibels above a jet engine. It was no use arguing about it. He was twenty years Katy's senior. It represented a generation gap in the world of music impossible to bridge. Besides, no one could be heard over the racket anyway. He tried to be a good sport and pretend the raucous music was pleasing. Ugh.

After his third drink, he excused himself for the restroom, instead inconspicuously making a bolt for the front door, and outside into the comparative quiet of the street. He leaned against the exterior side of the building several feet from the entrance, ignoring the vibrations through the wall and the continuing heat stored in its brick, watching crowds of people milling about on the sidewalk, moving in both directions in a confused mass, jammed in lines trying to get into clubs, standing round watching the crowd, and the inevitable hawkers, trying to steer people to their club with smarmy charm. It was Saturday night in Cabo.

He glanced over at the security guard leaning nearby, his large stomach protruding against the brown uniform shirt, dressed up with epaulettes on its shoulders and reverse sergeant stripes on its sleeves. He was gulping toward the bottom of a Tecate. It didn't look to be his first. A big guy, perhaps thirty, he looked vaguely familiar. He turned, sensing the Judge's gaze, then smiled in recognition. The Judge looked into the friendly eyes of Officer Gonzales, Chief Inspector Garcia's policeman told to stay with Ana on the roof. And now here he was, moonlighting as a security guard for Squid Roe.

"Señor Judge, how are you?" He raised his now empty bottle in a salute.

"Good. Muy bien," said the Judge, shreds of his high school Spanish floating back to his tongue somehow. "How goes the homicide case, Officer Gonzales?"

"It's confusing, Judge. There was no one on the roof. Or on any roof for that matter. I think the two old ladies… they just jumped."

"But two of them in one afternoon? The same place. Practically the same time. How could that be?"

"I don't know, señor."

Gonzales drew himself up against the wall to his full height. "I got in a lot of trouble, Señor Judge. First the Chief Inspector tells me to do one thing, then he tells me to do another. And now he says I screwed up. It's like he can't make up his mind."

"So, you're saying you didn't disobey any order?"

"Señor Judge. I swear I did exactly what I was told. The Chief Inspector told me to take Señorita Ana up the roof and then come back and stand in front of the stairwell door where he could see me, through the boardroom glass. In case he needed me, he said."

"Okay," said the Judge.

"Si. And then Garcia got all upset when I did what he asked. I'm a simple policeman, señor. I can only follow orders. It was all very stressful."

"That's interesting, officer, and definitely not what I was led to believe. If I wanted to reach you to talk some more, do you live in Cabo?"

"Just outside the main town, señor, in a small house in Jardínes del Sol. I have to go back to my post inside, but here, I'll give you my phone number."

The Judge thanked Gonzales for his card, steeled himself, and wished he had cotton in his ears, preparing to squirm his way back into the crowded Squid Roe.

His path was blocked by a young girl, looking directly at him with large eyes. She had black hair, done up in a sophisticated style, eyelashes too long to be real, thick racoon eyeliner, and bright cherry lips, complemented by rosy blush expertly blended along her cheek lines. She wore tight yellow shorts and a matching bandeau that outlined budding breasts not fully grown. She looked about fourteen.

"You're very handsome, señor," she said. "We could do some fun together, no?"

"No," the Judge said.

Her liquid brown eyes probed the depths of his. He saw a mixture of hope and desperation there. Young eyes already old, having seen so much in her short life. The Judge felt other eyes on him. He looked to the left where a young man, early twenties, forty feet up the street, was watching them with hard eyes.

"Where are you from?" asked the Judge.

"Guatemala. I am working my way to the U.S."

"Like this?"

"Romance is a very natural thing, señor. It's how we're built. Besides, I have a debt to pay off here before I can move closer north. This is my only way forward."

"But you're so young."

"Not so young I can't provide pleasure, señor."

The young man up the street yelled and waved his hand. Fear flashed across the girl's eyes. "I can't chit-chat, señor. Can we have some fun? Or no?"

"No," said the Judge, giving the girl a sad smile.

The girl turned and moved up the street toward the young man, spreading her hands open in front of her, indicating no transaction had been negotiated. He didn't look happy. The Judge shuddered, and tried to regain his equilibrium.

He pressed his way back into the crowded Squid Roe, feeling like a rugby player at the center of a 'maul', and edged toward the bar. He ordered himself a Dos Equis, a piña colada for Katy, and a vodka martini for Alan, then precariously balanced the drinks through the multitude, slopping drinks only here and there, mostly on people's feet.

As the Judge set the drinks down at their table, Katy was still whirling around its top, dancing up a storm. But Alan looked pooped. He'd collapsed into his seat, mopping his forehead with a now-wet handkerchief. He reached for the Judge's cold Dos Equis like a drowning man, knocking off a third of the bottle in a long gulp, ignoring the martini. Against his better judgement, the Judge downed the martini he'd ordered for Alan, and wondered if he'd have another headache tomorrow. He thought it likely. But it beat listening to the racket accosting him from all sides stone cold sober.

CHAPTER 16

The room phone rang sharply at nine the next morning. The Judge had slyly taken the other side of the bed, but it didn't help. Katy reached in her sleep to pick up the phone, and handed it across to the Judge without ever waking, apparently a skill picked up as a new mother.

"Good morning, Judge."

Shit! It was Chief Inspector Garcia again. Back for more blood like the lonely vampire he was.

"Chief Inspector, we really should stop meeting like this. People will begin to talk."

"We haven't met yet today Judge, but I expect you outside the lobby in thirty minutes. We are meeting with Miguel Cervantes this morning."

The Judge groaned to himself all the way to the bathroom. At least his head was kind of working today.

They drove along the main drag to the mall, parked in its expansive parking lot, then walked through the mall's soaring corridors, air-conditioned, lined with every possible shop and store imaginable, and back out into the blistering sun, facing the harbor.

The sea was a deep blue, quiet, with a multitude of boats rocking quietly in their slips, few people around this early. The air should have been wet from the moisture of the sea, but instead it was dry, hot, all the moisture sucked out by the surrounding desert that was Cabo.

They walked along the harbor to the Ruth's Chris Steak House. Garcia insisted on sitting outside for breakfast under an umbrella, expounding on the scenic picture of the boats and harbor. As they finished ordering breakfast (steak and eggs for the Judge; eggs, refried beans and tortillas for Garcia), the door to the air-conditioned inner dining room opened, a place the Judge now wished Garcia had chosen instead of the patio, and Miguel Cervantes strolled out. He wore khaki pants, brown loafers, and a lightweight khaki safari jacket without arms worn over a soft green silk shirt with a large collar and patch pockets, eyes hidden behind aviator glasses with silver rims. It was irritable how cool he looked; the lucky bastard had probably been hovering next to the air conditioner in there, waiting for the Judge and Garcia to melt. The Judge felt immediate dislike for the man, but couldn't say why.

Miguel whipped his aviators off with a flourish, surveyed the patio, pretending to just see them, and marched over to their table.

"So, Miguel, I think you met the Judge," said Garcia, standing to greet him.

The Judge remained seated, mostly out of petulance, reaching up with his hand to shake. Miguel had a firm handshake, matched with the obligatory direct look from dark oval eyes overshadowed by dark bushy eyebrows in a tan face. Miguel's smile was punctual, not friendly.

"Okay. So? What do you want from me?"

"Just answers to a few questions," said Garcia.

"Shoot. But let's keep it short. I have things to do."

"How'd you get along with María and Ana?"

"Great. I was the baby brother. They always took good care of me."

"Weren't you only half siblings?" asked the Judge.

"That's true. My father married my mother late in life, after María and Ana's mother had died."

"And are you fairly compensated for what you do for the company?"

"I am. They, María and Ana, took care of me. Of course, they needed my vote, and old Pablo's, to lock in control of the board once Luis, Roberto and Rosa came on board."

"Did you vote them onto the board?"

"No. They each got their shares from their grandfather's estate at twenty-five. That gave them each over ten percent of the outstanding shares, enough to vote themselves onto the board under the bylaws"

"How did you come onto the board, Miguel?" asked Garcia.

"My dad never changed his will when he married my mother. But his original will gave shares in ASAM to 'all' his children by blood in equal shares, without naming them. Each bloc was held in trust and then delivered to the offspring when they turned twenty-five. So, I was entitled to one-third of one-third of the outstanding shares on the day I turned twenty-five, the same as María and Ana. One day while I'm working in Mexico City in a bank, an abogado turned up at my window and said, 'Surprise, you're now the owner of 11.1 percent of ASAM'. I immediately quit my job, relocated to Cabo, and voted myself onto the board of directors."

The Judge said, "I understand the younger board members didn't have much say about running the business."

"No."

"And you were close to your half-sisters?"

"Yes. It's a great tragedy they're gone." Miguel shifted his gaze. "I hold you personally responsible, Chief Inspector."

"Me?" Garcia's face lit up in a deep pink.

"Yes, you. At least as to Ana. She should never have been on that roof alone. You sent her out there by herself, and she jumped, or got pushed, or whatever happened. It was stupidity on your part."

"But I instructed my officer to accompany her and stay with her on the roof."

"Yes, but he didn't, did he?"

"Well... no."

"The company is considering filing a lawsuit for criminal negligence because of the way you handled your little morality play. And your chief is very unhappy too."

Garcia seemed to melt smaller in his chair, hunching over, his eyes dark, angry.

"This is all off the point," said the Judge. "We're trying to find out what happened on that roof and who was involved. Perhaps someone sitting in the board meeting was manipulating María and Ana to jump off that building."

"Like an invisible hand?" said Miguel. "That's crazy, señor."

"Even so, did any of the people in the board meeting have reason to kill either of your sisters?

"No."

"No one was antagonistic toward them?" asked the Judge.

"Well, of course Luis. He was always yelling about how the junior board members were not fairly compensated. It got to be a drag listening to him rant."

"What about you, Miguel?" asked Garcia. "We heard there may have been some ill will between you and your sisters."

"That sounds like idle gossip. We got along great. I sat quietly in their board meetings and cast my vote as they suggested. And they paid me off handsomely each month; like a slot machine."

"Are you married, Miguel?" asked the Judge.

"No."

"Ever?"

"No."

"A girlfriend?"

"Several. I'm not gay if that's what you're getting at. How's that relevant to anything? That's really none of your business." Miguel glared at Garcia, presumably for permitting the Judge's question.

"Just wondered what your social life was like. Whether you had a domestic arrangement."

"Women are like fireflies. They twinkle for a brief time. Then they change, get old, fat, wrinkled, unattractive and clingy. But there's a new set of fireflies along every thirty seconds. And so it is with females. I spend my time with young women not over twenty-five, hot slender bodies, tight, not stretched by kids, lots of energy, barely broken in. I enjoy the sport of attracting them, sparking a romance, and getting into a relationship for a short ride. I even enjoy dumping them. Women are for trading, not keeping. No. I'm not gay."

"Explain what do you do at the company," said Garcia.

"I manage the consumer products division. Clothes, small appliances, tools, household items of all sorts, some manufactured in Mexico, some imported here for distribution. I also help with Luis' management of our high-tech parts operations, aircraft and space parts, self-driving car parts that are starting to be tooled. We have a great company; we don't need to chase some silly marijuana pipe dream."

"Miguel is something of a sportsman, Judge," said Garcia.

"I am. I race go-fast boats, I fly stunt-planes, I ride motorcycles, and I chase woman. I like 'fast'. How's that relevant?"

"Thank you, Miguel. Most helpful," said Garcia, quickly terminating the conversation before the Judge could ask anything further.

Miguel got up from the table and strode back through the door he'd come out of, back into the air-conditioned inner sanctum of the restaurant. No doubt heading for the air-conditioned mall.

"What are you thinking, Judge? No one snuck out of that board meeting and up to the roof. And at least for Ana, we're part of their alibi. There's no way any one of them could be directly involved, unless they had an accomplice."

"It's a puzzle, Garcia. What about your man, Gonzales? Do you trust him?"

"Mostly, yes. He's been with me six months. The Chief hired him because his father and the Chief are third cousins, or something. But he wasn't there when María fell. He and I were still at the station. And he wasn't on the roof when Ana fell. I was yelling at him through the glass into the corridor beside the stairwell. We're also his alibi."

"I think when we figure out the 'how' of these twin deaths, it will point us to the 'who'. When do you expect the autopsy report?"

"They're backed up, Judge. Perhaps next week. I may get preliminary information sooner."

"You've sealed off the nineteenth and twentieth floors, and the roof?"

"No one in or out."

"Good."

The Judge suffered through Garcia finishing his eggs and beans, hardly visible under the pool of salsa verde he'd ladled on. The Judge felt himself melting more and more into the chair, perspiration breaking out under his arms and in the constricted crotch of his puke shorts.

Finally, Garcia was finished, the bill was split and paid, and they trudged off the patio, out into more heat, which wrapped the town and harbor like a blanket, holding close the scent of burning charcoal, cooking bacon, lard-layered tortillas and drying fish.

"Can I go back to my hotel now, Inspector?"

"One more quick meeting, Judge, and then we're done for this morning."

The Judge groaned, took his slightly-used handkerchief out of the back pocket of his puke shorts, wiped his forehead, and wished he'd brought a hat.

CHAPTER 17

Garcia led the Judge south past the boats along the back end of the small Cabo Harbor and out onto Boulevard Paseo de la Marina, crossing over and down a block to a cantina and boutique claiming itself to be The Happy Ending. It was not quite eleven a.m., but a party was going on, the place half filled with mostly young people, including a bachelorette covey in skimpy bikinis, up and dancing on the bar to a raucous rendition of 'Toes in the Water' by a swarthy guitar player with a solid voice. Four young women, in tight two-piece outfits revealing more than necessary in the Judge's opinion, were slinging drinks behind the bar and to the occupied tables. One was sitting on an inebriated young man's lap, swaying to the music.

There appeared to be air-conditioning. Unfortunately, it was mostly absorbed by the crowd, twisting, dancing, clinking glasses, and chugging drinks. It was noisy, and it was hot. At least the Judge's shorts blended in here.

Juan Moreno, ASAM's corporate attorney, sitting at a table in a far corner with a coffee cup in hand, waved them over, remnants of a chocolate donut on a plate in front of him. A few dark crumbs appeared to have attached themselves to his narrow tie, bright red with clashing blue mini-triangles, fastened to his white shirt with an inordinately large tie clip, gold. He wore a grey polyester suit, the pants rumpled, perhaps slept in, the coat thrown over the back of his chair. His thick glasses sat on his beak-like nose, partially shrouding sharp eyes.

As they approached, Juan smiled, all thin lips and crooked teeth. He looked the caricature of an attorney, slippery, crafty, vulture-like, making the Judge want to check his wallet.

"I didn't know you were bringing counsel, Garcia. All lawyered up, are we?" His eyes seemed to dart here and there behind the glasses, never looking directly at either of them.

"The Judge is helping me on this murder investigation," Garcia said.

"Oh, murder now, is it? I thought they both just jumped. You shouldn't complicate things, Garcia. It only makes the world more difficult. You think they were pushed?"

"Something like that," said the Judge.

Moreno's thin nose shifted a degree or two to point at the Judge, assessing.

"How can I help?"

"We'd like a rundown on the board, who had disagreements with María or Ana, who was opposed to their interests, who had a motive to see them disappear," said the Judge.

The thin lips twisted into a tight smile. "Almost everybody else on the board, gentlemen. Of course, I can't divulge confidential information, but there's a lot of dysfunction on ASAM's board."

"Who do you represent?" asked the Judge.

"The corporation."

"Do you represent any of the directors individually?"

"No. I mean yes. Well… I mean I've represented Old Pablo for some time now. He's the one that brought me in as corporate counsel."

"So, you should have no conflict talking about the interests and attitudes of the other directors, excluding Pablo, so long as it doesn't pertain to privileged corporate matters."

"I suppose that's right." Moreno sounded doubtful.

Garcia said, "Señor, you'll tell us what you know over this friendly coffee, or I'll sweat it out of you at the police station."

Moreno paled.

"Okay. Okay…. There's a natural divide between the older members, Pablo, María, Ana and Miguel, and the younger members, Rosa, Roberto and Luis. This is accentuated by the way the shares are split. Pablo, María, Ana and Miguel control two-thirds of the stock, and as a bloc control the company. The millennials are a minority, and are treated as such. María was the leader of the senior group. Luis often speaks for the millennials."

Moreno's words were tumbling out over themselves now. He didn't want to be interviewed at the police station. The Judge was beginning to appreciate how different the Mexican justice system was from California's rules of supposedly fair play.

"Go on," the Judge prompted.

"The minority draw fees and salaries half or less of what the majority take, have more junior positions in running the company, and believe they are discriminated against. They are angry. There are also various family rivalries, slights and frictions that go back years, but still play a part in the interactions on the board. Everybody seems to have a grudge against somebody."

"Explain."

"Roberto's been stealing money and was caught by María. Pablo believes Ana cheated him out of a larger share in the company. Miguel holds a grudge for the way his mother was treated. Luis hated María for the way she's treated the millennials, and because he has a different vision for the company. Rosa is a tramp and was an embarrassment to María and Ana. There is bad blood between Miguel and Roberto, but I'm not sure why. Rosa has a strong dislike of Miguel; again, I don't know why. And so on."

"That must make your job tricky."

"It's like herding cats."

"How much does the company pay you in fees each year?" asked the Judge.

Juan glanced at Garcia. "I have to answer that?"

Garcia nodded.

"The equivalent of about two hundred thousand a year. They're my major client."

"So, you must have been upset when you heard they were considering other counsel?" The Judge was bluffing but he thought it worth a shot.

"Oh that," said Moreno smoothly. "That wasn't going to happen. Pablo wouldn't provide his vote to the bloc anymore if they fired me."

"I heard there was a new bloc forming," the Judge said, bluffing again. "Of course, now it's all changed."

"What? What new bloc? What did you hear? Tell me."

"I took it as idle speculation. Where do María and Ana's shares go now they're gone?"

"I have to tell the board that first. You're coming to the emergency board meeting in about an hour, I assume. I'll announce it there."

"We'll be there," said Garcia, before the Judge could get a word in about other commitments, on vacation, and so on.

The Judge asked, "Was there anything unusual about the board meeting, prior to María's death?"

"No. Luis and María were arguing quite aggressively, from either end of the conference table. Nothing unusual about that. The rest of us were just sitting there. Like watching a ping pong match. This consultant, Alan something, was there. A waste of money on him. The controlling interests weren't going to let the company go into the marijuana trade."

"But that may change now."

"We'll see. Come to the board meeting. It's not going to be all as smooth as Luis anticipates."

"Was anyone angry enough to kill María, and then Ana?" asked the Judge.

"I don't know. Any of them could be, I suppose. But none of them were on the roof. We are all in the boardroom."

"Suppose there was an accomplice?" asked the Judge.

"That's possible. But I thought, Inspector, you found no one on the roof each time? Are you sure they didn't just jump, each of them, bound in some silly suicide pack?"

"I doubt it, but our investigation is in an early stage. We'll get to the bottom of it," said Garcia.

"Do you know the police officer Gonzales?" asked the Judge.

Moreno looked startled, then guarded, then bland, in the space of two seconds.

"Ah, yes. He was the one that went up on the roof with Ana, wasn't he?"

"Yes. Do you know him personally?"

"I do corporate law, not criminal, Judge, so I don't know many policemen."

"That wasn't my question. Do you know Gonzales personally?"

Moreno paused, then responded. "Yes." In a muffled voice.

"How well do you know Gonzales, Senor Moreno?" asked Garcia, catching the scent.

"He's my nephew."

CHAPTER 18

The ASAM emergency Board of Directors meeting was held in a conference room in the second story of The Mall, Cabo's only mall, a structure so large and so windy the Judge found himself quickly lost in its maze. No one wanted to go meet in the resort where bodies flew off roofs. Besides, the two upper floors of the timeshare building were locked up tight and surrounded by wide yellow tape.

The Judge and Garcia ran into Alan Clark in the maze of small shops, and the three puzzled their way to the correct elevator, and then the correct corridor, and finally to the doors which opened into the conference room. The opposite side of the room was all glass, looking over Cabo's harbor, a potpourri of colors and shapes lit by the hot sun, some bright, some dusty: boats, masts, sails, carts, water taxis, and people wandering the harbor causeways in the heat. Three stories up, the view from the conference room extended beyond the harbor to the carpet of blue sea stretching to the horizon past the Arch.

A large granite slab served as conference table, surrounded by high-back leather chairs which tilted dangerously when the Judge lowered his bulk into one, causing him to jump forward to the edge of his seat lest he fall backwards. He felt awkward, tired, and still too hot. The air-conditioning didn't seem to work in the conference room any better than in the Happy Ending.

Alan Clark settled in on the Judge's left, next to Rosa Cervantes. Rosa looked more formal now in a pantsuit of grey, cut so tight that every crease and fold of her body seemed on public display. Her black hair was swept up into a long trail curling down one shoulder. She showed a smile filled with a row of perfect white teeth, first at Alan and then at the Judge, leaning forward to shake the Judge's hand again, the Judge unconsciously drawing his fingers back quickly lest she bite.

Next to Rosa sat her brother, Roberto. He looked as hung over as the Judge felt, large circles under his eyes, and a certain greyness to his skin making him look older than his thirty years. To the Judge's right, at the head of the table sat Luis Cervantes, tall, thin, tense, a slight victory smirk on his face. He was dressed in tan slacks and blue blazer over a starched white dress shirt, custom made with an enormous collar, open.

Across from the Judge sat old Pablo Cervantes, his eyes closed, one empty chair separating him from the head of the table and Luis, as if a divide. He wore a colorful madras shirt above black slacks. The Judge could hear his faint purring across the table as he slept, and he wondered who picked old Pablo's clothing out for him.

Next to Pablo sat Miguel Cervantes, the surviving brother to María and Ana, his eyes sad and downcast, his mind somewhere else. Perhaps reliving happier times with his deceased siblings.

At the other end of the table sat Juan Moreno, the company's corporate lawyer, upright and alert, his sharp eyes already studying the assembled surviving board members, calculating advantage behind his glasses. Behind him, in a chair against the wall, sat Chief

Inspector Garcia, his flip-top notebook open to take notes.

Luis obnoxiously pounded his pen against his water glass with venom, startling the room, shaking Pablo out of his nap with a start.

"Shall we begin? I have called this emergency meeting of the board, and I move that I act as chairman of the meeting. Do I have a second?"

"Seconded," said Rosa on cue.

"All in favor raise their hands."

The hands of Luis, Rosa and Roberto went up.

"Any opposed?"

The hands of Pablo and Miguel went up.

"Motion carried. Now, since we lost our CEO and our CFO yesterday, I move that the following officers be elected, effective immediately:

Myself, Luis Cervantes, Chief Executive Officer and President.

Rosa Cervantes, Secretary.

Roberto Cervantes, Chief Operating Officer.

Myself again, Luis Cervantes, Chief Financial Officer and Treasurer."

"Seconded," exclaimed Rosa, again on cue.

"All in favor raise your hands."

The vote was the same, Luis, Rosa and Roberto voting for, and Pablo and Miguel voting against.

"Well, I am glad that's settled," said Luis, satisfaction written across his face.

Alan Clark turned to the Judge and whispered, "Does that do it, Judge? Is Luis now in control?"

"Point of Order, Mr. Chairman," said the Judge, his gravelly voice echoing around the room, all heads turning. The corporate lawyer, pen suspended in the middle of writing a note, leveled his eyes at the Judge with antagonism.

"How are the shares of the corporation held now with the loss of María and Ana? Did they have a controlling bloc, and who do those shares go to now?"

Luis frowned, his eyes turning to their lawyer, unhappy someone was raining on the parade.

Moreno leaned forward in his seat, on the spot now. Darting a hateful look at the Judge for stealing his thunder. Clearing his throat. Deepening his voice as befitting an abogado.

"Well, yes. Technically before yesterday, María held 11.1 percent of the voting stock, Ana owned 11.1 percent of the voting stock, Miguel owned 11.1 percent of the voting stock, and Pablo owned 33.3 percent of the voting stock. Pablo, María, Ana and Miguel typically voted together, creating the working majority bloc. Rosa, Roberto and Luis each owned 11.1 percent."

"But who gets the stock that was held by María and Ana?" asked Rosa.

"That's the interesting part," said Moreno. "María didn't have a husband or children, so she left her stock in trust to a charity. Ana left a small part of her stock to her ex-husband, and the balance in trust for her daughter, an artist in Mexico City."

"So, what's that mean?" asked Luis.

"Here's the important part: recall that as a condition of the original transfer of the shares of stock to each of you, and to María and Ana, you all had to sign a Restricted Stock Agreement. That was specified in the wills of each of the two deceased founders, José and Antonio Cervantes.

That agreement provides that upon transferring your shares, by sale, by gift, upon foreclosure, or in this case upon death, your shares may be transferred, but the voting rights for your shares transferred cease for a period of five years. In the law, we say that the shares are being 'sterilized' for a period of time because they lack voting rights. So, the shares of each of you in this room continue to have voting rights, but María and Ana's shares are no longer voting shares."

"So what percentage of the current voting rights of ASAM do each of the people in this room own?" asked the Judge.

"The shares held by Miguel, Rosa, Roberto and Luis, each represent 14.2 percent of the now outstanding voting shares. The shares held by Pablo represent 43.2 percent of the now outstanding voting shares."

The silence that followed was thick. Finally, Miguel spoke up.

"So, Luis, you, Rosa, and Roberto, voting as a bloc, have together only 42.6 percent of the voting shares. Pablo and I still control the corporation, as we hold 57.4 percent of the voting shares."

"No!" hissed Luis, losing all control. "That's bullshit. That's not right. That can't be."

"I'm afraid he has a point, Luis," said Moreno.

"But we're the established board. We have control. I'm not calling any shareholders' meeting to elect directors."

The Judge said, "Typically the bylaws give any minority shareholder with a significant interest the right to call a new shareholders' meeting to elect directors."

"And it's the case here," said Moreno. "Besides, Pablo and Miguel acting together constitute a majority of the voting shares and can clearly call such a meeting."

"And that's what I'm doing," said Miguel. "I'm giving you all notice I'm calling a shareholders' meeting for fifteen days out, here, in this room, at ten a.m. You'll receive a written notice, sent out today by mail and email."

"Is that legal?" Luis' voice was going falsetto now as he rose from his seat, glaring at Moreno.

"I'm afraid it is."

Luis slumped back in his chair, despondent.

"Are your shares restricted like this too, Pablo?"

"Pablo nodded his head affirmatively."

"What happens to your shares when you die?"

"I have no kids, no wife, no heirs. In accord with my deceased brother's wishes, one half of my shares go to José's descendants, which now would be Miguel, and Ana's daughter in Mexico City. And one half to Antonio and Jorge's descendants, which would be Luis, Rosa, and Roberto. But the shares are sterilized on transfer, no voting rights, for five years, just like yours."

Again, there was silence in the room as this information was digested.

"That would still be better than now," said Luis, turning back to Pablo. "Are you going to die any time soon, Pablo?" His voice was flat.

Pablo blinked. Uncertainty showing in his face. He looked over to Miguel for support.

"Was that a threat?" asked Miguel, stabbing a finger at Luis. "Are you threatening to arrange for Pablo's death, just as you did for María and Ana?"

The meeting immediately descended into a shouting match, angry voices filling the air, making the Judge's head hurt. He stood up and walked out to the sanctuary of the corridor. Alan Clark rose and followed, allowing the conference room doors to shut behind them, closing out the flying invectives.

"This family is a little crazy," said the Judge.

"A little?" Alan raised an eyebrow.

"I don't think I can help you with any legal work here on your contract, Alan. At least until they decide who is going to run the corporation. And that may take a while."

Alan nodded. "I'm trying to stay neutral, Judge. But it's a tough balancing act. Also, I have an invitation for you and Katy."

"An invitation?"

"Yes. To a very swank cocktail reception for the Lieutenant Governor of the State of Baja California Sur, tonight, over in Palmilla. They've asked me specifically to invite you and your lovely wife. Apparently, word of a famous California judge in their midst has spread. Will you come?"

The Judge was trapped, and he knew it. Katy would give her eye teeth to go, and if he declined she'd sooner or later hear about it. Then he'd be in big trouble. The last thing he wanted was to use one of his few nights in Cabo to swan around some foreign cocktail party where they probably didn't speak English. But he was stuck.

"I'm sure Katy would love to go," he said.

"Great, Judge. Let me pick you up. Say nine p.m. in your lobby?"

"Okay."

Rosa stormed out the doors then, pointing a finger at the Judge, hissing "You should have kept your mouth shut, shit head. Now look what you've done."

The Judge spread his hands, palms up, expressing his bafflement. He suspected she needed someone to blame. He was handy.

Roberto and Luis walked out next, followed sixty seconds later by Old Pablo and Miguel, and, hidden behind them because of his height, Chief Inspector Garcia. Garcia walked up to the Judge for consultation, waving a small floppy notebook in which he'd been taking notes. "Most interesting recriminations, Judge."

"Yes, but do they get us any closer to a murder suspect? Has your office made any progress in determining what happened?"

"Some. They both appear to have been incapacitated with a chemical agent, perhaps in aerosol form, partly pepper spray and partly some other agent. Some chemical we suspect would have disoriented them. We just don't know what the other substance was, or how it was administered, or by who. Listening to the acrimony in this board meeting, maybe we heard the why."

Moreno, the company attorney, came out, locking up the conference room doors and slinging a briefcase over his shoulder. The Judge turned to him as he passed. "Counselor, if I may ask, who is ASAM's transfer agent?"

"Why?" asked Moreno.

"Just a thought I had. I suppose it's of public record somewhere if you don't want to tell me."

"He wants to tell you, don't you, Señor Moreno?" said Garcia.

"Of course," snapped Moreno. "It's an outfit called All-Mexico Stock Transfer Company in Mexico City."

"Are there any other arrangements or agreements regarding ASAM's voting shares, like a voting trust agreement, or a proxy coupled with an interest, or an out and out transfer of voting rights while retaining the equity interest represented by the shares?" asked the Judge.

"Not that I know of."

"Thanks, Mr. Moreno."

Moreno walked away.

"So, what else do we know so far about these deaths, Garcia?" the Judge asked.

"Just that chemicals were used."

"What about the cuts on the arms and hands?"

"No sign of plaster, paint or wood splinters in the wounds."

"And you're sure no one else was on the roof?"

"Yes."

"A puzzle." Said the Judge. They walked out into the heat together, the Judge feeling as though he'd just walked into the center of a hot-air balloon.

"We are going to interview Luis Cervantes at his ranch later this afternoon, Judge, you and I."

"Now wait a minute, Garcia. I've already given up enough of my vacation."

"This will be our last interview, Judge. I've already interviewed Pablo Cervantes. But I must insist you attend. I'll pick you up at three p.m."

The Judge shrugged, then nodded his head in weary acceptance, wishing he and Katy had gone to the Hotel Coronado for their vacation as they'd originally planned. Declining Garcia's offer to give him a ride to his hotel, he'd already seen way too much of the obnoxious little man, he flagged a cab with semi-working air and sped homeward for Katy and his air-conditioned hotel room.

CHAPTER 19

At 3:15 in the afternoon the Judge was rattling north through the back streets of Cabo, the Chief Inspector at the helm, displaying no better aptitude for driving than he did for inspecting. They paralleled the Pacific Coast for a while past the outskirts of town, then cut onto a bumpy dirt road, wafting a trail of dust behind as they climbed up a ridge and down its backside toward the beach. An old masonry wall appeared with two large carved doors set in its center, blocking the road. Garcia got out and identified himself at a squawk box. The doors swung open remotely, revealing a large expanse of verdant lawn, and a putting green, wrapping around two small lakes, one larger with a fountain, one smaller with an assortment of ducks and two swans who watched the car suspiciously.

The road was cobblestone now, meandering around one lake and then the other, then through a thick strand of bamboo and flowering plants that looked like a mini-rainforest, coming out on the other side to expose more sweeping lawns lined with palm trees, leading straight for one hundred yards to a turn-around centered with a large bronze of a boy riding a dolphin, splashing water down into the surrounding pond. The pond was filled with sleepy looking koi who watched the Judge with indifference, too lazy to move, as he got out of the car and peered at them.

At the other side of the turn-around sat a magnificent old Spanish-style home, its back to the adjacent beach and tide pools, all whitewash stucco and red tile. The house was two-story, with several dark wood balconies jutting out from second-story bedrooms. It was anchored on the left by a separate six-car garage with guest house over, and on the right by a fenced paddock with two thoroughbreds munching grass, ancient stables visible in the distance.

Luis Cervantes knew how to live.

As they stepped onto the porch, the front door opened, and a man beckoned them in, apparently a butler by the cut of his outfit. He identified himself as Andrés. The butler and Garcia spoke in Spanish for a minute, then the butler ushered them in, through the grand hall, across a formal dining room at the back of the house facing the ocean, out across a red tile patio and around an infinity pool, then down steps to the sandy beach. "Luis is snorkeling in the lagoon," said Garcia. "He'll be out shortly."

The butler gestured to a mosaic table and four chairs on the sand above the light surf, snuggled under the shade of a large yellow umbrella, and took drink orders.

"Dos Equis. Chilled!" said the Judge.

A man was slowly snorkeling across the small lagoon created by two rocky ridges running into the sea approximately one hundred yards apart, the one to the right curving around to blunt the face of the swells rolling in from the Pacific. He was obviously enjoying himself. He must be really cool, thought the Judge with more than passing envy, pressing his beer to his temple. He wished he'd worn his shorts. He could have waded.

Garcia and the Judge watched Luis snorkel for a few minutes, each lost in his own thoughts. Garcia likely thinking about his case, sweating how he would solve it and placate his chief. The Judge thinking about his romp with Katy the night before, wondering when he'd be cut loose from this babysitting duty and allowed to return to his vacation.

Suddenly there was commotion on the water. Luis came up from his floating belly position suddenly, upright in the water, kicking his legs like mad to raise himself higher in the water, whipping his tube and mask off, then flailing around with it in the water, cursing. He dove under the water, touching sandy bottom, then pushed off and up, squirting out some ten feet closer to shore, putting his head down in the water, swimming with all his might.

He gained his footing as the bottom shallowed, then kicked out with one leg behind him before charging through the water for shore at a dead run, yelling for Andrés at the top of his lungs.

The three ran down to meet him, Andrés leading the way. Luis flopped down on the wet sand just above the tide line, nursing his leg, which was ribboned with blood.

"Something attacked me," he gasped through clenched teeth. "A whole school of something. Piranha or something, swarming around, ripping pieces of flesh off my leg, trying to squirm up across my chest to my neck."

The Judge looked at Luis's left leg. It was pock-marked with bites, perhaps ten or so, nasty gaping little wounds where small chunks of flesh had been torn away. There was something odd about the pattern, what was it? The Judge's thought was interrupted by the need to move Luis to the shade. Garcia was too short, so the Judge and Andrés each got under one arm and helped Luis hobble over to the table and chairs and the shade. He collapsed, gasping.

Andrés ran to the house, returning with gauze bandages and disinfectant. Luis's leg was cleaned. Andrés pulled a sharp white bit of tooth out of one wound, and put it on a nearby plate. The Judge picked it up and examined it. It seemed to be a tooth all right, all white, sawed and jagged at one end. But its weight felt wrong, almost like metal. The Judge wondered idly if there was a fish swimming around with a gaping hole in its teeth, sort of a Lauren Hutton of the undersea world. He took out his handkerchief, wrapped up the bit of tooth, and tucked it back in his pocket.

Luis's leg was wrapped; then the Judge and Andrés walked him up the steps, back across the patio and around the infinity pool, and into the dining room where he settled on a dining chair. Four-fingers of a pale gold tequila were produced in a cut-crystal tumbler and downed by Luis in one gulp. It seemed to help.

"That's better, gentlemen," Luis said. "I'm sorry to get you all wet Judge, but I really appreciate your help. I don't know what happened out there. I was watching our local fish. Then suddenly I was jumped by these vicious small fish with lots of teeth. It was awful. Like piranha. Very aggressive. They weren't afraid of me. They only backed away when I could stand up and kick at them. If I'd been a little farther out into the lagoon when they attacked, who knows what would have happened. Ugh. It gives me the shudders just thinking about it."

Luis held out his empty tumbler, Andrés refilled it, and Luis emptied it again.

"Okay. It's okay Andrés. I'm better now. Let me quickly change, gents, and we can meet in the living room. We can talk there. It's air-conditioned."

Yes, thought the Judge. Oh, thank God, Yes!

CHAPTER 20

Garcia and the Judge settled in the living room, the Judge grabbing the seat closest to the air. Five minutes later Luis joined them. He'd changed into an expensive looking white linen shirt, embroidered on the pocket and cuffs, over dark blue designer jeans with a heavy tan belt, and soft leather slippers with a stitched design. The Judge noted how his narrow face emphasized his large dark eyes under narrow eyebrows; ranging eyes, they seemed to miss little. Luis seemed older somehow, older than his thirty odd years.

Garcia said, "So, Judge, Luis is one of our community leaders in Cabo. He's on the board of the Chamber of Commerce, on the Hospital Board, contributes his spare time to the Governor's Field Office here, and is the first one to provide a contribution or volunteer this estate for charity events. I only wish we had more young managers like Luis volunteering in our community.

Luis smiled. "I also play poker Thursday nights in the group with the Chief Inspector here and his Chief. They love to have me come because I play so poorly. It's always an expensive night."

"We are merely giving you lessons," said Garcia, smiling. "Expensive lessons they may be, but you improve with every hand."

"My playing may improve, but my wallet loses weight."

Luis smiled now too.

Garcia moved on to business. "Luis, as you know we are looking into the death of your two aunts. We suspect neither was a suicide. The Judge has some experience in homicides, so I've asked him to sit in on my investigation."

"Do I need my lawyer present, Inspector?"

"No. No. It's nothing like that. We just want to get your impression of how it all went down. We are talking to everyone who was there."

"Let's talk then. And Judge, I'm glad you're here. I want to help in any way I can."

"Where were you when María fell off the roof?" asked Garcia.

"In the boardroom with the others."

"Who was there when she fell, Luis?"

"Let's see. There was Rosa, Roberto, Pablo, Ana, Miguel, Moreno, the company attorney, me... and oh yes, Alan Clark."

"You're sure they all stayed in the room? No one left to follow María up to the roof?"

"No. No one left."

"And when Ana fell?"

"The same. And you and the Judge were there too, looking on. Such a sad mess."

"Did you have a good relationship with María, Luis?"

"We had our differences. No secret about that. But she was my Aunt. She was family."

"What were the differences about?" asked the Judge.

Luis turned to the Judge. A flash of irritation at being questioned flickered, then was quickly buried in a bland smile.

"She was the CEO, and thereby the ring leader in paying everyone their salaries and bonuses. The trouble was she was paying the older members lavish compensation, while forcing the younger members, Rosa, Roberto and me, to work for chicken feed. They voted themselves each a quarter-million-dollar bonus last year, while we got just eighty thousand a piece. It wasn't right. It wasn't fair."

"Were you upset she refused to consider your proposal for becoming a marijuana producing company?"

"Not particularly. I'd brought Alan Clark down to present the opportunity to the board. Thought it could be a significant play for us. But the senior bloc didn't want to move forward. I knew it was a little too forward an idea for old Pablo and my two aunts. But I thought Miguel might see the wisdom in it."

"So, when you were yelling at María in the board meeting, it wasn't about marijuana?"

"Oh, I may have rattled her cage a little with the medical marijuana proposal. María was something of a throwback to an earlier time. She had no vision for fresh marketing opportunities, new methods, new products. She wanted to do things the way they've always been done. No automation, no expansion of plants, of products, of markets. I tried to talk to her about the lower cost per unit I was getting in the plants in my division. How it was building our cash flow and increasing our profits and market share. She wouldn't listen. But when we were yelling, it was over the way Rosa, Roberto and I are compensated by ASAM."

"Which division of ASAM do you run?"

"The high tech one. It's small, but it's important. The division builds products of the future. Airplane wing components for Boeing. Radar and electronic systems parts for Northrup. Missile parts, drones, smart car parts for the self-driving car prototypes. María's division was selling boxed cereal for Christ sakes."

"And you're successful? You said you keep the costs down?"

"I've got very low costs per unit from my people, and high quality."

"How do you do that?"

"I've inserted a lower wage base in my division, taking on a significant number of less skilled workers, along with a regiment of training to bring them up to speed. And I use a buddy system, matching each unskilled worker as an apprentice with a journeyman worker. I've set up my three division plants in rural settings with free housing on site for the employees. That way they have the chance to opt for an extended work schedule, earn more money, and keep the plant wheels turning twenty-four seven. It's dropped labor costs dramatically. And we're getting fewer part rejects and returns. My throughput is better as well."

"And María wasn't happy that your division was so successful?"

"I think she was jealous. She didn't believe my labor rates, calling them fictitious. She was a stubborn old lady with a fiery tongue and no management sense. It's better for the company she's gone."

"As in dead?" asked the Judge.

"No. As in no longer CEO."

"So, you were stymied in building the company business, and paid peanuts while Señora Cervantes and the senior board members sucked out the cash?"

"That's pretty much right, Judge."

"Doesn't that sound like a good motive for murder?"

Luis bit his lip. "No one on the board had any hand in this, Judge. We were all jammed in that damn boardroom."

"If your division is so profitable, Luis, why go into marijuana?" asked the Judge.

"My division has small sales. But if we move into marijuana, it could be entirely different. Marijuana is going to be a twenty-three-billion-dollar business in the United States alone. Our farms are stretched out around small towns up and down the Mexican side of the U.S. border. It's the perfect crop for us. If we snap up only ten percent of the market, that's over two billion dollars. That sort of revenue is a hundred times what ASAM is doing now."

"But marijuana's still illegal under our Federal Law."

"That will change and we both know it, Judge. Your populace wants their weed. It's going to happen. The politics of marijuana are already underway. You gringos don't have enough jobs to keep your people employed. So, you need to keep them occupied. You're going to dope them up and leave them in the sun."

Garcia said, "Señor, I see a problem with your plan. Our own laws only allow for businesses to grow marijuana with a THC content of one percent or less. Most U.S. grown marijuana has THC concentrations ten to twenty-five times higher. How do you plan to compete?"

Luis smiled. "Laws will continue to change here as well as in the U.S., Señor Garcia. It just takes someone with vision to see into the near future. And our company can be the future, if only the board members will listen. I have the younger board members with me. I just need either Pablo or Miguel to push this through."

"Or you need Pablo to die, his voting shares sterilized with no vote," said the Judge."

"I never said that."

"You implied as much at the board meeting."

"I was angry. I said lots of things I didn't mean."

Garcia asked, "How was María's relationship with the other board members?"

"Old Pablo and Ana thought María walked on water. Miguel got on with her I suppose. I don't think they were close. Rosa, Roberto and I were unhappy with the compensation arrangements, which were totally unfair."

"And how about Ana? How was Ana's relationship with the board?"

"The same. She supported the unfair compensation."

"Do you smoke weed, Luis?" asked the Judge.

"Occasionally. But I prefer Jack Daniels."

"Do you think marijuana is harmful?"

"Perhaps, Judge, I've done my homework. Did you know that long-term marijuana use is linked to lowered motivation, impaired daily ability to function, and sometimes anxiety, panic attacks, respiratory illnesses and even increased heart rate and risk of heart attack," said the Judge. "Marijuana smokers often have the same respiratory problems as tobacco smokers. Marijuana has four times the tar, three to five times more carbon monoxide and over fifty percent more carcinogenic hydrocarbons than cigarettes. Three or four joints is equivalent to twenty cigarettes."

"So why would you grow such a crop?"

"I'm a business man, Judge. If marijuana's what the U.S. market wants, and it's legal, I think ASAM should be in the business of providing it to our North American cousins. Let the Yankees smoke themselves into oblivion. ASAM could be the next Phillip Morris, trade on your New York Stock Exchange, it could coin money and create economic growth for Mexico. It would be good for everyone on this side of the border."

"But what about the damage to Mexican smokers from using Marijuana?"

"I didn't say I was going to sell it in Mexico."

"Oh,… I see." The silence hung for a moment.

"Doesn't Luis have a beautiful home here, Judge?" Interceded Garcia.

"Yes. It looks like you've already made lots of money, Luis."

"Some, Judge. I've been fortunate. Our father left Rosa, Roberto and me small trust funds. I've taken mine and played your American stock market. I'm up at the crack of dawn every morning during the week trading stocks, options and futures. It's addicting. It gets into your blood. And as you know, your New York Stock Exchange has had a very good run. It's provided the down payment for my home here on the beach, and it helps me pay expenses and contribute back to the Cabo community."

"You've been very fortunate," said the Judge.

Luis smiled. "Fortune favors the fearless."

CHAPTER 21

That evening the room phone rang exactly at nine p.m., the desk announcing Alan Clark was in the lobby, as prompt as his word. Katy and the Judge marched with Alan out of the lobby and across the turnaround toward a waiting SUV, the heat settling about them like a cloud. Katy swished beside the Judge in a long green silk dress with a Miss Saigon cut, slender with curves, thanks in no little part to some elastic undergarments the Judge saw her wiggle into, flattening her still pouchy stomach. Females were tricky creatures.

The Judge had hoped to wear his puke green shorts and a white dress shirt, but Katy would have none of it, forcing him into beige slacks and a blue blazer which he said he'd carry, but be damned if he'd wear.

"Tonight, I have a date," Alan said proudly as he opened the passenger door. "An old friend who happens to be down here on vacation for a couple of days, just like you two. Can I impose on you two to take the very rear seat?"

Alan held the door while Katy and then the Judge bent and climbed their way to the back of the SUV and its third set of passenger seats. Then Alan settled in the second row of seats and waived the drive to start.

As the driver took them to pick up Alan's date, the Judge wondered if it was the cute little Mexican girl Alan had been flirting with in Cabo Wabo the night before. A pretty thing, bright and new, attracted to

127

Alan's apparent wealth, if not his age. Some part of the Judge had been a little envious at Alan's freedom to flirt and partner up on the dance floor with multiple females, not married and under tow like the Judge. Then again, the Judge wasn't much of a dancer.

They pulled up the main thoroughfare through town, all lights and scrambling traffic, Mexican style, dodging jaywalkers here and there, then turned right, toward the beach and the line of fancy resorts ringing the surf. They bounced across a river bed, paved and pretending to be a road, the Judge holding the ceiling with one flat hand so as not to hit his head. Then up through fancy wrought iron gates, checking in first with a guard in a crumpled uniform and long moustache. Finally, they pulled into the roundabout of a frothy-looking resort, pink and orange stucco with large porticos.

Alan dashed into the lobby, and reappeared with a tall brunette on his arm, difficult to see in the soft light. Too tall to be the Cabo Wabo girl, and she walked like an American.

Difficult to see, that was, until the sharp point of Katy's elbow went slashing into his ribs with venom. It startled him out of his enjoyment of the SUV's frosty air-conditioning stream, making him yelp.

He looked closely at the woman on Alan's arm.

Oh Shit! It was Barbara!...

Barbara and the Judge had been an item of sorts some years before he'd met Katy. Item, hell, they'd had a passionate affair behind her then husband's back. Images of wild nights on a fur rug fireside in Vail, and a tangle of legs and twisted clothes in the back seat at the Seattle Airport parking lot, flashed though his mind.

Like daguerreotypes lifted to light from an old box in a dusty attic.

The affair had ended when the Judge insisted Barbara either run away with him, or mend fences with her husband. Barbara decided economic issues took precedence over love, at least until her then hubby made partner in his fancy accounting firm, which was supposedly imminent. Since she wouldn't end her marriage, the Judge ended the relationship.

Unfortunately, the Judge seemed destined to run into Barbara periodically, the last time in Silicon Beach the year before. Worse, Katy invariably seemed to be there when Barbara turned up.

Katy took a dim view of Barbara. Was it because Barbara was beautiful? Or perhaps oversexed? Barbara exuded a feminine sensuality that hung like musk in the air when she entered a room. Perhaps it was because Barbara was still infatuated with the Judge. Or because Barbara was now single and on the prowl for her next husband. 'Marrying up', as they called it in Beverly Hills, a blood sport with Barbara. But the Judge suspected it was mostly a territorial thing between females. Unfortunately, he was the territory.

Barbara wore a sequined dress of gold that shimmered as she walked, tight across her hips and butt, swooping low in front to display a little more of her enhanced breasts than the Judge thought the law should allow. She bent to get into the front seat, damn near falling out of her dress, to Alan's clear satisfaction and Katy's sharp intake of breath in the backseat. Barbara waved her small gold clutch purse about in front of her, perhaps as a shield to fend off Katy's cold stare.

"Hi, Judge. Heard you were coming tonight." She winked at him, implying a double entendre. "And Katy. So good to see you." This said with a studied lack of conviction.

Oh boy, thought the Judge. This was going to be a rocky evening.

Alan tried to maintain chatty conversation as the SUV took them along the great coast highway that connected Cabo to San José del Cabo, known as the Los Cabos Resort Corridor, punctuated periodically by grand resorts facing the sea. He appeared oblivious to the drop in temperature with the arrival of Barbara. Katy was tight-lipped but smoldering, eyes narrowed, drilling a hole in the back of Barbara's brunette head.

The party was at a private villa in Palmilla, ranked the best resort in Baha California. Flanked by secluded sands, aquamarine waters and pristine fairways, Palmilla was a specular enclave of the rich and the powerful according to Alan. They drove through a large private gate after inspection by two guards, squared up in uniform and tight on reviewing identification, then wound their way up a narrow road through the Palmilla Villas. The car took them to the top of the tallest hill in the resort, lying under a carpet of stars and a slender moon casting a small silhouette on San José Bay at their feet. Roofs of lesser villas stretched out down the hill to both sides. The dark sea held an indistinct horizon in a 180-degree arc, split only by the spike of pale yellow across the water.

The Villa itself had a grand gate with a doorway cut in it, manned by a cluster of five Mexican marines in formal dress, carrying automatic weapons. A tall Mexican in a pale green chauffeur's uniform stepped out of the shadows to open the passenger doors, directing them toward the gate, from behind which the sounds of a small mariachi band rippled above the noises of a large cocktail party.

But more security clearance was required at the gate before they could step through onto a large stone terrace, anchored at one end by an infinity pool extending out beyond the cliff edge and overlooking the sea below. The residence, landward from the pool, was large and magnificent, stone and stucco, with long sliding panels of glass opening to the view from living room, den, dining room and four massive bedrooms.

A large crowd partly occupied the house and oozed out over the patio to the very edges of the pool. Brightly dressed women, mostly young like Katy, and casually dressed men, mostly old like the Judge, chatted with animation and verve, drinks in hand, while young Mexican girls in stiff starched whites passed plates of munchies and bussed drinks.

Alan plowed into the middle of the crowd, seeming to know many, with Katy and Barbara in tow, leaving the Judge a straggler behind, blocked as the crowd opened to accommodate Alan and two beautiful women, then closed again before the Judge could follow.

The Judge glimpsed Katy, turning back on tip-toes, looking for him in their wake, catching his eye, sticking her tongue way out, bringing her white teeth down softly on top, a universal sign of biting her tongue. The evening was deteriorating rapidly.

And the Judge was hot again. Dumped from the air-conditioned car, stuck on the crowded terrace, hemmed in on all sides. The heat lay like a blanket, though it was now ten p.m., the sun gone for some time.

The Judge tried to maneuver closer to the open sliding doors to the house where a swath of cool air seemed to pour from hidden air conditioners of no doubt gigantic proportions. He could hear the faint hum, and feel a slight vibration through the terrace stone as compressors churned to perform the herculean task of cooling the house with all its doors open. But the packed crowd made it impossible to get near the doors.

There'd been mosquitos buzzing around them as they alighted from the car, sensing the chance for soft American flesh into which to sink their proboscises.

But there were no insects on the patio. Only the faint scent of DDT, rising like a cloud from the ground and foliage, wafting through the moist night air, coloring slightly the taste of assorted puff-pastry hors d'oeuvres passed around the patio on large silver platters. The Judge wondered whether he'd be sick.

He turned to his left, adopting a flanking tactic to elbow his way to the cool air, and ran smack into Chief Inspector Garcia, standing with a younger man, chatting in Spanish. The Judge stuck out his hand instinctively, muttering, "Hello."

Garcia took it to shake reluctantly, not particularly happy to see the Judge. But the Judge's path was tightly blocked moving forward, and now back. He was trapped, and he knew no one else. Alan and the girls were nowhere in sight, consumed by the mass of humanity. Likely now ensconced in the house sitting next to the air conditioner vent.

Lucky bastards.

The younger man with Garcia turned to size up the Judge, glancing expectantly at the Chief Inspector for an introduction.

Garcia introduced the Judge to Señor Martínez, giving his title with a flourish, apparently as was the custom. "Señor Martínez is the Chief of Police for all of Cabo San Lucas." Garcia's boss.

Martínez was young, likely mid-thirties, tall, thin, with an aquiline nose and pale white skin that emphasized dark arrogant eyes now regarding the Judge with faint amusement.

"Nice to meet you, Judge. I've heard about you. An amateur detective of sorts from Los Angeles as I understand. Often getting in the way of legitimate police investigations and procedures, sometimes tainting or destroying evidence, making it more difficult for authorities to do their work. Are you going to... how do you Americans say it... 'gum up the works' down here too?"

It was the final straw. The heat, the mass of humanity, too much chili verde on his fried eggs at lunch, the wafting fumes of DDT, and damn Barbara showing up, the harbinger of domestic strife to come when Katy got him alone in the hotel room and vented. It was all just too much.

"You are the one who Garcia talked to yesterday on his cell after the first death of María Cervantes?" asked the Judge.

"Yes."

"You're the one who suggested a replay of where everyone was at the moment of María's death?"

"Well yes."

"So, you're actually responsible in part for Ana's death. Sort of a two-for-one murder for the perpetrator?"

Martínez's head snapped up, his eyes narrowing.

133

"We don't know it was murder, señor. We have two deaths, but nothing to suggest foul play. They likely each chose suicide for personal reasons. Almost a suicide pact. It was no one else's fault." Martínez was turning pink now, controlling his temper with difficulty.

"No one except the person who laced their face with pepper spray, blinding them, disorienting them. Then forced them each off the roof, over its edge, with a sharp blade, slashing at their hands and forearms."

"You are all they say in your country, señor. Trouble! This is not California. We handle investigations and people differently here. I think you're not so welcome in our town. You should consider departing back to California before something untoward happens."

Martínez turned on his heel, straight, proud, his mouth grim, clearly offended by the blunt gringo. Garcia turned away as well in unison with his boss.

Fine, thought the Judge. Now I have absolutely no one here to talk to.

CHAPTER 22

The Judge felt a bump, and then a tug at his elbow. He turned to see Barbara standing almost wedged against him in the crowd. Somehow, despite her enhanced figure she'd managed to shimmy her way out of the house and through the patio crowd to the Judge's side, leaving Alan and Katy behind.

The dancing brown eyes gave the Judge a mischievous look, twinkling. The soft smile was all Barbara. God, she could turn on the charm when she wanted.

"How are you, Judge? You're looking pretty good for yourself. What's it been, eight months?"

She was spot on. Practically to the day.

"You're looking good yourself, Barbara. How goes the quest for a new husband? Any candidates?"

"Oh, well. You know how it goes, Judge. Lots of competition in West L.A. So many men seem only to care how few years a girl has on her. They don't give credit for experience, maturity, and natural talent in the bedroom honed to a fine skill." Barbara rolled her eyes for emphasis. "I understand you have a new son."

"Yes. Little Ralphie. Cute little guy. Eight months old."

"Not into kids myself, Judge. They ruin your figure for starters. Make your boobs saggy, your stomach flabby and checkered with stretch marks, your feet larger, ruining your shoe collection, and steal calcium out of your bones, setting you up for osteophytosis when you're old. The first year you're a wreck, with no life and no sleep. For the next twenty you're full of anxiety about them, meanwhile shoveling out money for food, clothes, soccer lessons, medical, college, and listening to them talk back more and more with each growth spurt. Finally, they go off to shack up with someone, never quite right for them, never quite good enough, and you see them twice a year on holidays. What's the point?"

"It's life, Barbara. It's living. It's sharing all the experiences with them along the way."

"Not the experiences I'm looking for Judge. But how about you? How's your sex life?"

"Barbara!"

"Has Katy recovered from all those pregnancy hormones, healed up, and gotten her sex drive back?   I could always 'pinch-hit' for her, you know."

"We've had this discussion before, Barbara.   I don't need any pinch-hitting."

"Sorry to hear that, Judge.   We were great together.   Remember that orange grove we pulled into off the Four-oh-five one night? Or me in that beautiful kimono, and nothing else, at noon, in the middle of the gardens at the Tokyo Hilton? We've had some great times."

He had to smile.   Barbara's lively brown eyes searched his, finding what she wanted there, memories of a past that tied them together forever. Barbara had been a wild ride... all the way. They'd shared the most intimate parts of their bodies, joined, panting, gasping, heaving together like some single organism, higher and higher, cresting together and sliding down the back side of ecstasy. La petite mort the French called it.

Not surprisingly, they looked at each other differently, shared a common bond, indulged themselves in memories of past revelries. Yes. Once lovers, forever different between a man and a woman. Some part of her was in him still, and some part of him was in her for sure.

He smiled at Barbara at that thought, then felt other eyes boring into the side of his head. He glanced to the left to find Katy on tiptoes, staring at him across the crowded patio, watching his repartee with Barbara. He blanked his face quickly, too quickly. Caught!

"We've both moved on, Barbara. Fond memories are great to hold and reminisce about occasionally, but I'm firmly committed to my new life."

Barbara pouted, but quickly slid into her public happy face as the Judge felt a shift in the atmosphere around them. Suddenly there Katy was, tucking her arm territorially through his so there was no mistake to whom he belonged. Showing all her teeth to Barbara in a smile that was more grimace then friendly. He'd no doubt pay further for engaging in this little tête-à-tête.

Alan Clark magically appeared at the Judge's other arm, like the Cheshire cat in Alice, all smiles and excitement. Tugging the Judge starboard, toward a small knot of men in expensive looking suits, enjoying cigars and softly talking while they studied the view across the infinity pool to sea.

They seemed to know Alan, parting and making room as Alan dragged the Judge over and thrust him into the middle, excitedly making introductions. The Judge found himself presented to Ricardo Díaz, the Lieutenant Governor of the State of Baja California Sur. The Lieutenant Governor was older than the Judge, shorter, wizened, like a dried fruit, paper-thin skin laid over a network of fine blue veins. Tired, worldly eyes examined the Judge with interest.

"So nice to meet you. Can I call you 'Judge'? It seems everyone does, except for those few detractors who use mean little names."

The Governor's English was flawless, right out of Stanford.

"It's tough to please everyone, sir. But it's a pleasure to meet you."

They smiled at each other and shook hands, two public faces hiding a variety of emotions. The Judge sensed he was well-known and not particularly well-liked by this Lieutenant Governor. The tension in the way the man had stood up and back when the Judge arrived, his hands clasped grimly behind the back now the shaking was done, the hooded look in the man's eyes… all these suggested caution and suspicion.

"Thank you for the invitation to this fine party, señor," said the Judge.

"Por nada. We are always happy to socialize with our American cousins."

There was an awkward silence and then Alan pulled him away, claiming it was time for margaritas.

The evening wore on, as cocktail party evenings do, everyone getting a little sloshed, a little more passionate in their opinions, and a little muddier in their thinking. The Judge settled himself on a balcony rail to watch from the side for a while, balancing his hors d'oeuvres plate with one hand on one knee and holding his drink in the other, wishing he had a third hand so he could actually eat.

Networking parties were all much the same. There were the aggressive networkers, fliting around like moths from cluster to cluster of guests, introducing themselves, collecting cards, flitting off again, determined to meet everybody. Sometimes they were paired up as wingmen working together. Sometimes they were apart but in sync, one going clockwise, the other counterclockwise, touting their skills and those of their partner in quick sharp stabs to those who would listen.

There were the more passive networkers, pitching their tent in one corner or another, often in calculated spots to see the most traffic. Perhaps at the end of the bar, or by the security-covered entrance where people arrived, or the Judge's favorite, the kitchen door where the hors d'oeuvres came out, always a popular place to hang if the food was good. Setting up like snake oil salesmen, waiting to snare passersby who might be sold their product or service, or know someone who could be.

And there was the bureaucracy, all eyes and ears, dreadfully aware of their relative rank and the pecking order, swanning around and through the lower castes, nibbling at the heels of higher ups, trying to be noticed and curry favor.

Katy was engaged in animated conversation with the wife of someone who'd been introduced as the wife of the supervisor of the small U.S. State Department office in Cabo, and was comparing notes on new babies. Now that she was an accomplished member of the motherhood club, she could talk for hours about their new offspring with other new mothers, rehashing each nuance of development over the last six months.

Alan Clark reappeared at his elbow again all Cheshire smile, in his element and enjoying it. "Hi, Judge.

I've snagged an invite for tomorrow afternoon to tour ASAM's airplane parts plant. Want to join me?"

The Judge considered. He might like to go for many reasons, not the least of which was two older women who'd sailed off their rooftop while he'd helplessly watched. But would Katy approve such a side venture? He was doubtful. He was already in trouble over Barbara; did he want to pile more coals on the fire? Finally, he said, "I'd like that, Alan. Can Katy come too? I'm sure she'll be interested in airplane parts."

Alan looked doubtful she'd have an interest, but responded, "Sure." Then he squeezed himself out into the ebb and flow of bodies, spying someone else he thought he might know.

The Judge settled back on his balcony, feeling no need to meet anyone else, giving up on reaching the interior of the house and its blasting air conditioner. Alan returned later, having exhausted all possible contacts to meet, and himself in the process. The Judge waved Katy over. Alan dived back into the crowd to rescue Barbara, cornered by two older gentlemen flirting and trying to get her number, dragging her toward the front gate and motioning for them to follow. It was time to go.

But Barbara disengaged and swung a little unsteadily back to the house, using a side door that had escaped the Judge's attention. The Judge and Katy reached Alan at the gate where he waited for them.

"Are we ready to go?" asked Alan.

"We are," answered the Judge.

"Where's the other person in our group?" piped in Katy, apparently unwilling to use Barbara's name.

"Barbara's in the bathroom. Should be out shortly. I'll have the driver bring our SUV."

"Okay," said the Judge, planning to quickly get Katy into the back of the SUV and hopefully limit further social contact with Barbara. But it wasn't to be. Barbara arrived into the midst of their little group just as the SUV pulled up. And she was drunk. She walked with a distinct wobble ahead of the Judge toward the SUV's open door. When she tripped and started to fall, the Judge reacted quickly, stepping up behind her, wrapping his arms around her torso to stop the fall, hands settling naturally across each breast.

"Oh, Judgee," she slurred. "You haven't held me there for so long. It feels so good." Straightening, then leaning back against him, her tush naturally pressing against his loins at the front, sending sensations of fire down his legs and up his belly.

Suddenly small determined hands shoved between them, pushing Barbara forward and away, one hand going to her head, forcing it down, the other firmly on her back, propelling her into the open rear door of the SUV, as though a cop making an arrest.

"Stay away from my husband!" hissed Katy.

Barbara's head was spinning, unstable. Katy's push was too hard, sending Barbara to her hands and knees sprawling across the forward passenger seat of the SUV, ratcheting her tight sheath dress up around her waist, displaying bikini cut panties and a lot of flesh, her long legs still sticking out of the car.

It was too much. Barbara started dry retching across the back seat.

Katy stood back, appalled.

The Judge produced his handkerchief, reaching in, cuddling Barbara's head with one hand, holding her across her breasts again with the other, sustaining her while she dry-heaved for 30 seconds. It seemed an eternity.

Then he gently wiped her face with the handkerchief, helped her up to a sitting position on the seat behind the driver, and rolled down the automatic window for her. She hung there, one arm and most of her head hanging out into the hot night air, white-faced, trying to calm her breathing.

"Sorry, Judgee," she muttered, trying to regain control of her body, people clustering around at the curb outside now, staring at the drunk American woman, wondering who she was.

The Judge got back out of the SUV to stand by Katy, who was silently fuming.

Alan rushed around them and climbed in next to Barbara, putting his arm around her, trying to comfort her.

"Tanks, Ally Baby," she muttered. "Car's steep off the ground."

Katy and the Judge got in and squeezed their way to their back seats, the Judge sitting behind Barbara at Katy's insistence. The Judge glimpsed something silver, a flask, in Barbara's hand. He caught the scent of Tanqueray mingled with Pure Grace Nude Rose by Philosophy, Barbara's signature fragrance. The gin lent a certain medicinal element to the perfume's floral woody smell.

They roared off down the twisting lane leading off the hill, surrounded on each side by the dark foliage and here and there a smattering of soft lights in gardens and windows.

"Judgee, you still back there?" Barbara called over her shoulder from the center seats.

"I'm here Barbara." Noncommittal.

"Kay. Wanted to be sure you weren't left. Is your child-bride there too?"

"I'm here," said Katy. "I'm not a child bride. You're drunk. You'd best put your head back, close your mouth, and sleep it off." Katy's voice was cool.

"Barbara just had a good time," said Alan. "She's a bit exuberant."

"Fuckin' A, Ally. Have you ever done it in a SUV?"

Alan blinked. "Err… no Barbs."

"Let's. Right now."

"We have company behind us Barbs, and no modesty panel behind the driver. They're watching and listening to us."

"Don't bother me Ally, more the merrier says I." This came with a wave of her hand over her head and a giggle. "Maybe they'd like to play too."

The Judge peeked sideways at Katy, bolt upright, arms folded, eyes smoldering, blood giving her face a pink glow. She turned to him, sensing his eyes, and silently mouthed:

"Stupid drunken ho! Can't believe you were sleeping with her."

The Judge was glad he wasn't in a place where Katy could speak openly and he'd have to respond. He simply spread his hands, palm up, and gave his best boyish smile, hoping it would carry the day.

Katy glared back, not amused.

That's when Barbara said, "Let's get this party going." Then she started to sing.

"Mine eyes have seen the glory of the coming of the Judge;

He is trampling in my vintage where my grapes of life are lodged;

He hath loosed the fateful lightning from his firm and mighty cod;

His truth is marching on."

The last line was sung with volume and raising octaves. She paused there, waiting for reaction.

But it had gotten terribly quiet. The driver was now craning his neck around intermittently, to see what would happen next. Alan was appalled, jaw dropped, mouth open, hardly breathing. The Judge's face was transitioning from pink to purple as he fought to control his anger. He didn't dare look at Katy.

"Alright Barbara, stop it right now." The Judge used his deep judicial voice. The one reserved for troublemakers in his courtroom. "You're not that drunk and we both know it. You're just trying to make trouble. Now sit up, act your age, and be quiet."

"Ahhh, Judgee, you used to be a lot more fun. Before you met the child bride. You've gotten 'old' on me."

Katy suddenly grabbed a magazine from the side compartment in the door, 'Cabo Life', rolled it up, leaned forward, and started boxing Barbara's ears and head.

"Ahhh, Ahhh… Eeeee!" Barbara screamed. Throwing her hands over her ears, ducking forward and away from the light blows, then sliding left to collapse her head onto Alan's lap for protection.

Katy took a swing at Alan with malice, barely missing as he ducked.

"Okay, Katy. It's okay. You can stop," said the Judge, snatching the magazine away. "I'm sure Barbara's sorry. She'll be quiet now."

In the middle seat Barbara sobbed into Alan's lap, her narrow shoulders shaking, large tears running her mascara and puddling, leaving widening spots on Alan's slacks.

Alan looked back at the Judge, mouthing: "What do I do now?"

"Just hold her," the Judge mouthed back, wincing a second later as Katy's skinny elbow shot into his ribs with force, constricting his air supply and sending a spasm of pain up his side.

Alan ringed Barbara's head with one arm, stroking her head and hair with his other hand, murmuring, "It's okay, Barbs. It's okay."

They reached the Judge's hotel first.

"Sorry, Judge, Katy. I'd normally get out to say goodbye, but it'd be a little embarrassing what with this suspicious spot on the front of my slacks. Besides, Barbara is asleep on my lap."

Katy bolted from the SUV and the Judge followed, Katy neither speaking nor looking at the Judge as she marched in through the lobby and over to the elevators, leaving him far behind. It would be a bleak night.

CHAPTER 23

The next morning the room phone rang. The Judge shook himself awake and picked it up, expecting to hear Garcia again. Instead he heard the golden tones of Alan Clark, asking if he'd recovered from their night of revelry.

"That depends on whether Katy is speaking to me today, Alan."

"I'm sure it'll be find. Are you enjoying your Cabo vacation?"

"What vacation? The good Chief Inspector has been running me around like a wagon."

"Yeah," said Katy from their balcony where she was apparently catching the weaker early morning rays from the sun. "You tell him, Judge."

"Don't you secretly enjoy the attention, and the puzzle of it all, Judge?"

"Certainly not." And then in a whisper, "Not while Katy's eavesdropping from the balcony."

"I just got a call from Old Pablo, Judge. He's desperate to talk to us. Well, really to you."

"About what?"

"I don't know, but he sounded quite rattled."

The Judge sighed. "Where? When?"

"Ten-thirty a.m. At The Office. You'll love the place. Right on the beach."

Katy stepped into the room and stood to listen now at the Judge's shoulder.

"Okay, Alan. I'll come," muttered the Judge.

"Bring Katy, Judge. Pablo still likes young females. We'll be better received if Katy comes. And remember, we're touring the ASAM Plant this afternoon."

Katy snorted at the outright sexism, but yelled over the Judge's shoulder into the phone. "I am coming for sure. There nothing to do in the hotel room without the Judge." She gave the Judge a licentious wink.

The Office turned out to be a restaurant partly on the sand, just to the east of the harbor, a favorite watering hole and food joint for visitors and locals.

Pablo met them at the front door, looking tired and something else… was it fearful? His hands seemed to shake slightly, despite an obvious effort to control them. He wore white linen shorts draped around his skinny butt and hips, beneath a silk long-sleeved sport shirt, blue and white checked, pulled down low past his barrel chest and protruding stomach, and a white golf cap, covering his bald pate.

They walked across a raised cement platform that made up the upper dining room, down wooden steps onto the sand, and were shown down further, to the last row of tables nearest the water.

Pablo slipped off expensive Italian loafers to reveal white gnarled feet and set them on the end of the table, tucking his toes into the warm sand. They sat down at a table ten feet above the edge of the tide, the table's top sloping a little from the grade. The Judge and Alan sat on the down side with their backs to the surf, placing Katy next to Pablo on the high side, looking out to the surf and the bay.

The tide was slowing edging up the beach, making a soft swishing sound periodically below them. An umbrella was pulled over, shading their table from the sun. It was all very... relaxed.

"So here we are, Pablo," said the Judge. "What's up?"

Pablo leaned low across the table, whispering, his words coming in quick gasps, his hands shaking now uncontrollably.

"I saw death.... He came for me."

"What?"

"Death, he came for me last night. I caught a glimpse of him sneaking up on me. Just out of the corner of my eye. I dodged. I ran. Like the wind. Got into my hacienda. Slammed the door. He lingered for a while, watching me through the glass. Then he disappeared. It was a very close thing. I'm sure he'll be back!"

"Slow down, slow down, Pablo. Tell us slowly, from the beginning. What happened?"

"It was just after dark. I was on my patio at the back. I usually have my cigar and my tequila just after sundown. My housekeeper does not allow me to smoke in my hacienda. She's very strict. So, I have to smoke outside."

"She's the one who picks your shirts?" asked Katy.

"How'd you know, señora?"

"How much tequila did you drink?" asked the Judge.

"Well, you know. Some. It keeps me going, helps me sleep. I drifted off in my patio chair, as I often do. It's the best time of the day."

"What happened next," asked Alan.

"I was dozing there, on my patio. But then I sensed something. Like the air had become compressed or something. Like I'd dropped into a sinkhole of air. It was beating against my temples. My eyes flew open, I looked around. Out of the corner of my eye I saw Death, his red eyes staring at me, swinging down to gather me up. I didn't wait for him. I dived low off the chair, skinned my knees, crawled into my dining room, slamming the sliding glass door behind me. Then I collapsed. My heart was pounding so hard I couldn't breathe. My pulse was racing, making my arms ache. I thought I was having a heart attack. Then Death came up to the glass and glared at me, hovering there for seconds, figuring how to get me. I screamed for my housekeeper. She came running. With my nitroglycerin. Saved me."

"Did she see Death?" the Judge asked.

"No. As soon as she came, poof, he disappeared. She said maybe I was dreaming. A nightmare or something. But it was no dream, señor. My housekeeper helped me through the cocina, out to my garage. We got into my old pickup, and she drove. We roared away. We went to the emergency room, then to the Grand Solmar Land's End and she checked us in. I'm not going back to my hacienda. He waits for me there. I'm so scared."

"Tell us more about what Death looked like, Pablo?" asked Katy.

"Death?"

"Yes."

"Like a cat."

"A cat?"

"Yes. I hate cats. I've always been allergic to them. And afraid. When I was younger my brothers used to tease me about it. But I got even. I used to torture and shoot cats for fun in our neighborhood. But now Death has come for me in the form of a cat. For revenge."

"Perhaps it was a real cat you saw," said Alan.

"No. It was Death. It was no regular cat. Its paws never touched the ground."

"It was a floating cat?" asked the Judge.

"Yes. He was shrouded in black, ready to grab my soul and carry me off. His mouth snarling, his forelegs outstretched for me, sharp claws waiting to sink into my flesh... and his eyes. Oh, my God, his eyes. Fiery red eyes from Hell."

Katy, the Judge and Alan looked at each other. Alan subtly rolling his eyes.

"And you think I can help somehow?" asked the Judge.

"You're a very wise man, señor. I've read about you. The board all got copies of your resume and newspaper clippings of your exploits. You're an American judge, educated, with vast experience. I talked to my priest, he didn't believe me. I talked to Moreno, the company lawyer, he didn't believe me. I hope you'll believe me. And that you'll know what to do."

"Have you talked to Chief Inspector Garcia?"

"No. He reports to his police chief, and his chief is a man with divided loyalties, so that makes the Chief Inspector the same. They will not protect me from Death."

Pablo's lips turned into a grim line as he stared past the Judge's shoulder into the breakers, reliving the night before.

"You believe me, don't you señor? What shall I do?"

"Either you had a very bad nightmare, or you saw what you saw, Pablo. I think you were wise to leave your hacienda and go to a hotel. For now, I would stay there. What's more, I wouldn't tell anyone where you're staying now. Don't tell your family, don't tell the Chief Inspector, don't tell anyone, and don't let your housekeeper tell. Stay there for a few days. Meet people elsewhere, but don't tell them where you stay. Give me a chance to figure this out."

"Yes, señor, that's what I'll do. I knew you'd have sound advice."

"Now I need a favor from you, Pablo."

"What can it do?"

"Tell us more about ASAM."

"What?"

"Tell us more about the company you helped to build. It may help us sort things out."

Pablo looked dubious, but replied, "As you say, señor."

"Can you tell us about your position on moving into the medical marijuana business?" asked Alan.

"And tell us about the man who started it all," chimed in Katy.

Pablo let go of his black thoughts long enough to produce a shy smile, mostly aimed at Katy, showing yellowed teeth with nicotine stains, crinkle lines breaking out around his small brown eyes, his beaked nose pointing higher, indicating new interest in the conversation. "My brothers and I started the company a very long time ago. It was José's dream. My brother, Antonio, and I went along. They're both gone now. I was the youngest. I know I'll disappear soon. It's life. But not now, I'm not ready."

"What was the initial business?" asked Alan.

"We drilled for oil in Mexico. We were wildcatters, as you say. And we struck a lot of oil. Fate smiled on us. We moved into refining and then distribution as well."

"Did you ever sell drugs?" asked Katy.

"Hell no. Back then there was no drug problem. Or at least not much of one. There were no cartels. No drug epidemic in your country. No violence in our country. Not like now. This drug business is the worst thing that's ever happened to Mexico. It's made us into a place of violent warfare."

"But it's legal to sell marijuana in California now, Pablo," pressed Alan. "Surely if there was a good business opportunity to make serious money with the crop in cross-border sales, you'd consider it."

"These younger people think I'm too old, Señor Clark, as do you. That I don't understand. But I understand just fine. There are no short cuts. We wade into this marijuana trade, we throw away sixty years of what our company's about. We become no better than the scum that run drugs. Running marijuana that we know is Federally illegal in the United States. And for what? So, our lazy next generation can get a little more money out, a little earlier, that they haven't earned."

"But surely if everybody's in the trade, you don't want to be the last one to the market. They project thirty billion dollars in U.S. sales of marijuana in the near future."

"I've no interest. One of the few things on which I and my two nieces agreed. God rest their souls."

"Who do you think is responsible for their deaths?" asked the Judge.

Pablo's hawk-like nose swung around to point at the Judge, his eyes narrowing. "Are we sure they didn't just jump? Some say it was a double suicide."

"Come now, Pablo. Your two nieces, suddenly deciding on the same day to jump off the same building? That's way too much of a coincidence."

"Maybe María fell, an accident. And then Ana was so distraught she just jumped out of grief."

"You really think that's what happened?"

"No…. You're right of course. Someone killed them both."

"Any idea who?"

"Or how?" chimed in Katy.

"No… Maybe Luis. He's the one trying to drag us into this marijuana business. They were standing in his way. He's an asshole. He always hated us."

"Why?" Katy asked.

"Because we were the controlling bloc, María, Ana, Miguel and me. We wouldn't pay the kids the big salaries they thought they were entitled to."

"Not like the salaries the controlling bloc got," said the Judge.

"Of course not."

"Including you?"

"Yes, including me. But I own a third of the company. These kids, Luis, Roberto and Rosa, each own only eleven percent. Besides, I've been around since the beginning. A lot of the relationships that make this company work are mine."

"Who else might have a motive?" asked the Judge.

"No one I can think of."

"Perhaps Miguel?"

"Miguel was part of our voting bloc. He took care of us. We took care of him. He'd have no reason."

"Miguel is María and Ana's half-brother," said the Judge.

"Yes. My older brother, José, was a swinging bachelor after his first wife died. But then he married the club dancer. Jesus, she had nice tits. Could dance too. I always liked her. More than just a bar girl. A real artist. We all got hard in that club when she came on and started to dance."

Pablo gave Katy a leer.

"Course my brother let his little head do the thinking for his big head. Always a mistake. He didn't need to marry. He had the money to provide her with everything she could want. But when she got pregnant with Miguel... Jesus, she threw such a fit, bullied José to up and secretly marry her."

"So, Miguel got shares in the company too."

"Yes. When Miguel reached twenty-five, a third of José's shares in the company, eleven percent of the total outstanding shares, were turned over by José's trust to Miguel. He immediately put himself on the board. Had the votes to do so. We made a pact to vote our shares together, keep control of the company in our hands. And that has worked quite well right through today."

"What about you, Pablo? I understand you and Ana didn't get on?"

The old man sat back in his chair, a congenial smile blanketing his face, like a poker player looking at his new hole card.

"Ana and I didn't have the best of relationships, it's true. She was the accountant. Always a bean counter. And a meddler. Always getting in other people's business."

"Was there something specific that made your relationship strained?"

"Yes. You see, originally José founded the business and owned it all. When our middle brother and I came in, we split the stock three ways. We each got a third. After my brother, Antonio, died, José promised he would bequeath enough of his shares to me, so I'd have control when he passed. There was a will drawn up to that effect. And José signed it. But there was only one document. I never got a copy.

Ana, the accountant, was appointed Executor of José's estate, and conveniently couldn't find that will. It disappeared. I had an angry confrontation with her. She was a tough bitch. Just laughed in my face. Said I could suck wind. Blamed me for introducing my brother to the dancer. Said María and she would control the company. I could either play along, or watch from the outside looking in."

"So, you didn't get any additional shares?"

"No. She screwed me over."

"And María went along?"

"Yes."

"Were you angry enough about being cheated out of the shares to arrange for the death of your nieces?"

Pablo just looked at the Judge, his expression communicating, 'What a stupid question.'

It was then the Judge felt cold on his feet. Cold and wet. The tide swept in and around him under his chair, soaking his feet, softening the sand under the back

155

of his chair. He felt the back of the chair sinking into the suddenly wet sand, down, farther, farther…. Suddenly he was doing a painfully gradual backward fall, as the chair slowly tipped itself over onto its back in the wet tide. It was too late to scramble out, too much lead in his butt. His feet along with the front of the chair tipped high into the air, 225 pounds carrying the chair ever backward until he landed in a slow splash, sea water sluicing around him.

They all laughed at him. Even Katy. They seemed to think it outrageously funny as he scrambled up out of the foamy sand, the back of his shirt and puke green shorts soaked.

He looked at himself in disgust.

Katy beckoned a waiter over and ordered him a double Cadillac margarita, extra extra strong.

CHAPTER 24

Alan showed up at their hotel at one in the afternoon with a Sprinter work van, labeled with the name ASAM on both sides, driven by a young local with a wide smile underneath friendly brown eyes, dressed in white linens offsetting his brown skin and dark floppy hair. He looked to be someone in a brand-new job, excited to be driving the gringos north, chatty about his country and full of eager questions about theirs. The van was new, its rear compartment stacked with boxes that read Bolts and Fasteners, bound for the ASAM plant.

They set off on an hour and a half drive north, Alan up front in the passenger seat and the Judge and Katy in the back, up the Pacific Coast of Baja, up to Todos Santos, the ancient colony city above Cabo, pushing twenty miles North beyond its boundaries. They eventually pulled off the main highway, down a dusty dirt side road, and up to and along cyclone fencing with spooled barbed wire on top, stopping finally at a security kiosk in front of a high gate. They produced their passports to verify their identity to three alert guards, dressed in freshly pressed khaki and carrying automatic weapons, and soon were waved on.

They wound their way through a banana plantation for perhaps a quarter of a mile, and finally into a large parking lot sprouting a huge two-story industrial building at its other end, corrugated metal in grey and black. There was another perimeter fence around the building, and another security check outside its lone gate. They walked through the gate, and then through a metal door into built-out office space at the front of the building: beige carpet, white plaster walls with pictures of various airplanes, and a wood counter, heavily varnished, made from a single tree, running down one side. The office smelled crisp and clean, with a hint of new paint.

A rotund lady behind the counter gave them a friendly wave, obviously expecting them, then buzzed her boss, who was out a side door like Jack Flash to greet them, all hand-shakes and toothy smile. The plant manager introduced himself as Tomás Castillo, and openly gave Katy an appreciative look. The Judge decided he didn't like this plant manager much.

"Nice to meet you gentlemen, and to have you visit our plant. Miguel Cervantes was here last week doing his quarterly inspection and Luis Cervantes will be here tomorrow. This seems our month for visitors."

They settled in Señor Castillo's office for an orientation, sharing strong Mexican coffee and a selection of donas, buñuelos, churros, and sopapillas. The Mexican dona was a donut-like fried dough pastry, dipped in chocolate, and proved to be surprisingly good. Señor Castillo loaded them down with numbers, revenues, profit margins, principle customers, vendors, and numbers of various parts manufactured and assembled in the plant. He exclaimed proudly, "We produce some of the lowest cost air frame parts in the world."

They were led out of his office and up a flight of stairs to the second story, through another locked security door, and found themselves out on a catwalk overlooking the cavernous two-story space of the building filled with large tail and fuselage constructs in the process of fabrication and wiring, silver outside and bright green on the inside, heavy blue, red, yellow and purple wiring streaming from their open ends like confetti. The air was tinted with traces of phosphine and arsine from several acetylene torches in use, giving it a distinct garlic-like smell. Sounds echoed across the vast chamber from twenty assemblies in progress at work stations spaced across the cavern.

Skilled workers in white overalls swarmed around each assemblage like ants. Other workers, apparently less skilled, dressed in dusty blue overalls, rushed around bussing parts and sweeping the floors where bits of wire, cable and aluminum debris fell periodically in assembly. The white-garbed workers looked happy enough, chatting with partners on the line, joking with supervisors. The blues looked more... something... perhaps subdued?

Security personnel stationed at varying intervals along the assembly line looked up at their little party suspiciously. A couple stopping to admire Katy's legs from below. The Judge wondered what was so secret it required pervasive security.

They were led further along the catwalk, and then down stairs in the middle to the first floor of the building to get a good look at the fuselages and tail assemblies. Behind them at the back of the plant floor, several short work benches contained smaller assemblies in process: radar antennas, radio equipment, drones, and units that looked to be part of conveyer belt installations. One bench contained a robot, on large roller wheels, arms extended with screwdriver hands. Here too, each white-clad skilled worker had a second 'gofer' worker in blue, assisting in bussing parts, sweeping the floor around the station, and holding pieces together for riveted assembly.

The plant had the feel of army organization, each person drilled with his job responsibility, tight discipline, each task broken down into its smallest components, a body for each component. The wage rate must be very low, mused the Judge, since so many people were in play.

The Judge inquired about a restroom, feeling a need to reprocess coffee, and the donas, which were sitting in his stomach in a less festive way than one would have anticipated by their appearance. The chocolate icing had been part mole, and the dough had been heavy in grease. The fried eggs smothered in verde sauce earlier in the morning hadn't helped.

Señor Castillo frowned slightly at the Judge's request, but called a security guy over and in rapid Spanish instructed the man to escort the Judge to the baño and stay with him. The security man led the Judge around the corner of one line of benches and to a side wall where a small metal room jutted out onto the plant floor. Inside were four toilet stalls, two sinks, and an industrial size shower, the Judge supposed for hazardous spills.

The security guy took a position inside by the door, but the Judge waved him away, saying he'd be a while, demanding privacy. The guard shrugged and wandered off.

The Judge had just settled into his stall, perfuming the air with a blast of ill-wind, when the door opened in the stall next door and someone settled there. All the Judge could see were dirty white tennis shoes and the bottoms of dusty blue overalls. The Judge returned to his concentration, only to be disturbed again.

"Señor, are you there?" whispered the new neighbor in a thick Spanish accent.

"Errrr, yes. And busy."

"You are from outside?"

"Yes."

"American?"

"Yes."

"Please, please help me señor. Trabajo de esclavos here."

"Esclavos?" asked the Judge, uncertain of his Spanish.

"Slaves, señor! They keep us locked here as slaves to work."

"I don't understand?"

"Like a prison, señor. A prison for people who've done nothing. I am from Guatemala. I gave them money. They said they would take me to the U.S. Instead I'm imprisoned here. Three months now. There are others too."

"How many?"

"Everyone in azul... blue."

"It's like a forced work camp?"

"Si, señor. If you cannot get me out, will you call my wife and tell her I'm alive? My name is Felipe Martínez. My wife and nomos, they must think I'm dead. In some ways, I am."

A small scrap of paper was thrust under the stall panel, a name and number scribbled on it.

"I'll see what I can do," the Judge whispered. "I'll call the police."

"Oh Dios, no, no, don't do that. They're the ones who sold me here. Call Mexico City, señor."

The front door to the restroom opened, banging against the adjacent wall; then someone pounded on the stall next to the Judge.

There was the slush of a quick flush; then a hasty exit from the stall, and two sets of steps marched from the room.

The Judge finished his business quickly, dousing his hands with water at the dirty sink, there was no soap, and bolted out the door.

A tall scrawny security guy was walking a shorter equally skinny man in his early thirties, dressed in dusty blue, toward a bench at the back of the factory floor. The man in blue looked over his shoulder once, his face contorted in fear. The Judge had little doubt who'd been the Judge's brief stall mate. It hadn't been the security guard.

The Judge put a bland expression on his face, stuck one hand in a pocket, feeling the scrap of paper there, and sauntered back to his little group, clustered around a bench mid-floor where Castillo was explaining the nuances of elevators and stabilizers on airframe tails.

Señor Castillo was running out of steam, having been talking non-stop since they'd walked into the plant. He suggested a return to his office and some mid-day refreshment, spinning on his heel and they rapidly retraced their steps up the stairs to the catwalk and across the second story to his office.

They settled around his desk to a platter of frosty lime margaritas which mysteriously appeared with salted chips, salsa and guacamole, Alan Clark running his mouth again at how modern and efficient the plant was.

Señor Castillo preened more with each new compliment, all smiles and congeniality.

"Are these workers all hired locally?" asked the Judge.

"Oh yes. We hire and train people from our local community."

"And the ones in blue too?"

"Of course. All local labor." Señor Castillo looked at Alan, hoping he would start a new topic of discussion.

The Judge pressed on. "Are there labor unions?"

"Oh no. These employees are well paid and well treated. They have no need of a union."

"Do some live here on the plant property?"

"Err... yes. A dorm on the other side houses some eighty people."

"All blue workers I suppose?"

"Why yes, how did you know?"

"Can they leave whenever they want?"

Señor Castillo gave the Judge a deprecating smile. "Of course. This is not a jail."

"Can we go back to their dorm and talk to a few of the blue workers?"

"Err.... No. I don't think that's a good idea. Besides, they only speak Spanish. I understand you don't?"

"It's true. But Señor Clark here speaks fluent Spanish."

"We run a tight ship here, Judge. We can't have tourist visitors disrupting our work week. It's not permitted."

Señor Castillo folded his arms across his chest, signifying the discussion on this point was closed.

"Are you familiar with Mexico's law against human trafficking. I understand it provides for thirty years' imprisonment and huge fines if one is caught."

The friendliness evaporated from Castillo's face, his lips turning into a grim straight line, his eye glittering at the Judge with malice. One hand coming up, forefinger pointed at the Judge's chest, gesturing. If it'd been a gun, the Judge was sure Castillo would shoot.

"This is not the states, amigo. I understand in your country debutants can flap their lips all they want and say stupid things. This is Mexico, señor. People treat one another with respect. For those who don't.... Well, they sometimes disappear, never to be heard again."

Katy gasped at the blatant threat.

Alan jumped up, pasting another smile on his face, pulling the Judge by his arm out of the chair. "Well, Señor Castillo, it's getting late. It's time for us to go. Thank you for the tour. We'll be off now."

Alan hustled them out of the office, across the parking lot to their van, flagging urgently at their young driver sharing a cigarette with a security man at the corner of the building. They all clambered in and the car sped off, reaching the front gate and cruising through without a stop. They turned south at the main road, retracing their steps toward Cabo. After twenty minutes, the Judge adjusted his rear seat back to a tilt into the storage compartment, planning a short nap.

There was a high-pitched yelp behind him, the seat bouncing off a lumpy blanket in back that now moved. A small head with black curls shoved out from beneath the blanket, glaring at the Judge.

CHAPTER 25

The face was of a young girl, perhaps 14, dark hair, dark eyes, petite features displaying indígena ancestry, her face framed by the top of her blue overalls. Fear-filled eyes were set into dark circles, and the grim line of her mouth belied her apparent youth, hinting at experiences that had aged her beyond her years.

"Pull over, pull over," Alan screeched to the driver. The van rattled to a stop on the unpaved dirt beside the road. The driver turned back in his seat to stare, worried now there was an extra person in the back.

All eyes turned to the girl. She looked at them calculatingly now, deciding whether they could help. Finally deciding she had no choice.

"Trabajo de esclavos, Señor."

"A slave," said the Judge.

"Si. Ayúdame! Help me. Get me away."

Katy reached over, putting her hand on the girl's trembling shoulder.

"It's okay. No one will hurt you here."

"Can't go back. Don't send back."

"We won't send you back." Said Katy.

Alan caught the Judge's eye, shaking his head slightly, disagreeing, mouthing the words, "It might not be that simple."

"What's your name?" asked Katy.

"Cristina. Cristina Reyes."

"Where're you from?" Katy asked.

"From Honduras, Téguz."

"But right now. You work at the plant?"

Fear spread again across the girl's face again.

"No go back. Bad men. No go back."

"No. You won't go back. You're with us now. They mistreated you?"

Anguish showed now. The girl started to cry.

Katy patted her arm some more, coaxing out more information.

"My family paid money, me go to America. But lies. Steal money. Dump me here. Esclava!"

"They don't pay you to work in the plant?" asked the Judge.

"No. Food, bed only."

"You worked on the floor of the plant?" asked Katy.

"Si. Azul. And worse. Esclava sexual. At night guards come. Sometimes one. Sometimes two. Sometimes three. This came out in a rush.

"Slow down, slow down," said Katy.

"Forced sex. How you say… rape. Awful. Unnatural. Not like God meant. Treat me like animal. Like perro… dog. Night after night. Different men. Handed around. Bastardos malignos y ladrónes. I… I… can never be wife now, never be a mother. God failed me." Small tears streaked down her cheeks again, etching lines in their dust. "Can you send me back to Téguz? To my family?"

She put her hands over her face then, making a small keening noise.

Alan leaned over to the Judge and whispered, "She must go back, Judge. We can't become involved. We can't know about any of this. This will destroy my relationship with Luis, with ASAM. And it's not safe information to have. If they find out we know, like the plant manager said, we could just disappear."

Katy, catching snatches of Alan's whisper, turned to glare at him, her chin up, eyes flashing. Cristina seemed oblivious to their whispers, lost in her own personal sorrow.

"We're not taking her back, Alan," the Judge said. "Driver, let's move out. Back to Cabo."

The driver looked doubtful, thoughts of objecting crossing his face, but he finally turned back to the wheel and swung the van back on the road. They tottered off again. Now it was Alan who looked scared. "This is not going to end well, Judge. Not for any of us. This is a serious miscalculation. I wish we hadn't come."

"But we did, Alan. We're here. And Katy's right, we can't just abandon this girl."

The van rocked around a steep curve on the highway, then the driver slammed on the brakes suddenly, skidding to a stop in front of an army truck parked perpendicular to the road, essentially a road-block. Three soldiers stepped forward from the brush at the side of the road, all khaki and camouflage, automatic weapons at the ready, faces obscured by the brims of their khaki patrol caps, looking hostile from what little could be seen.

The girl dived back under the blanket, which started to visibly shake with her fear. The driver turned in his seat to them, his face a pasty white, words failing him. He looked like he might be sick.

A sergeant rapped on the driver's window and signaled him to roll it down, then leaned in to chat, eyeing Katy in the backseat in a way that made the Judge uncomfortable. They spoke briefly, then the sergeant barked, "Okay, everybody out. I want you lined up against the side of the truck and I want to see your passports… now."

They clambered out and did as they were instructed. One of the soldiers opened the rear compartment. Cristina was still and silent under the blanket, which had stopped shaking. But the solider took a careful look. When he lifted the blanket Cristina made a little screeching noise, covering her face with her hands.

The soldier grabbed her by her hair and hauled her on her knees out the back of the van. There was a Spanish tirade between them. Finally, the soldier looked at the sergeant, who nodded toward the army truck. The soldier pushed Cristina over to the back of the army truck, instructing her to put her foot on the low tail gate running board. He then laid both hands flat on her rounded bottom displayed through blue overalls, and with a large grin boosted her into the back of the truck. This provoked another tirade of Spanish from Cristina.

"She's with us," Katy said. Her chin coming up, trying to stare down the sergeant. "She's with me."

"Not any more, señora. She's wanted back at the ASAM Plant. She has to go back."

Katy's face turned red. She was barely controlling her anger.

"She's a slave back there. It's against the law of your country. You can't take her back. They'll just abuse her some more. It's wrong."

Alan was turning red too. He looked like he was having trouble breathing.

The sergeant just looked at Katy for a second. "This is Mexico, señora. Not your country. We do things our way here. She goes with us. You go on. Back in your van now. Vamoose."

"But... but... it's not right."

"Come along, Katy," said the Judge, putting his arm around her shoulder and guiding her back toward the van. "There's nothing we can do here... right now. Let's regroup and consider our options."

Alan bolted ahead of them and into the van, like a rabbit finding a hole. Katy flounced her hair, gave the sergeant an intense look, gave the Judge a similar look, seething now, then marched over and crawled into the van.

Their last sight of Cristina was of her in the back of the army truck, huddled in a corner, knees up, head down, hands over her face, her body shaking slightly with small sobs.

A corporal pulled the truck back, and their driver gunned the van down the highway, quickly putting space between himself and the army.

Katy was beyond angry. "It's so unfair, Judge. How can you let them take her back? How can you just stand by?"

"Their county, their army, their guns, their rules, Katy. What could I do?"

"Something, anything. Not just stand there like a dope."

The Judge bit his tongue. Katy had a mouth on her when she was riled.

"We'll get back to Cabo and we'll make some calls, Katy. Perhaps something can be done."

"This is awful Judge. To watch that girl just taken away, back to those animals.

Alan said, "Modern day slavery is a lucrative business, a one-hundred-and -fifty-billion-dollar industry world-wide, and growing, Katy. You get in the way and you just get rolled over."

"It's true." said the Judge. "Experts testified in the case ahead of mine earlier this year. In Mexico, it's number three after drugs and arms sales. Mexico is a source, a transit path and a destination country for large-scale migration flows. This creates a large pool of easily victimized people. "Over sixteen thousand children are trafficked annually in Mexico."

"I've read about it too." Said Katy. Women, men, girls, boys, lured from poor rural regions in Southern Mexico and Central America with false job offers to urban, border, and tourist areas, then caught up and enslaved using violence, threats, deception, debt bondage. People forced to provide labor against their will; or sex, or both… But it's personal now. Now I've met Cristina. I never thought I'd be a part of it."

"You're not part of it, Katy," said the Judge. "There's nothing you could have done, no way to stop the army from taking Cristina back."

"If we don't speak out now, Judge, denounce it for what it is, then we are a part of it. We allow them to perpetuate this ugly system. How many of the domestics, the gardeners, the street beggars, the construction and factory workers, and the agricultural workers, are secretly slaves, held in captivity, forced to work for a pittance with no hope of freedom?"

Alan said, "Sometimes these people have a better life than they would have had back at subsistence level on some poor farm."

"That's bullshit, Alan, and you know it. They work because they have no choice, no freedom, no out."

"We'll find something to do somehow, Katy," said the Judge. "We won't just turn our backs on Cristina, or on my friend in the toilet." He produced from his pocket the snatch of paper he'd received in the restroom and passed it around for inspection as he told what he knew of Felipe Martínez's story.

They were silent after that, each lost in their own thoughts as the van spurred farther south, back to Cabo.

CHAPTER 26

It was almost seven p.m., and the transition out of the air-conditioned van and across the un-air-conditioned lobby was painful for the Judge. Jesus, didn't it ever cool in Cabo?

Initially the room was no better, cleverly engineered so when Katy took the key card out of the wall box to leave the room, it turned off everything, including the air. God, he hated crafty engineers and bean-counting accountants. They seemed to rule the world, making it an uglier place for everyone.

He sat down in the chair under the ceiling air vent and consumed a well iced gin and tonic, Sapphire, the first damn civilized thing he'd done all day, while he watched Katy pace back and forth across the room like a caged lioness. She was still stirred up about Cristina. They suspected everyone wearing a dusty blue uniform at the ASAD plant was forced labor.

"Okay, honey, why don't I call that Lieutenant Governor guy, Díaz, we met at the party last night, and report what we saw today?"

"Good, Judge. You do that. And how about Chief Detective Garcia, why don't we call him too?"

"Err... the Chief Inspector and I don't get along too well."

"Do you trust him, Judge?"

"I don't know, Katy. I just don't know."

"I kind of like him, myself. I know he's arrogant and stuff, but so are you dear. Your Chief Inspector is cute, so so short, and with his big mustache."

"Katy!" The Judge was scandalized now, and a tad jealous. He knew she was teasing him, but he couldn't help himself. "I hope you like me more than you like Chief Inspector Garcia."

She just smiled at him, pleased at how easy it was to push his buttons. He suspected she, and most females, considered men simple creatures. And he supposed they were. Controlled by hormones, and sexual and territorial instincts, as much as, or more than by logic and intellect.

They tumbled into the bed together, mostly exhausted, sheets only, enjoying the cool air flooding the room, drifting off to sleep in each other's arms. But the Judge's sleep was troubled. A terrified Guatemalan girl kept running through his dreams, pursued by a clutch of angry goats, snorting and pawing the ground with animal menace. He awoke several times, his pulse pounding, his head aching. It was a relief to get up at five the next morning and pursue legal work on the computer while Katy slept blissfully on.

They stayed in their night clothes, him in his pajama bottoms festooned with small red crabs, a joke gift from her last Christmas, she in a frothy lace negligee, until ten, lingering over room service breakfast on the terrace, looking out to sea. Finally, the Judge produced the business card of Lieutenant Governor Díaz and, taking the room phone, dialed the Lieutenant Governor's office. A pleasant girl answered the call, and when he gave his name and asked to speak to the

Lieutenant Governor, he was surprised to be put right through.

Katy listened over his shoulder to his half of the conversation as he laid out the events of yesterday at the ASAM plant.

"Yes," said the Judge. "Katy and I, and Alan Clark, we can all testify to the facts I've just given you. At least two people held against their will, essentially forced slaves, the woman also a sex slave, at the ASAM plant. Something needs to be done, and at once."

"Yes, I know the plant's manager name. It was Castillo."

"I was shocked as well. I don't think they knew we were going to visit."

"Good. I'm relieved you'll take it from here. Please let me know what happens, will you?"

The Judge hung up, proud of himself. "There, Katy, it's done. Now perhaps we can go on with our vacation. The Judge turned to catch a pillow, full in the face. This precipitated a desperate pillow fight, accompanied by screams, growls, threats, and darting about the room to reload pillows, ending in sex, as it often did. Much later they stuck their heads out of the room, the Judge testing the late morning heat outside.

The Finisterra was a large resort built along the beach facing the Pacific Ocean on the downslope of a ridge dividing the western side of Cabo from the sea. Built in a giant horseshoe facing the water, five stories high, it was mostly large one-bedroom suites with sunny balconies looking out over two pools in the center, one with a swim-up bar, de rigueur for Cabo resorts. Beyond stretched the blue Pacific as far as the eye could see.

They settled in for lunch beside the pool, well shaded from the heat, the Judge sporting his puke green shorts again, despite Katy's ribald remarks about their origin, his appearance, and length of use. They downed margaritas with verde'd eggs, cheese tacos, and frijoles con arroz, watching a noisy exercise class of mostly chubby Americans in the pool, trying to exercise water-bound to Latin music blaring from speakers and the commands of a skinny Mexican sadist. The Judge knew he should join in. God, he hated exercise.

Alan Clark found them there, by the pool. He must have called their room, then started a search of the resort grounds. There seemed no escape from the guy. Katy stiffened immediately, still riled from Alan's position on the run-away girl the night before. But the Judge greeted Alan warmly, flagging a passing waiter to get him a drink.

They did social talk for a while, the weather, the food at the hotel, news back in the states, how much Barbara enjoyed meeting up with them the other night. At this Katy looked at the Judge behind Alan's back and rolled her eyes. Finally, Alan smoothly got around to the real reason for his visit.

"You haven't told anyone about yesterday... and... you know, the runaway girl?"

"Does it matter?" asked the Judge.

"I received a call from someone high up in the company."

"Luis?"

"No. Not a board member, but high in that division."

"Who?"

"I'm not at liberty to say, Judge. But he made it very clear that we could all be in serious jeopardy if word leaked out. He said the company would handle it internally. That we should tell no one."

"Bull shit!" Katy muttered.

"What did he mean, 'serious jeopardy'?" asked the Judge.

"He didn't elaborate. But I took it to mean 'personal harm.'"

"You mean he's threatening us!" Katy's voice rose an octave.

Alan looked from the Judge to Katy.

"Katy, we're in Mexico," Alan said. "Not back home in the U.S. Different rules. We can't just run to the local cop on the corner and complain about slavery. Or about injury to ourselves should people decide to get rough. We must tread lightly."

"What you mean is do nothing, Alan. Do nothing that will spoil your sweetheart consulting gig with ASAM. This all about you, Alan. Not about that poor little creature, Cristina, we abandoned to the army yesterday, so they could haul her back to Hell."

"Hey guys, lets calm down," said the Judge. "Alan, it's too late anyway. We've already reported it to the Lieutenant Governor."

Alan's face turned a pasty grey.

"Shit. That was a mistake, Judge. Perhaps a critical mistake."

"We felt we had little choice, Alan. We couldn't stand by and do nothing."

"I wish you'd talked to me first." Alan sighed. "Well, it's done. We can't do much about it now. It'll likely blow over okay. But for God's sake, don't tell anyone else."

"You're asking us to publicly keep our mouths shut until we're back in the U.S.?" Asked the Judge, ignoring a display of Katy pointing thumbs down behind Alan's back.

"I don't know that we can do that. Besides, the ASAM board needs to be informed. Ultimately, it's their responsibility."

"For God's sake, Judge. What do you think the fight was really about between María and the rest of the board? The board already knows all about it, and they are struggling with it."

"You mean they condone it?" asked Katy.

"I didn't say that."

"What are you saying, Alan?" asked the Judge. "That some of the board are for operating with slaves and others of the board are opposed to it?"

"That's about the size of it Judge."

"And the new majority? Where do they stand?"

"I've already said too much. Got to run now, Judge. Got to make an appointment. I'll call you later." Alan bounced off his sun-lounger and bounded away, waving a hand over his shoulder.

The Judge watched him go with a sense of disquiet. This vacation, supposed to be about relaxation, fun, and partying in the sun with Katy, was rapidly going downhill.

CHAPTER 27

After Alan's departure, they'd returned to the room and its air conditioner, sleeping, making love, sleeping some more, hanging out all afternoon. Katy caught up on badly needed rest, a condition seemly symptomatic to the first six months after an offspring's arrival. Later they ordered champagne from room service and watched the sun go down into the Pacific, leaving a bright golden puddle on the edge of the horizon, its yellow tentacles streaking across the undulating waves and disappearing into the foam of heavy surf churning the sand at resort's edge.

Then they'd gone down to the steak house covered by a huge palapa between swimming pools. The Judge had a Mexican steak, polished off with a Dos Equis. Katy tried the fresh lobster, the specimen as ugly as ever, staring angrily at the Judge out of lifeless beady eyes, as though threatening to crawl off its plate and onto the Judge's lap in full attack.

Katy used her words, mostly talking about Ralphie, their new eight-month old. The Judge vaguely understood the baby was growing, rolling over in its crib and trying to pull itself up on furniture. It would be a Holy Terror soon. Katy missed nothing, catching every detail of development, week by week, day by day, almost hour by hour, on which she elaborated with a fusillade of words.

The Judge listened to her description in living color; each little nuance of how Ralphie was trying to stand by pulling himself up, was trying manfully to crawl, and would bring any and every object within his reach to his mouth. He'd heard it all before of course, blow by blow, but it gave her joy to tell it. And he listened each time with satisfaction, pleased to be included in her experience. They had a full set of new ties together now, a new focus that would provide a lifetime of discussion, and likely a fair amount of angst. He smiled at the thought.

The Judge ordered a fresh beer and they wandered down to the beach, leaving their sandals on the last patch of patio before the sand. Walking close to each other and the incoming tide on the hard-packed sand, hand in hand, the night air warm and moist.

The waves crashed and cracked beside them, like some huge monster's maw, daring them to step closer, but they kept their distance. It was exhilarating to take a little risk, daring the surf to come farther up the sand for them, but this wasn't a surf to be trifled with.

It was a dangerous beach, always. No swimming allowed. Periodically each year the waves suddenly crashed further up the beach, engulfing some unsuspecting tourist, collapsing upon them with the weight of water, dragging them out to sea in its powerful jaws, crushing them in its churn and roll, ultimately perhaps spitting them back lifeless up on the sand. Deaths happened often enough here that the Cabo authorities declined to issue specific numbers on fatalities on the beach. Fatalities weren't good for business.

Suddenly, over the roar of the surf, the Judge heard something out of place. What? A high batting noise, growing louder, almost like the stubby wings of a bat, flapping against gravity, sustaining its little rat body in flight. Louder still now.

The Judge turned to look behind them, some instinct motivating him to put his arm around Katy's shoulder. The beach was dark, empty. Only the distant lights of their resort, five hundred yards back.

Then he saw it. A small dark shape materializing out of the night from the sea, a huge misshapen insect the size of a small dog. Low, fourteen feet off the deck, swooping down at them in a forward dive... fast. It was on top of them before he could react, two long antennae in front with wickedly sharp rotating blades, seeking their exposed flesh.

He pulled at Katy and they ran. But it was too fast. They couldn't outrun it. Suddenly there was a hiss. Looking over his shoulder he saw a cloud of grey vapor swirling toward them, spit at them as though from some hungry dragon. Settling over their heads!

In desperation he pushed Katy forward, stopped, and heaved the Dos Equis bottle at it with all his might, sending it somewhere into an arc above the thing's head.

There was a grinding, crashing sound of glass against shell, and suddenly the thing turned sideways and unsteadily limped off over the surf, disappearing into the night.

But the cloud descended upon them like a net.

The Judge's eyes, burning intensely, closed involuntarily and started to tear. He coughed, choked, hardly able to breath, trying to drag Katy away from the cloud. His face and arms were on fire. He could feel the bile rising in his throat, his stomach starting dry heaves.

"Blink rapidly," he mumbled to Katy, his voice caught in his throat, rough and anguished, barely audible over the roar of the surf.

They stumbled further south down the beach, away from the cloud, hardly able to see the sheer rock that now appeared to their left, funneling them ever closer to the surf, the cloud drifting menacingly with them in the light breeze like an avenging blanket. The Judge could feel himself becoming disoriented, unable to think clearly, unable to react, unable to even determine direction, finding it difficult to lift his feet, blind panic settling into his consciousness making it difficult to move or think. He shook his head hard, trying to make it work again.

They were suddenly engulfed in a giant wave, tumbling down over them with the weight of cement, swallowing them whole, then throwing them against the rock face with the force of a freight train. Searing pain flashed through the Judge's shoulder from the impact, numbing his arm and hand. Katy was dragged downward and nearly torn from the Judge's arms by the retreating current; trying to hold her, he stumbled and almost lost his own footing to the onslaught.

The Judge opened slits for eyes, feeling the water still up to his shorts, seeing another ten-foot wave towering over them, then slamming down.

CHAPTER 28

They were submerged again, this time for what seemed an eternity. The Judge pushed and clawed his way back to the rock face, dragging Katy behind him, throwing one arm over a protruding rock and hanging on with all his might as the wave receded.

They desperately hobbled along the rock face to its end and then up the beach to higher ground, collapsing on the sand, gasping for breath and rubbing their eyes. They lay there on their backs, coughing and sputtering up a mixture of sea water and something else. Something disorienting which made them sick to their stomachs. They were soaked, sanded, bruised and bleeding, still mostly blind from the remnants of the grey cloud in their eyes. They felt for each other, the Judge wrapping his arms around her, holding her tight, Katy softly whimpering, shaking. After a while the Judge staggered to his feet, helped Katy to stand, and they moved shakily higher up the sand, away from the churning surf.

They made their way unsteadily back toward the hotel, staying high up on the beach where the sand was soft, squishy, slowing their progress. Katy flinched each time a particularly big wave crashed, its power transmitted into vibration under their feet. She had a nasty bruise on her cheek, and was limping noticeably, favoring her port foot. The Judge was concerned she might be in shock. But her shaking had subsided.

The Judge had sand everywhere inside his salty-soaked clothes. As he walked, it rubbed his skin raw where his thighs joined his torso, and inside the elastic band of his Polo underwear. His hair was filled with sand and it was under his nails. He damn well had sand up his butt. His raised adrenalin was partly a concern the attacker might come back, but mostly anger over this attack on his wife. Someone would pay. Someone would pay dearly.

They reached their room, an oven inside as the air conditioner had gone off with their departure and the removal of the room card from its slot. The Judge put Katy into a cold shower, fished around on his nightstand for Chief Inspector Garcia's number, and called his direct line. It was 11:45 at night.

The Chief Inspector's line rang and rang. No answer. Finally, after an interminable amount of time, voicemail came on in Spanish.

"This is the Judge. It's urgent I talk to you as soon as possible. My wife and I have been attacked. Nearly killed. We've made it back to our hotel, but I don't know how safe we are here. I need your help."

The Judge hung up, wondering if the little asshole would bother to call him back. For all he knew, Garcia might be behind the attack. Nothing was what it seemed in Cabo.

They locked and chained the door, locked the sliding glass balcony door, and crawled into bed to hold each other. Katy took two Tylenol and drifted off to sleep. The Judge lay there staring at the ceiling for a while, wondering what sort of mess they'd walked themselves into, then let his eyes close briefly. When he next opened them, he discovered blinding sunlight focused in through two cracks in the blackout curtains pulled across the balcony's glass door. It was morning, and late morning at that.

Katy was there in the room-provided bath robe on the phone, talking softly so as not to wake him. He vaguely realized she'd been making calls for some time. She smiled at him, terminating her conversation and reaching up to throw the curtains open with a flourish, crashing bright sunlight into his eyes, making him squint in pain. "Get up, get up, hubby. You need to call your special friend, the Lieutenant Governor of all of Baja California Sur. Tell him what's going on. Get him to put a stop to this shameless trafficking."

He got up, nodded his understanding, fished again on his nightstand for the Lieutenant Governor's card, and dialed the number. The very efficient secretary answered again, immediately switching from Spanish to English, not sounding surprised at his call.

"Is Lieutenant Governor Díaz in?"

"In but unavailable, Mr. Judge."

"When will he be available to speak?"

"I don't know Mr. Judge. I can't honestly say."

"I, we, my wife and I, were attacked last night on the beach here in Cabo, nearly drowned."

"Oh, Dios mío! Are you okay?"

"We're banged up but okay. No serious injuries. But only by chance. We could have died last night."

"That's terrible. What can I do?"

"Tell the Lieutenant Governor I need to speak to him right away. That it's urgent."

"I'll tell him, Mr. Judge. But he is very busy. He is not taking calls today."

The Judge thanked her and hung up. Why did he feel he was getting a run-around? This didn't bode well.

The Judge turned to see Katy watching him, her eyes narrowed and cynical now. "They're all in on it Judge. All bastards."

"Now Katy, we don't know that. Díaz is a busy man I'm sure. But I've been thinking. Perhaps we should cut your vacation here a little short. You could head back to Los Angeles this morning. I could stay on and sort things out a little."

"Not a chance, Judge. I'm not leaving without you. And I made a commitment to that girl, Cristina. We need to see she gets help."

"What about Ralphie, dear? He's missing you dreadfully I'm sure. And your folks are getting on in years. They may be running out of energy. Perhaps you should go back, for him... I mean to check on him?"

Her chin shifted up toward the ceiling.

"I miss him terribly. But I'm sticking with you on this one. We Thornes can't be bullied."

The Judge sighed. They were in way over their heads, in a country not their own, with limited rights, few contacts, and no certainty on who could be trusted. He knew enough about his wife to know there'd be no reasoning with her today. Her dander was up. She was nothing if not a fighter. Particularly when she felt cornered, as they both now felt.

The room phone rang. It was the front desk announcing they had a visitor. The phone downstairs was handed over and Chief Inspector Garcia came on the line.

"Hello, Judge. Are you alright? I got your message this morning and came over immediately. Do you need medical assistance?"

"We are a bit scraped and battered, but alive. It was a close call."

"Why don't you come down and have breakfast and we can talk."

"Yes, we'll come now. To the big palapa, by the pool."

The Judge quickly pulled on his puke shorts, the only thing handy, shaved, doused his throat with mouthwash, and headed down, leaving Katy still in the room, scrambling to get dressed and catch up.

Chief Inspector Garcia was sitting at a small table by the pool in front of the palapa under an umbrella, sipping coffee. He nodded as the Judge approached. He looked pleased the Judge had called him for help. The Judge could see it was... satisfying.

"Your message said you were attacked last night, Judge."

"We were. By a flying insect-like creature."

"By an insect?"

"Insect-like. It was not an insect."

"What was it?"

"A damn drone..."

"You were attacked by a drone?"

"Yes. On the beach. It was built with long outstretching arms carrying spinning blades. It belched a cloud of pepper spray and a nerve gas on top of us, blinding, disorienting, making it difficult to think. Then it drove us into the surf."

"The surf can be deadly here."

"Yes. We damn near drowned."

"How'd you get away?"

"I fouled its props with a well-thrown beer bottle. We were lucky. Luckier then María and Ana."

Garcia sat up in his chair, alert.

"You think this drone of yours was used to kill the Cervantes women?"

"I do. The smell of pepper spray. The cuts on their hands and forearms."

"From the blades."

The Judge nodded."

"Of course," Garcia said, "A drone. How modern. But who, Judge? Who has such a drone?"

"ASAM!"

The name hung there between them for ten seconds like an epitaph. It was as though Garcia didn't want to hear the name, didn't want to acknowledge the company's involvement.

The Judge pressed on. "I visited the ASAM plant near Todos Sandos. It's their airplane parts division. They build drones there. I saw them. Look there and you'll find the drone used to drive María Cervantes, and then Ana Cervantes, off that roof."

Garcia sat back in this seat, sipping his coffee, eyes narrowed, digesting this information.

"There's something else too, Inspector."

"What else?"

"That ASAM plant is using slave labor as a part of its work force."

"That's a serious charge. You know this for a fact, señor?"

"I do. I had contact with one of the forced laborers in the plant. He asked me to help him get away. And later we met a young girl, perhaps fourteen, who stowed away in our car just before we left the plant in a desperate effort to escape. She was held captive as both a worker and a sex slave."

"Where's the young girl now?"

"Your army barricaded the road and took her into custody. They were doing ASAM's bidding. Taking her back."

Garcia's eyes narrowed again.

"You think this is why you were attacked? To shut you up?"

"I think it likely."

"Who knows about this forced labor?"

"I do," said Katy, marching up to the table. "And Alan Clark. And of course, Señor Castillo, the slimy plant manager. And yesterday we called the Lieutenant Governor."

"I see," said Garcia, chewing on one lip.

"And now the Lieutenant Governor is ducking my calls," said the Judge.

"I'm just a lowly policeman, Judge. In our system in Mexico, I have limited powers. But it sounds like you've opened your mouth to the wrong people. But I didn't say that, and you didn't hear it from me."

The Judge just looked at Garcia, anger in his eyes.

Garcia put his hands out, palms facing the Judge. "Understand I don't condone human trafficking, Judge. But the reality is that Mexico is a destination country for men, women, and children fleeing from the south. And occasionally such people find themselves caught up as victims of forced labor, or even sex trafficking."

"I've been talking to people on the phone this morning, Chief Inspector." Snapped Katy. "Mexico is already on the Tier 2 Watchlist of our State Department's annual Trafficking in Persons Report. "It's a designation given to countries that do not meet minimum international standards for stamping out this ugly practice."

"You have to understand, señora, most cities in Mexico have a Zonas de Tolerancia where prostitution is allowed. This has made Mexico a huge destination for sex tourism, and a that has inevitably led to some forcible exploitation of girls as sex workers."

"There's nothing inevitable about it, Garcia," said Katy.

"Hasn't the government adopted new laws, Inspector?" chimed in the Judge.

"Yes, in 2007. And the government has increased its anti-trafficking law enforcement efforts. Our Federal Secretariat has assumed leadership of our Interagency Trafficking Commission and the Congreso de la Union has created its own Trafficking Commission. The number of human trafficking investigations and convictions has been very, very low, which suggests there's not much of this activity in Mexico. We believe the Tier 2 designation is unfair."

"Bullshit!" said Katy. "Investigations and convictions are low because of governmental ineffectiveness and payoffs to local law enforcement, judiciary, and immigration officials. I've been talking to the UN people this morning. Dishonest officials extort bribes and sexual services from trafficked adults and children. They extort payment from irregular migrants. They falsify victims' documents and threaten victims with prosecution or deportation, so they'll forgo official complaints. They accept bribes from traffickers. They facilitate movement of victims across borders and deliberately ignore commercial sex and forced labor locations where they know trafficking is taking place."

"Señora, it's not nearly as bad a picture as you paint. Mexico is coming to terms with its human trafficking issues."

"Coming to terms? Your law was passed in 2007, and trafficking is still a growth industry! How can this exist in the twenty-first century, Inspector, in Mexico, in an otherwise modern country?"

"A modern country in many respects, señora, but perhaps not so much in this."

Katy leaned forward now, jabbing a finger toward Garcia. "I've been doing my homework about your country, Inspector, and the powerful criminal cartels. Women and children, and to a lesser extent men and transgender individuals, all exploited in sex trafficking. Forced into labor, human beings shipped across the US border, people used like cattle in your plants and fields."

Garcia spread his hands. "I'm sure what you've been told is overstated."

"Like hell! It's systemic in Mexico, and it's modern day slavery. Your own Labor Secretary admits organized crime networks are behind the recruitment of laborers put to work and exploited in agricultural, manufacturing and commercial industries here in Mexico."

"'Exploited' is a strong word, señora."

"Last year, Inspector, contractors ran ads on the radio in Jalisco State, seeking workers for a tomato-packing plant. The ads offered a reasonable wage, and room and board. But when applicants arrived they were thrust into overcrowded housing and paid only half of what had been promised, much of it delivered in vouchers redeemable only at a company store where products were sold at high markups.

One colleague I communicated with this morning actually spoke to one victim, a man named Valentin. Valentin went to work at the site with his wife and children. They were housed in a tiny room with two other couples who also had children. The camp food was rancid and rotten. They were held and worked at the camp essentially as slaves. They were told they could leave the camp if they wanted to, but the foremen discouraged it, and in the end, forbade leaving. Several people tried to escape, he said. Some succeeded; others were captured, brought back, and beaten before the assembled camp.

Finally, one worker escaped, made it all the way to Jalisco's state capital, and filed a complaint with Mexico City's Special Prosecutor. The camp was raided, and the camp's five foremen were arrested. Nearly three hundred people, including forty teenagers, were held against their will in slave-like conditions, just so some greedy evil... fuckers wouldn't have to pay people a living wage to sort and pack their Goddamn tomatoes! Sorry, Inspector, there I go, using strong words again."

"Well... that's an unfortunate situation, but it was just an isolated incident, señora."

"Oh? What about the cucumber fields and packing plant in Colima?"

"The what?"

"Forty-nine indigenous Mixtecs, recruited by a local Mixtec gangster. Upon being transported to the worksite, the Mixtecs were subjected to unsanitary bathrooms and latrines, a lack of proper food, and no potable water except what they could get from a single distant well. Children worked barefoot in packing lines. Workers were provided no proper protection against extreme temperatures and dangerous fungicides and pesticides. Pay turned out to be based on piecework, resulting in many workers paid so little they could never reach minimum wage. The corporate employer set up a company store where prices were jacked to the ceiling. And workers were restrained from leaving. I'm told the rescue of those forty-nine makes it four-hundred-and-fifty-two people rescued from slave-like conditions since the beginning of this year around the Colima area alone.

And Inspector, these appalling stories go on and on. Two-hundred members of the Rarámuri indigenous tribe were freed two months ago right here, in Baja California Sur. They'd been forced to work under shameful conditions on the potato harvest.

And what about the Mexican and foreign men, women, and children, forced to work for the cartels? Forced to act as lookouts, forced to work in the production, transportation and distribution of illicit drugs, and sometimes forced to act as assassins. What about the big, supposedly legitimate companies, who engage in forced labor? Making their bottom lines look better at the expense of their enslaved employees. Companies like ASAM!"

Garcia threw up his hands in defeat.

"Okay, okay. It's a problem here in Mexico. We are working on the it, but you are right. Trafficking is difficult to stamp out."

"What can we do about this girl, Garcia, this Cristina?" asked the Judge. "And the man in the bathroom stall at the plant, Felipe. How can we at least help them?"

"I don't know. It's not my assignment right now. My assignment is the twin murders of the sisters."

Katy said, "You can go to your police chief? Or to the Governor of Baja California Sur, since we seem to have no luck with the Lieutenant Governor."

"It's our system here in Mexico, señora. Everything runs on personal relationships, personal favors, and small payments along the way. I wouldn't know who to trust. If I start making waves... at a minimum I'll be out of a job, and worst case I'll have my own personal drone chasing me."

"But, but... what about our embassy, Chief Inspector? Can't we go to them for support and help for Cristina and Felipe? Or the President of Mexico? Or the United Nations Task Force on Human Trafficking?"

"You seem to have plenty more ideas than I do, señora. But if you pursue this, I'm afraid you make yourself a target. In fact, it sounds like you are seriously at risk already. And unfortunately, there's little I can do."

Garcia was silent for a few seconds, thinking.

"I would do this, Judge, but understand you didn't hear this suggestion from me:

There's a man, Santiago Lopez, here in Cabo right now. On vacation like you. He is a well-known news reporter for the daily Veracruz newspaper, La Opinión. And his cousin in Mexico City is the Vice Chairman of the Mexican Congress Commission on Human Trafficking. He's staying at Palmilla. You should talk to him. And now, today! But for God sakes don't mention my name. Tell him all you know. If he writes a story about it and the information about ASAM is made public, it is possible there may be less incentive to do away with two talkative Americans."

Garcia stood up, spreading his hands, indicating it was all he could offer.

"Be very careful from here, Judge. It may be time for a quick flight back to California. There are large sums at stake. And the people involved are ruthless."

CHAPTER 29

As soon as they got back to their room, the Judge called Palmilla, the resort where the cocktail party had been, and asked for a guest, Santiago Lopez, who was with La Opinión. The front desk put the call through to the room, but there was no answer. When voicemail came on, the Judge said, "I am a retired Judge visiting Cabo. I have a matter I must discuss with you, Señor Lopez. It's of the utmost urgency and I'd like to talk to you today." He left his hotel number and his email.

They traded emails through the balance of the morning and early afternoon, the Judge becoming more specific with each email, and more desperate. His final email said he had valuable information relevant to human trafficking in Baja California. Señor Lopez agreed to meet at the main bar of Palmilla at four p.m. for a drink.

The Judge left Katy in the hotel room, under protest, and taxied across the boot of Baha toward San José and Palmilla, repeating his earlier trip now in sunlight, watching the bright blue coast slide by punctuated periodically by one resort after another.

The main bar at Palmilla was adjacent to the dining room of the resort, modern, soft lavender lights, steel bar and stools, lots of silvers and greys in wallpaper and upholstery, complemented by dark wood paneling here and there. It could have doubled as a trendy bar in New York.

There was only one customer in the bar, perched on a stool, a small slight man, Mexican, late forties, huddling over his lone drink, a Jack and Coke. He wore tan shorts and a blue striped business shirt, tails-out, sleeves rolled up, skinny brown feet dangling sandals on the ends of his toes under a barstool just a tad too tall for him.

"Are you Señor Lopez?"

The man glanced sideways, squinting at the Judge in the dull light, then nodded slightly. The Judge piled onto a stool beside him, towering over Lopez, taller and unfortunately heavier. He'd become the typical fat American, the Judge thought, looking across the stacked bottles behind the bar at himself in the mirror.

"I'm the Judge. We spoke by email."

"Yes. You are a man in trouble."

"How do you know?"

"I'm a newspaper man. I smell it on you. Not fear quite yet. Not yet. But anxiety. It'll turn to fear later. It's the way of these things. I've been a reporter a long time."

"Then you know I'm hoping you can help."

"Yes. Don't we all hope that? It's easier to hope than to admit we're alone."

"Can I tell you my story?"

"Better get you a drink first. Here."

The man smacked his hand flat on the bar, making a slapping sound. The louvered partial doors at the other end of the bar swung open and a chubby Mexican appeared like Jack out of his box, dressed in grey slacks and white dress shirt, sleeves rolled up, ready to take a drink order. The Judge ordered rum y Coca, tall, with lemon and sparse ice. Lopez nodded his approval.

A small middle-aged woman stepped into the bar, decked out in a short pink dress, displaying strong muscular legs beneath, raven hair cut short, and soft brown eyes which settled on Lopez. She made a bee-line for him, throwing her arm around his neck and giving him a kiss. Lopez brightened perceptibility, a smile spreading across his face, the tension lines disappearing.

"This is my wife, Alicia, Judge. Isn't she beautiful?"

Color rose a tad in Alicia's cheeks at the compliment. She extended a delicate hand with long fingers to shake the Judge's hand, smiling, cocking her head toward her husband for information.

"The Judge may have a story for me, honey. I'll just be a few minutes. Go get us a table and order us some wine. I'll be there shortly."

She gave the Judge another soft smile, then disappeared around the end of the bar into the dining room.

"Isn't she wonderful? Twenty-three years together, and my pulse still races when she walks into the room. Don't know what she sees in an old goat like me. But she loves me, Judge. You married?"

"Recently. And the problem I have appears to be my new wife's problem as well."

Lopez just nodded. By unspoken agreement they waited, silent, until the bartender set the Judge's drink down in front of him and disappeared again behind his louvers. Then the Judge launched into his story. He started with the tour of the plant, not naming its corporate owner, then described the note passed to him in the restroom, the later discovery of the 14-year-old Cristina stowed away in the back of their van, the army blockade of the road, and the resulting re-capture of Cristina.

Lopez listened intently, scribbling a few notes on a napkin.

The Judge next described the attack on the beach by what he believed to be a drone, and the huge waves that nearly swept the Judge and Katy out to sea.

Lopez nodded, seeing it all in his mind's eye, then stared into space for a time, considering the information, and its source.

"You left something out, Judge."

"Did I?"

"Yes. The name of the company that owned this plant?"

"Yes. It's ASAM."

Lopez looked up sharply. He clearly knew the name.

"You're sure, señor?"

"Yes."

"I see."

"Is this a story of interest to you, Señor Lopez?" asked the Judge. "And perhaps to your cousin, who I understand is Vice Chairman of the Mexican Congress Commission on Human Trafficking."

Lopez was silent again for a time, staring off into space. Finally, he turned back to the Judge. "Sorry, Judge. Not trying to be coy. Just considering the ramifications of your discovery, and the consequence of my delving into it."

"What's that mean?"

"Mexico can be a very dangerous place. It was ranked the world's second-deadliest conflict zone in 2016. There were twenty-three thousand killings in Mexico that year, second only to the Syrian Civil War that left fifty thousand people dead."

The Judge paled.

"And it's a particularly dangerous job to be a newsman in Mexico today, señor. One must be careful, just to stay alive. If one does too many stories, or maybe just one wrong story, or the wrong people are involved, a newsman can be gunned down."

"But the government... the police... don't they protect you?"

"Not like one would wish. In fact, sometimes they're part of the problem. You see, Mexico is going through a freedom of expression crisis right now."

"How so?"

"So many horrible things, all this year. Javier Valdez, one of our most beloved newsmen, correspondent for the daily La Jornada and a co-founder of the regional weekly RíoDoce, was shot on a busy street in broad daylight. His body, his trade-mark straw hat partially covering his head, was just left to lay on the street for a time, roped off by the police.

Another columnist was shot twice as he left a restaurant with his wife and son. A journalist and mother of three was fatally shot eight times outside her home while she was in her car with one of her children. A rolled-up piece of cardboard was left with the words 'being a tattletale'.

A freelance journalist who founded La Voz de Tierra Caliente, was killed at a carwash. And another columnist was shot twice near the city of Cordoba in Veracruz.

More than one hundred newspaper and media journalists have been killed, or simply disappeared, since 2000. Many deaths have been confirmed as related to the victim's journalist work. Most crimes have been improperly investigated and remain unsolved. Very few perpetrators are ever arrested or convicted."

"That's scary."

"It is. So, you see why I'm cautious?"

"Yes."

"Human trafficking is a sad story here in Mexico, señor. Forced labor, forced prostitution, inhuman treatment by human beings of fellow human beings. It is a discouragement for us all who would like to believe in the higher qualities of man."

"You've done stories on trafficking before?"

"Yes, of course. I've tried to shine a light on this… 'industry'. At the beginning of the year I did a story about a typical victim, let's call her Yolanda. Sexually abused by a relative for as long as she could remember, rejected by her mother, Yolanda was twelve, waiting for friends in a Mexico City subway, when a boy selling candy came up, telling her somebody had bought her chocolates. A young man of twenty-two approached, introduced himself, chatted her up, made a date for the next day to drive to nearby Puebla. He picked Yolanda up in a bright red Firebird Trans Am the next afternoon. She was very impressed.

The young man said he loved her. A week later Yolanda moved in with him. She was only twelve remember. For three months it was wonderful. He bought her clothes, shoes, flowers, more chocolates, and treated her well. He seemed to have plenty of money. She finally asked him what business he was in. He told her. He was a pimp.

A few days later he told Yolanda everything she had to do for him, to pay him back for the clothes, the meals, the good times, the roof over her head. He explained the sexual positions, how much she needed to charge, the things she had to do with her client and for how long. How she was to treat her client, how she had to talk to him, how she had to pretend to sexually climax with moans and yelps so the client would give her more money. He took her to Guadalajara for a week and put her in service. She'd start at ten a.m. and finished at midnight. Twenty men per day for a week. Some men would laugh because she was crying. She said she'd close her eyes, so she wouldn't see what they were doing. And try not to feel anything as they used her.

Toward the end of the week, a john gave her a hickey. Her pimp was angry when he spotted it. That's when she said she wanted to quit; to leave. This made her pimp even more angry. He beat her with a chain, punched her with his fists, kicked her, pulled her hair, spit in her face, and burned her with an iron. It was two weeks before he could put her back in service.

After that she was sent to brothels, roadside motels, streets known for prostitution, and even homes. There were no holidays or days off, and after the first few days, she was made to see at least thirty customers a day, seven days a week.

Yolanda was working at a hotel at one point. She'd turned thirteen. The police showed up and shut the place down. She thought she and the other girls would be rescued. But the police took the girls to several rooms and shot video of them in compromising positions. The girls were told the videos would be sent to their families if they didn't do everything the police then asked them to do. Yolanda said what the police then did to them was disgusting. Most of the girls were not even fully developed, all were frightened, sad, crying. Several were only ten years old. It didn't matter to these police.

When Yolanda was fifteen, she gave birth to a baby girl, fathered by her pimp. He threatened to hurt the baby if Yolanda didn't obey him. He took the baby away from her a month after it was born. She was not allowed to see her baby for a year.

Yolanda was finally rescued for real during an anti-trafficking operation in Mexico City. She was sixteen. Her ordeal lasted almost four years. By Yolanda's estimate, she'd had sex with strangers some forty-three thousand times, up to thirty men a day, seven days a week, for almost four years."

"That's awful."

"It is. But I'm afraid not atypical. It highlights the brutal realities of human trafficking in Mexico. And also in your country, señor. In the United States. Human trafficking has also become a trade so lucrative and so prevalent that it knows no borders. The trade links towns in central Mexico with cities like Atlanta, New York, and your own Los Angeles."

"Will you look into my story, Señor Lopez? Consider doing an article on ASAM and its practices?"

"I'd like to. I should. But I want to see the sun come up each day also. Can you blame me?"

"No," the Judge said, disappointment in his voice.

"Who is directing this trafficking at ASAM? Do you know?"

"I don't know who's at the top. The plant manager's name is Castillo. He's clearly involved."

"Let me think about it, señor. I'd have to move quickly if I wanted to verify what you say and then expose it. Before ASAM moves everyone to some other plant, covers their tracks. Either way I'll certainly call my cousin. I think he'll be interested to hear about ASAM and its clandestine activities."

The Judge sat back on his stool with some small relief. This was at least something. He hoped this was the beginning of a solution to the pickle he and Katy were in. As he did so, shifting his angle to the bar, he saw the partial shutters at the other end were open perhaps six inches. The barman was standing there, peeking out, eavesdropping on their conversation. The Judge hoped this was casual curiosity. Not someone prepared to peddle what he'd just heard to the wrong people.

The Judge thanked Lopez and they both got up. Lopez, over the Judge's objection, insisting on taking the tab. They shook hands, Lopez looking the Judge in the eye and saying in a low voice, "Be careful. This is not California, Judge."

Lopez swung around toward the dining room, brightening again at the prospect of seeing his Alicia. The Judge turned and left, feeling just as lonely and isolated as when he'd arrived.

CHAPTER 30

Promptly at seven a.m. the next morning the phone rang in their room, waking the Judge out of a nightmare of sorts, ugly mosquito looking robots diving out of the sky, swarming around his head, as though in some steampunk version of Pearl Harbor. He awoke in a cold sweat, cold because the air was still turned up full tilt, and scrambled for the phone, unfortunately now on Katy's side of the bed.

The gravelly tones of Chief Inspector Garcia didn't bode well, nor did the command he meet the good inspector immediately in the lobby. He threw toothpaste and brush into his mouth briefly, gave up on shaving, jumped into jeans and a rumpled shirt hanging over a room chair, and felt his way out of the room and down toward the elevators, hoping coffee would miraculously appear at the end of his march.

Inspector Garcia was pacing impatiently in the lobby, quashing the idea of coffee, and without discussion escorted the Judge out to a waiting black sedan, shiny and new, the words POLICE DEPARTMENT – CABO SAN LUCAS, emblazoned in small gold letters on its doors. They roared off, leaving a cloud of exhaust, hauling ass down the cobblestone lane through the resort to the street, scattering the hotel housekeeping people walking up the road to begin their shifts.

Garcia turned to the Judge without a smile, and stabbed his finger toward the town. "My Chief wants the murders of María Cervantes and Ana Cervantes solved now, today. No delay. I've decided to enlist your efforts again."

"Where are we going, Garcia?"

"Back to your ASAM plant. Where you saw the drone. Let's see if it, or one like it, is there."

"At the plant?"

"Yes."

"Look, I'm on vacation, Garcia. I've no interest in running around the countryside and…."

Garcia held up his hand, palm outward, into the middle of the Judge's face.

"This isn't for discussion, señor. You're going to help me. And if we're successful, perhaps you and your bride will no longer be targets for a disappearance."

The Judge snapped his mouth shut. Garcia had a point.

They rattled over the same course north as before, traveling at a third again the speed, whizzing through toll booths and around traffic with impunity, everyone seeming to know it was a police vehicle and immediately steering clear. Neither man talked much, accepting the uncomfortable silence between them as a given.

Two-thirds of the way north, Garcia's cell phone rang. He took the call, listening to a report from someone, the line of his mouth growing tighter as he listened. Hanging up, he turned to the Judge with a burr in his voice, "There's a seafarer's word for you, Judge. You're a Jonah."

"What'd I do now?" the Judge asked, spreading his hands to indicate his confusion.

"That was my Chief. The newspaper man, my friend. The one I assume you saw yesterday."

"Lopez?"

"Yes. Our Señor Lopez. Gunned down this morning outside a breakfast restaurant near Palmilla, in front of his wife and his two small children. Four shots to the chest. Died at the hospital."

"Shit," said the Judge. "I spoke to him, met his wife, just yesterday afternoon."

"Yes, señor, I'm sure you did."

The Judge slumped back in his seat, pale now, the enormity of his position hitting like a brick. A part of him wanted to reach for his cell phone and buy tickets for he and Katy on the first flight out of this desolate, miserable little place.

"This has got to be stopped, Garcia. For several days I've been sitting in the belly of this conspiracy. They attempted to drive us into the sea and drown us. It was only pure luck that we ended up back on the beach."

"Like Jonah, Judge? In the belly of the fish for three days, then thrown up onto the shores of Nineveh?"

"Yes. Like Jonah."

The Judge stared out the window for a time, wondering how a simple vacation had turned into such a mess. Finally, he turned back to Garcia.

"Are we wise, Garcia, tumbling into this plant like this? Just you, me and the driver. They have a ton of security people carrying guns around the perimeter and inside. We might be gunned down too."

Garcia gave him a superior look, stretching himself a little taller in his seat. "I want that drone identified, Judge, and the person who used it. It would be their error to start trouble."

They'd reached the bend in the road where the army truck had been three days before, the spot empty now. Five minutes further up the road, a new army truck and a jeep sat at the side of the road, the back of the truck filled with sleepy looking soldiers with automatic weapons. The sedan paused briefly while Garcia huddled out the window with a Captain in the jeep, then sped off again, the military falling in behind. Apparently, Garcia knew his adversaries, and how to play the hand, mused the Judge. It was his country.

The front gate of the plant was just as before, except the security personnel took one look at the little caravan and immediately stacked their weapons against the side of the little booth and stood away, almost at attention. Two soldiers from the truck jumped out and took up stations at the gate, assuring no one would come in or go out.

They drove through the plantation and into the parking lot of the plant, Garcia hopping out of the sedan and marching for the door to the office, leaving the Judge to scramble out the other side and catch up. Garcia bulled his way into the little office and pointed an accusing finger at the rotund receptionist sitting behind the counter.

"Quiero al gerente de la planta aquí." He pointed at his feet. "Now." He made it sound as though she were personally responsible for not having the manager front and center that instant.

Her fingers flew over her small keyboard, calling one location after another, desperately trying to track the manager down. Finally, she reached him, apparently at the back of the plant, because she hung up and whispered, "Cinco minutos." Looking hopeful.

"Harrumph!" was all she got from Garcia.

Three minutes later Castillo came rushing through the shop door, out of breath. He'd apparently run all the way.

Garcia looked suitably attended to, flipping out his badge and shoving it into the face of the panting manager.

"English please, señor, for my friend. You know the Judge already, I understand."

Castillo nodded dumbly, slowly recovering his breath and his toothy smile, worry in his eyes.

"Perhaps we could sit down in my office, Inspector," said the manager, gesturing toward his door. "Juanita, cerveza por favor."

"No," said Garcia. "The Judge and I want to see the plant. Let's go."

They marched up the stairs and out on to the catwalk above the plant floor. The Judge spotted the difference immediately. Everyone was very busy as before, but everyone had white overalls on. There were no blue-clad workers.

"They're gone, Castillo. All the blue workers. The forced slaves. They're all gone."

Castillo burst in to a large political smile, spreading his hands palm up and out, looking like a crocodile suddenly caught on dry land.

"We only have skilled workers here, Judge. Independent, skilled workers. We have no slaves."

"But when I was here, half the plant was dressed in blue overalls. Unskilled labor, forced labor, forced to toil here for scant wages or none at all, no hope of leaving. Slave labor."

Castillo turned to Garcia. "Do you know what he's talking about Inspector? I haven't a clue. Americans are so… emotional."

The Judge started to say more, angry now, but Garcia held up his hand, stifling their exchange.

"We're here about murder, Castillo. The murder of María Cervantes and Ana Cervantes. And an attack on the Judge last night. By one of your drones."

"I don't know what you are talking about, Inspector."

"The Judge has drawn this picture of the drone that attacked him last night. Does this look like one of yours?"

Castillo took the sketch, his face turning pale. "Well, maybe. Doubtful though. If anything, it might bear a vague resemblance to Station 32's drone. But I'm sure it's not. No. Definitely not one of ours."

"Let's see the Station 32 drone, señor."

"That's top secret. You don't have clearance."

"NOW!"

Castillo capitulated, looking scared. "Yes, yes. Okay. This way. Let's go down on the floor and see."

They climbed down metal stairs to the plant floor, and Castillo led them to the back of the plant and off to the left where a partially assembled drone stood atop a wide work bench like an overfed praying mantis preparing to jump. It was one of the ugliest things the Judge had ever seen. Shaped like a pod, with a circular helicopter rotor above, and rocket fins at its stern for getaway flights. A nasty looking video camera at its front acted as a single cyclops eye, and a row of nozzles below suggested a mouth, no doubt for spraying gas. It rested on long, spindly, insect legs. Various spikes with sensors jutted out here and there across its skin, and in front, two long pincer arms extended out threateningly.

"That's it all right," said the Judge. "Except at the end of the pincer arms were sharp buzz sawblades, whirling while it was in flight."

"No. It couldn't possibly be."

"Yes. It is. Does it come with a cutting blade attachment?"

"Err, well, not exactly."

"You mean 'yes' Castillo, don't you?" said Garcia.

Castillo nodded reluctantly.

"There is as an option."

"What does the controller look like?" asked the Judge.

Castillo picked up a modified iPad from the work bench and handed it to the Judge.

"Range?"

"Short. About twenty blocks."

"How many of these creatures do you have here?" asked Garcia.

Castillo called a technician over. They conversed in Spanish, while Garcia eavesdropped. Castillo's complexion paled again, almost matching the technician's white coat.

"One is missing from their inventory, Judge," said Garcia. "Missing about a week. They had four completed units here. Now they have three."

"How convenient."

Castillo gave the Judge his toothy smile again, spreading his hands palms up.

"Who had access to this missing drone?" asked Garcia.

"Just Pedro here, the technician. He has the master key to the inventory room for the completed drones."

"Pedro, I've read drones are sometimes used to herd sheep. Is that true?" asked the Judge.

"Si, señor." Pedro was now balancing his weight on one foot and then the other, looking around the plant over the Judge's shoulder, avoiding eye contact.

"How's that work?"

"Drones can be set to guard a perimeter, or a block of space. They then herd livestock back into the confines of the space if they wander past the set boundaries."

"Set with automatic instructions?"

"Si."

"Can a drone be set to herd an individual sheep, say, in a specific direction one wants it to go in?"

"Si."

"Automatically, pre-programed?"

"Si."

"Can a drone be programed to return to its base or a set landing spot after it completes such a task?"

"Si, señor."

"Programmed to hover at a high altitude for a period, until it's needed?"

"Si."

"How long can it stay aloft?"

"With spare tanks, depending on its size and weight, and its flight characteristics, perhaps up to ten hours."

"What about submersible drones? Ones that swim?"

Pedro looked startled. "Those are confidential, señor."

"Not for us, Pedro. Tell me all you know, and now," said Garcia.

Pedro sighed. "They're based on drone swarm theory. Very small drones, the size of a small fish, with steel jaws. They can be released underwater in a group and then controlled as a swarm, maneuvered to a specific location, and used to guard a perimeter."

"Or attack a target?" asked the Judge.

"I guess they could be used for that. They are controlled by remote, like other drones, but operate almost as a single unit, as a swarm."

"Like piranha?" asked the Judge.

Pedro was looking very uncomfortable now. "Yes. I suppose."

"And you manufacture these here?"

"Only a few, on an experimental basis."

"Can we see one?"

"They seem to be misplaced right now. I was doing an inventory count last week and I couldn't find them. It's a single box of prototypes, easy to lose in our lockup."

"How many fish drones?"

"Perhaps six."

"Fully operational?"

"Well, pretty much. One could pilot them as a swarm underwater in a pond or something."

"Or in a sea lagoon?"

"I suppose."

Garcia turned and barked at the plant manager. "Pack the three remaining drones up. Put them in my army truck out front. And no further drones leave this plant until I advise you. Understood?"

"Si, señor." Castillo almost saluted, some color returning to his face.

"Put Pedro on the truck too. We'll talk to him some more back in Cabo. And I'll expect to see you in my office as well, Castillo, at one p.m. tomorrow."

Garcia imperially swung on his heel and started to walk to the front of the plant, leaving the Judge to trail behind again.

"What about the forced labor people, Garcia? What about the sex slaves? What about Cristina? And Felipe Martínez? We can't just abandon them. Just because these bastards set up shop with their victims somewhere else is no reason to look the other way."

"Not my department, Judge. I'm only interested in murder," said Garcia, waving his hand, pushing air away from his head as though it were all nonsense.

And so they left. The Judge fuming, arguing to at least peek into the dormitories behind the plant, to no avail. Hustled into the SUV and carted off, back to Cabo, Garcia simply ignoring him.

As they pulled into the back side of the town, something nagging at the edge of the Judge's mind took flight, blossoming into a full flung idea. "Garcia, can you call your office and get a telephone number for me?"

"Whose number do you want?"

"All Mexico Transfer Agent."

"Who? Who's that?"

"The transfer agent for ASAM shares."

"Oh." Garcia took his cell out and called to get the number, then punched it into his phone and pressed call, handing the phone to the Judge.

"Hello. I understand you are the transfer agent and the keeper of the shareholder records for ASAM. I need some information on outstanding shares. Can you help me please?" The Judge was routed to another person and repeated his request.

"Who am I? I represent Alan Clark, one of ASAM's key consultants, and he has asked me to check on an issue regarding its shares."

"No, I need the information now. I don't have time to submit paperwork, or obtain board approval for release of information."

"Okay, then, perhaps you'd like to give the information to Chief Inspector Garcia of the Cabo San Lucas Police Department."

The Judge handed the cell back to Garcia, who barked his identity and title into the phone. "Now that you know who I am, let me talk to your supervisor, por favor." He snapped. Thirty seconds later Garcia lapsed into Spanish, speaking staccato fashion into the phone, his voice rising with each sentence, clearly snarling over the voice of the supervisor in the transfer agent office. Garcia went silent for a few beats, listening, then handed the cell back to the Judge. "Tell them what you want."

The senior supervisor on the other end of the line, older and terribly apologetic, listened with bated breath to each word now as the Judge spoke.

"I want to know if anyone has filed with your office an irrevocable proxy, or a proxy trust, or any sort of document or agreement that affects any ASAM shareholder's right to vote his shares, or assigns voting rights to another party."

"Let me look," said the clerk.

A minute and a half later the clerk was back, suggesting the Judge take a pen and pencil.

"A proxy coupled with an interest was filed for all the ASAM shares owned by Roberto Cervantes, granting the irrevocable right to vote all of his shares in ASAM to his designated agent in perpetuity."

"And who is Roberto Cervantes's designated agent?"

"It doesn't give a name. It just appoints someone else to determine who the designated agent is to be."

"And who has the power to appoint the designated agent to vote the shares?"

"A Juan Moreno, Attorney at Law. ASAM's Corporate Counsel."

CHAPTER 31

The Judge was unceremoniously dumped at the front door of the Hotel Finisterra, as if excess baggage now he'd served his purpose in identifying the drone. It was three in the afternoon.

He mentally said to hell with Garcia and his murder case, determined to move on to enjoying his vacation in this never never land of Baja, looking forward to dinner with Katy. It was hot in the lobby, and hot in the elevator and hot in the hallway, and unfortunately hot in the hotel suite, Katy having gone somewhere and taken her key card out of the pocket beside the door, shutting down the air-conditioning.

Katy must have been gone awhile, otherwise the suite would still be cool. Her cell phone and passport weren't on the bureau; perhaps a little shopping, a blood sport for her; a ritual he detested.

As he stood by the wall, trying to crank the air up to its maximum, the phone rang. A pleasant voice sounded over the phone, with a slight hint of a Mexican accent, asking to speak to his wife. "Katy's not here right now. This is her husband, the Judge. Can I take a message?"

"Yes, of course. This is the U.S. Consular Agency in San José del Cabo. Katy was here this morning, seeking help for a young lady she met, and she believes is a victim of human trafficking in Mexico. I promised to get her a Mexican government contact in

Mexico City who might be able to help. Can I give you the information?"

"Yes, please."

"José Ramiro is the Senior Staff Attorney for the Congressional Commission on Human Trafficking and Enforced Labor. We've referred matters to him before; he's very dedicated to his job."

He rattled off a telephone number which the Judge jotted down.

"What time did my wife leave your office, if I may ask?"

"About eleven a.m."

"Thank you." The Judge hung up.

He stretched out on the bed and pretended the temperature was cooler, drifting off into a troubled sleep, the tension in his body slowly receding, occasionally startling himself awake with a random snore. Finally, he shook himself awake, stood up, and stretched. The clock by the bed said six p.m. Katy should have been back. But she wasn't. The Judge was concerned.

He took out his cell phone and dialed Katy, despite their mutual promises not to use their cells because of expensive Mexican cell rates. There was an immediate dull ringing from the closet beside the bathroom. Three steps and the Judge was looking inside the closet, at the wall safe there, rumbling with the ringing from Katy's cell phone. She'd left her cell in the safe. Damn.

The Judge opened the safe with the code, always his birthday, and pulled out her phone, her passport, and her purse. She'd come back to the room, put her things in the safe, then left again. He grabbed his hat and headed for the pool, expecting to find her asleep under an umbrella. But both pools held no Katy, nor did either restaurant around the pools, nor did the lobby bar or the restaurant on the upper level of the resort. The Judge was frantic now.

He returned to the room and checked his computer. There was no email from Katy. His phone had no text from her either; of course not, he had her phone. He sat there for a while, letting the cool air waft over him from the overworked conditioner, trying to think.

He called down to the lobby to asked if there were any messages. It turned out a package had been left at the desk for him. He asked them to send it up immediately.

He paced the room for twenty minutes until a bellhop arrived with a small square box wrapped with brown paper and string, collected his tip, and scooted out. The Judge looked at the package, rolling it around in his hands. There was no indication of the sender. There was only the Judge's name in printed letters on its top. The Judge had a bad premonition. Taking a big breath, he tore the sting and paper off, and opened the box.

His heart stopped. Nestled inside was a patch of soft aqua material and elastic. Katy's bra!

CHAPTER 32

The Judge charged about the room like a bull, cursing Mexico and all its inhabitants, raging. He finally forced himself to take deep breaths, to calm his pounding heart, lower his blood pressure. He splashed cold water on this face and sat on the edge of the bed again, trying to think.

He took Chief Inspector Garcia's card from this pocket and dialed the Inspector, forced to leave a message when Garcia didn't answer. He took the note he'd made for Katy from the U.S. Consular Agency in San José del Cabo, dialed the office, and after several minutes of fighting with an after-hours switchboard, was patched through to the same pleasant voice, now sounding tired, the sounds of food preparation echoing in the background, likely his kitchen.

The U.S. Consular guy was appalled, but had little to give in concrete help. He said the best he could do was move an urgent message up through State Department Channels, over to the Mexican counterparts, and down to the local police, the Federal police, and the Mexican Army, seeking all assistance. It sounded like a bureaucratic thicket that would take time. He promised to start making calls immediately.

After that the Judge just sat on the bed, holding his head in his hands, rocking slowly back and forth, distraught, uncertain what else to do.

Forty-five minutes later the Judge was pacing the room again. It was coming up on nine p.m., and an orange and pink sunset had faded now to black; black sky, black water, black mood. The Judge finally settled in a balcony chair, brooding at the occasional whiff of white and corresponding crack of sound that confirmed the surf was still there, still turbulent, still dangerous.

It was then the room phone rang. The Judge desperately snatched at it.

"Señor Judge, we have something we think you might want. She is unharmed. But you need to come pick her up right away, before something untoward happens."

"Where? When?"

He hastily scribbled down an address, and a name: Hernando. He dashed for the door, taking the stairs down two at a time, the elevators being too damn slow, threaded through a crowded lobby now bustling with late-night check-ins, and squeezed past a couple just alighting from a cab, throwing himself into its back seat, cutting off another couple waiting in line.

He shoved his scribbled note under the driver's nose, muttering, "Pronto."

"Si, señor. I know it well," said the driver, thrusting the taxi into gear.

As they sped down the main drag of Cabo, the driver called over his shoulder.

"Señor, this is not the best place. It's not so nice. It's in the Zonas Rojas. There are better places for you right here, downtown. Across from Cabo Wabo is a fine place. Much younger, prettier girls, and very accommodating. Perhaps you should try there first."

"No. Just take me quickly. What's the Zonas Rojas?"

"It's supposed to be where the government has issued permits for certain clubs in a designated area of town, called the Zonas Rojas, Red Zone. The girls are required to go to a doctor every day before going to work. If a girl is caught working on the street the cops give her a hard time and take all her money, but if she sells her favors at one of the clubs in the Zonas Rojas, it's legal."

"Why do you say, 'supposed to be'?"

"Like anything, the law says one thing but in practice it's another. This is Mexico, señor." The driver smiled.

"How so?"

"In the Zonas Rojas only about one in ten of the girls are registered. And only a quarter of the clubs have licenses. I recommend you stay here in town. It will cost you about a hundred-fifty for the works. If you want a room, there's a room charge too. You'll get all the touching, blow job, hand job, fingering and positions you want, and a massage. Of course, all this must be negotiated beforehand. You know, señor, to avoid miscommunication."

"And what's it like where we're going now?"

"Cheaper, señor. But it's more for local men. I don't think you'll be as happy."

"Get me there quickly."

"Si, señor."

They wound through the back streets of outer Cabo, always northward, always higher on the mesa. There was no moon and the streets were dark, the street lights disappearing after a few blocks from the center.

Finally, the cab driver slowed, then stopped at an unlighted intersection. A small market, closed, on one corner, a worn looking two-story building on the other, white washed, with blue paint running waist high along its walls. A small neon sign over its door proclaimed, El Ratón.... The Mouse. There seemed to be no one around.

"I will pay you a very big bonus, señor," said the Judge. "But I need you to stay here and wait for me. If I don't come back within thirty minutes, I need you to call the number on this card. Tell the gentleman I'm in need of help." The Judge handed the driver Inspector Garcia's card.

The driver took the card, nodding his understanding, looked at it, gave a low whistle. "You know some important people, señor."

The Judge got out of the taxi, crossed the dusty street, more dirt than pavement, and pushed at the front door of The Mouse. It swung inward, and he stepped in.

"EEK!" Two girls screeched together, one pointing to the Judge as he stepped inside, "What a handsome vaquero."

The place was dim, flooded with fuchsia from overhead spots that left dark patches in the corners and indistinct shapes at the handful of tables. The smell of stale beer invaded his nostrils.

Concrete walls and ceiling were painted a dusty red, as was a supported dance pole in one corner, surrounded on two sides by mirrors, and strobe lights not yet turned on. A portal in the left wall led out to a large open-air patio under the stars. Rickety looking wooden chairs and tables were spread here and there, some occupied. A narrow wooden staircase curved up beside the patio's portal, leading to a second floor.

In the middle of the opposite wall ran a small bar, punctuated at one end by a jukebox, its multi-colored lights flashing, chumming for coin. On the other end, a pool cue rack hung on the wall, and in front a small pool table. It was a long way from the posh clubs of downtown Cabo.

Four women leaned against the bar in various stages of undress, young but large, whale-like, two beckoning the Judge over with fluttering hands, the other two eyeing him with commercial interest. Three men, assorted ages, lingered at separate tables in the middle, two with young señoritas plying drinks. Beer. At the third table, a healthy young female of sizable proportion was performing a lap-dance on a scrawny young man, buried beneath her in his chair, barely visible around her soft edges. He seemed to be enjoying himself, her swimsuit top off and wrapped around his neck, his nose buried in her boobs.

The Judge was the only gringo.

As his eyes adjusted to the light, the Judge could see other shapes in the darkened corners huddled at tables, some just watching, some in negotiation. The place was ramshackle and depressing.

The Judge pulled a dusty chair out from an empty table in the shadows and took a seat, sweating profusely now from the heat and the tension. Katy wasn't in the room.

One girl from the bar ambled over, settled uninvited in the empty chair across from the Judge, sending out a cloud of cheap perfume that engulfed him, impeding his breathing. He wondered if he would be sick.

"Hi, señor. Nice to meet you." She stuck out a small meaty paw to formally shake hands.

She looked to be early twenties, sparkling brown eyes in a broad brown face, full ruby lips, long sleek black hair cascading across her shoulder and over one of her prodigious breasts, encased in an ivory transparent top. She wore tight pants, bright purple, so tight they looked like a second skin.

"I'm looking for someone," said the Judge.

"I know everyone here, señor. Buy me a drink and I'll help."

He nodded his okay.

She waved her arm in the air, and a tired old man toddled over, white wispy hair, ragged jeans, light blue shirt matching his crinkly blue eyes, wearing a white apron covered with stains. He held two glasses of beer in one hand, and a disreputable looking washcloth in the other, with which he gave the tabletop a perfunctory wipe. Then he shoved the beers down on the table.

"The smaller one is mine, señor," said the girl. "They don't want me to get too drunk." She giggled. "Would you like a lap-dance. I'm very expertise."

"No. No. I need to meet someone here."

"Well, now you've met me. Trust me, I'm all you can handle and more. You don't need to meet anyone else."

"No, this is business."

She pouted for a moment, real disappointment showing in her eyes. "Who do you need to meet?"

"Hernando."

She jumped back in her chair as though having touched something hot. Fear creeping in around the edges of her eyes. She looked around nervously, nodded mutely, stood, and tried to effectuate a nonchalant attitude as she crossed the room to the stairs and went up.

Sixty-seconds later another female flounced down in the abandoned chair, wearing a string bikini under a sheer cover of pink mesh. Thinner than the other one he'd met, younger, more attractive, she had an engaging smile and a devil-may-care look in her eyes. She looked like she enjoyed her work.

"I'm Alisa, señor. Will you buy me a drink too?"

The Judge waved his hand in the air, summoning the relic of a bartender again, who produced two more beers even though the Judge hadn't started his first.

"I am waiting for someone," said the Judge. "Your friend has gone off to get him."

"That's okay, dear. When the cat's away, the mice will play, si? You look very tense, baby. Have your beer and then we can loosen you up a little. Just for fun. For free."

"I'm not here for that."

"Of course you're not. But you're an American male, si? An American bull. You have certain needs. I understand. I know how to help."

She reached over and put her small hand on top of his.

"We can fix this together. It's how we're made. It works every time." She gave him a big smile.

"No. You don't understand. I'm married. I'm…"

"Don't worry, baby. No charge. Let me just sit on your lap for a moment. All will feel better. No more tension." Her hand moved under the table to rest on his thigh.

"No." His voice was too loud. Heads at the other tables turned. It got very quiet. There was suddenly tension in the room. Then someone marched over and plugged a coin into the jukebox. The sounds of the Beach Boys, singing 'Barbara Ann', pervaded the space. Everyone relaxed. Except for the Judge.

"Why do you do this work?" asked the Judge.

"Oh señor. You want to hear my sad little story?" Alisa rolled her eyes, smiling again.

"Yes."

"This is my truth, amigo. I don't tell everyone. I have two small niñas, two girls, two and four, and a bad husband. He beats me, drinks all the time, doesn't work much, we live with his mother who has a little store and treats me like shit. I am as you Yankees say, 'stuck'. So, I work here, I save my money. He doesn't know what I make, I hide it. When I have enough, my niñas and I will leave, go to Mexico City. I'll get a real job, and the niñas will go to school."

"It must be hard."

"It is. But it's my chance. People look down on us, on what we do. Call us ugly names. But I like sex. It's a natural thing. And without this opportunity I would be stuck with my abusive husband forever. I am fortunate for this job, the owners treat us sexoservidoras like family, and soon I'll be off to my new life."

She sat back in her chair, her fantasy brightening her face. The Judge wondered if it would work out that way. Life had the habit of throwing you rabbit punches continuously.

The other girl had returned, suddenly appearing behind Alisa's chair, not happy her seat was filled. There was a harsh exchange in quick Spanish, then Alisa bolted from the chair and moved quickly back to the bar, the first girl taking her place.

"Hernando is coming," she said.

"Good. I'll just wait here. I don't want company."

She looked disappointed, reluctantly raising her bulk and sliding from the table again. Stalking back to the bar. Not looking back. Pissed.

Three minutes later a tall thin Mexican came down the stairs, slowly, cautiously, surveying the room carefully. He looked at the Judge last, nodded almost imperceptibility, headed for the Judge's table. He had on green golf pants, faded from use, and a white shirt, freshly pressed. Mid-thirties, his gaunt face was elongated, matched by a long narrow nose, punctuated by a thin mustache and pock-marked from old acne. His small eyes shifted continually, evaluating his surroundings. Like a weasel, thought the Judge.

He settled into the chair across from the Judge, the Judge barely controlling his anger, his desire to reach across the table and grab the man by the throat.

The man sensed the Judge's rage, putting his hands up, palms outward.

"She's okay," he whispered. "Nothing has happened to her. I'm just a messenger. Don't shoot the messenger, señor."

"What do you want?" hissed the Judge.

"Nothing, señor. You can have her back now. This is just a warning."

"A warning?"

"Si, señor. I'm asked to point out to you this is Mexico. You're not in your California anymore. Things are different here. Culture is different. Laws are different. The way things are done is different. It does no good to meddle down here; to stir things up. You cannot change anything. You can only make trouble for yourselves."

"And?"

"And you and your lady are to stop crusading about human trafficking in our country. It is our country. If there is trafficking, it is none of your concern. Besides, many people wish to be what you call 'trafficked'. What you see as slavery they see as opportunity. These women here might be called trafficked. But they are here of their own free will. It is their ticket to a better life. You have no right to judge unless you stand in their shoes, see their lives as they see them. And that you can never do."

"Where's Katy?"

"Follow me, señor. But slowly, quietly. This is a fine old club. We don't want to disturb the patrons, or make the staff feel uncomfortable."

Weasel got up from his chair, slowly, turned, and moved back to the stairs. The Judge followed. The second story had a long corridor lit by small faint bulbs, tattered carpeting, and small bedrooms at intervals on each side, some doors open, some closed. The smell of sweat and sex and condoms hung like a blanket in the hallway. As they passed the first room the Judge heard the universal sounds of sex behind its closed door, mattress springs creaking in a steamy rhythm, a high female voice moaning with excitement, then a final male grunt, more gasp than yell, followed by silence.

Weasel led the Judge to the last door on the left, and gestured for the Judge to enter, which he did.

In the half light of a shielded bulb he saw Katy sitting dejectedly in her aqua panties on a bed, arms folded defensively across bare breasts, an older duenna sitting quietly beside her. Katy looked up, caught the Judge's blue eyes blazing at her, jumped for him, throwing her arms around him, clinging, beginning to softly whimper.

The duenna handed him a dirty blanket, which he wrapped around her protectively as he whispered, "Did they hurt you? Did they do anything to you?"

"No. No, Judge. For God's sake get me out of this hole."

He turned with her, her salty tears wetting the front of his shirt, and walked her through the door, down the corridor, down the steps, across the club floor, and out across the half-paved road to the waiting cab, gently helping her in.

"Get us out of here!" he snarled at the cab driver.

CHAPTER 33

The Judge drew a hot bath, helped Katy out of her panties, and eased her in, adding liberal amounts of bubble bath supplied by the hotel, trying to make her feel whimsical in the warm tub.   It was uphill work.

She was emotionally damaged. Her taken-for-granted secure world no longer secure. Suddenly she was just another leaf twirling around in the storm, subject to the happenstance of fate and luck, captive to events, currents and people around her, people who could snatch her up in an instant.

And beneath that he sensed something else. What? Anger?... No. It was more. It was rage.

He gave her a sleeping pill and curled up around her in the bed, protective, as she nodded off into a troubled sleep, tossing and turning, whimpering occasionally.

He was so very glad to have her back.

He popped out of bed at his usual six a.m., California time, did some legal work on this computer, and gazed over at Katy occasionally. She was now in a deep sleep.

He ordered room service for ten a.m. Everything. Three juices, omelet, fried eggs with verde sauce (his personal favorite), bacon, sausage, ham, fried potatoes, refried beans, three kinds of pastry, corn tortillas, and double orders of steaming coffee and tea. He wasn't sure what she'd want.

She awoke with the clatter of the cart, set up out on the balcony facing the sea, the breeze wafting in the smell of fresh coffee as he uncapped the pot. She slipped into a hotel robe and wandered out to the balcony, settling in a chair beside him, silent, brooding, focused on the distant blue horizon above the churning surf.

He poured her coffee with a little skim milk, the way she liked it, and passed the mug over. She took it in both hands, cradling the heat through the porcelain, smelling its aroma, then softly sipping.

They sat like that for a while, drifting. Finally, he spoke "How are you?"

She looked at him then, anger rising again in her eyes. "I want to bury those sons-of-bitches."

"It might be better to let it go. Pack up and head for L.A. Let them keep their crazy country."

"No, Judge. No. That girl. Cristina. She deserves our help. Fuck these people. They're destroying lives, multiplying human misery. Scavengers. They're a scourge on our entire race. It makes all of us poorer, all of us worth something less. It must be stomped out wherever it appears, without exception and without restraint. It must be hounded out of existence. It must end."

The Judge sighed.

"I have the feeling that means you don't want to go home quite yet."

She turned to face him then, aqua eyes ablaze, raging again.

The Judge nodded. It was her call.

He passed her his scribbled note from the U.S. Consular office guy in Cabo San José: containing the name and telephone number of the Senior Staff Attorney for the Mexican Congressional Commission on Human Trafficking and Enforced Labor. She took the note, looked at it for sixty seconds, thoughtful, stood up, abandoning the well-laid breakfast, and headed for her cell phone.

He wasn't the only person who was pig-headed in this family, he mused. Then, realizing he was famished, he dug into her abandoned breakfast with relish.

From the balcony, he heard Katy carrying on sequential conversations, a couple obviously conference calls. She seemed to get some traction in Mexico City. Touching buttons, triggering nerves, stirring up bureaucrats. And not just in Mexico. He heard her talking to someone from a group called The Coalition to Abolish Slavery and Trafficking. He also heard California Against Slavery, and another group called Anti-Slavery International in the U.K. He shuddered to think what his telephone bill would look like. She was stirring up a wildfire. He just hoped it didn't back around and consume them.

Two and a half hours later she reappeared on the balcony, exhausted, dark circles showing under her eyes, looking ruefully at the remains of their breakfast, well picked over by the Judge.

"Let's go have lunch by the pool, Judge. I'm in need of a stiff drink and some protein."

They wandered down by the pool, she outfitted in her new bikini, lavender, with spangles, too skimpy for the Judge's taste. But she was proud of the way her figure was bouncing back from delivery of their son, and he would not complain. Double margaritas were ordered with tacos, fajitas and nachos. Her appetite had returned. And there was new sparkle in her eyes.

"So, what's it all mean, Judge? First someone tries to kill us on the beach, then they turn around and give you a soft warning by kidnapping me?"

"It wasn't a soft warning to me, Katy. But yes, a puzzle, isn't it? Someone killed María and then Ana on that rooftop. They are culpable and vulnerable, and they know it. If we'd simply been swept out to sea by a rogue wave off that beach, it would have been an unfortunate accident, taking the heat off. It was easy play for them with their modified drone. It would have been billed as a tragic accident. And it almost worked."

"Did you hear back from your newspaper guy, Santiago Lopez?"

"Not from him, but about him. Unfortunately, Katy, he's dead. They gunned him down the very next morning after I talked to him, in front of his wife and two small children."

"Oh my God, Judge. I'm so sorry. I didn't know."

"Whoever this is, they play for keeps, Katy. We're damn lucky to get you back yesterday. I don't want you leaving my side again until we walk off the plane at LAX."

"Well let's make a deal, Judge. You focus on the murders. Figure out who killed those two poor women; hand the culprits over to Inspector Garcia so they fry. I'm going to create such an outpouring of attention on forced labor and human sex trafficking in Mexico they're going to think they've had a blow torch shoved up their collective asses."

"You're sure you want to play it this way?"

"I am."

"Okay. But whatever you do, you need to do it quickly, concentrated, so they have no opportunity to strike back. It's got to be a blitzkrieg."

"I'm working on it Judge. You go solve your murders."

They ceremonially clinked their margarita glasses, now empty and in need of replenishment.

The Judge wondered then if they were being foolishly optimistic and naive about what they could accomplish. He felt a tinge of queasiness when he considered the personal risks and the stark ruthlessness of their opponents. But Katy was on a tear; he knew she wouldn't be stopped. It was up close and personal now.

CHAPTER 34

They trooped back toward the room through the intense heat, both from above and blasting up under their feet from the reflective concrete surface of the pathways. The Judge had a fleeting fantasy of wading into the pool, shorts and all, and up to the shaded swim-up bar for a piña colada, but pushed it aside. Katy was all business now, no longer on vacation. There was no time for swim-up bars.

When they reached the room, Katy went back to her cell, contacting the United Nations, the State Department, and talking more with the Special Prosecutor Office for Human Trafficking in Mexico City. She also spoke to the editorial staffs of El Universal and Milenio, the two largest newspapers in Mexico City. The Judge could see she'd be at it all afternoon.

About three p.m. the room phone rang. The Judge picked it up to hear the voice of Chief Inspector Garcia, who was downstairs and wanted to talk. The Judge left Katy in the room on her cell and headed down.

He could see as he approached Garcia across the lobby that the man was not happy. His face was practically pink. He was restraining himself, with difficulty, from yelling at the Judge as he approached. They settled in a small nook off the lobby, and the Judge took the high ground.

"Where the hell were you yesterday, Garcia? Christ, Katy was kidnapped. I called you out of desperation. You never showed up, never returned my call, stonewalled me as though I didn't exist. Are you part of this network of bribes and favors which makes human trafficking big business in Mexico? Were you told not to come?"

Garcia looked like he would be apoplectic. Turning redder, almost gasping for breath, finally getting out, "I was here, you idiot, but you had gone. No note, no message, no return call. You just wasted my time, señor."

"You could have called me back Garcia."

Garcia glowered at him.

"Anyway, Judge, I understand your precious Katy is back, so that all worked out."

"What do you mean it worked out? They kidnapped her right out of our room, subjected her to emotional and psychological abuse, forced her to disrobe in front of three jeering thugs, kept her in a dirty room in a brothel for eight hours without food, insinuated they were going to press her into sexual service. She was a wreck when I finally got to her."

"But unharmed physically."

"Barely. How do you know I got her back?"

Garcia's coloring shot up again.

"Jesus, Judge. My Chief's switchboard started lighting up like a Christmas tree about ten-thirty this morning. Calls from the Special Prosecutor in Mexico City, calls from the Governor, from the Lieutenant Governor, from the mayor, from the major Mexican newspapers, from your Department of State, from the U.N., from various do-gooder groups around the world and inside Mexico.

Your wife has created a fuckin' shit-storm of controversy. She's even alleged our Army was involved, that it colluded with the traffickers. The Chief got a call from the Deputy Commander for armed forces in Baha California. And he wasn't happy. He's a man you don't cross."

The Chief Inspector was clenching and unclenching his fists now, his mouth just a grim line.

"And?"

"Tell her to stop. She's got to stop. She's shaking a tree that's best not shook."

"We both know it's too late for that Garcia. She's shined a spotlight on your cozy network that traffics in people. There's going to be a mother of an investigation, and I hope many heads roll."

Garcia sighed, took a deep breath, visibly trying to calm himself.

"You two are a playing a dangerous game, Judge. You're gambling this investigation she's ginned up will stop further retaliation against you two personally. But you may have miscalculated. Have you considered the risks if you're wrong?"

It was the Judge's turn to clench his fists. Garcia was right, of course. Their safest course would be to let it go, grab the first plane back to Los Angeles. Had it been his decision, that's what he might have done.

But it was Katy's decision. She was the one who had suffered, been humiliated. Their twenty-year age difference mattered in such things. She still had the principles of youth, unbent by the cynicism of too much experience and the caution of old age. He admired her for it. He couldn't just trash her decision, shut her down. And in the end, he knew she was right. One had to fight for what was right, sometimes at great personal sacrifice. It was the way of humanity as it tried to totter forward, in hit or miss fashion, toward something better than the present.

"I want a guard for her, Garcia."

"What?"

"I want a guard for Katy, while we're here in Mexico, until this all blows over. Someone I can count on. Someone that's clean."

Garcia sighed again. Nodded reluctantly. "Okay, let me see who I can find."

"So, what's happening on the murder case?"

"Who's had time?" said Garcia, spreading his hands.

"We need to get to the bottom of it, Garcia. And I'd like to help."

"Help however you like, Judge. I encourage you to do so. I'd much rather have a murder case to present to the Chief, than spend my time fighting this back-fire your bride has set."

"Are the upper floors of the timeshare building and its roof still cordoned off?"

"Yes. Tightly sealed."

"And you searched the roof carefully?"

"Yes. Nothing."

"Your men immediately sealed off the timeshare tower and the grounds after María fell?"

"Yes."

"No one in or out through the point of your complete search of everyone at the scene?"

"Yes."

"And the grounds were immediately searched?"

"Yes."

"No one out of place outside? No one who didn't belong?"

"No."

"And this was all done instantly as Ana went up on that roof?"

"Yes."

"So essentially the time share building was sealed off from the time Ana went up onto the roof, playing her part as María?"

"Yes."

"And after Ana fell, there was no one on another roof?"

"No. Not that we could find."

"Anyone else in the other buildings connected with the timeshare project?"

"No."

"You found no one who seemed strange or out of place?"

"No. Just timeshare owners and vacationing tourists. All accounted for, all seemingly innocent."

"So, either the killer of María slipped away before you sealed the site, which means there was a second killer who killed Ana, which seems highly unlikely, or there was just one killer who was still there, still on site, saw his opportunity to pick another board member off, and took it."

"That makes sense, Judge."

"Yet the only non-unit owner people on site were in the boardroom and in the sales office a floor below?"

"Yes."

"And was there anyone down a floor in the sales office who was connected to either María or Ana?"

"No. There were you and your wife, a young couple recently married, and four sales staff, all vetted, all with no apparent motive to attack either of the deceased."

"What about the boardroom? It was searched?"

"There's nothing to search, Judge. Just underneath the conference table and in the wine cabinets."

"Suppose we assume that someone at the board meeting was responsible for the two deaths."

"Yes, Judge, and if we do?"

"Then there's only one person who'd have had the opportunity to manipulate a drone from that meeting."

"Who?"

"I'd have to show you. Why don't we call another meeting there, back in the boardroom, put everybody back in the same positions, and see what happens?"

CHAPTER 35

It was five p.m. in the timeshare tower on the 20th floor. They all trooped into the boardroom like delinquent children: Miguel Cervantes, the surviving child of José Cervantes, the oldest brother; the clique of Luis, Rosa and Roberto Cervantes, the grandchildren of Antonio Cervantes, the second brother; and old Pablo, the surviving third brother. Behind them followed Alan Clark, Officer Gonzales, and Juan Moreno, the ASAM attorney.

The attorney still looked shifty, Alan was all smiles, his usual charming self, and Gonzales just looked dense. Garcia, the Judge, and a second police officer to keep order, were waiting for them. The Judge had placed placards with names at the seat where María had sat and Ana had sat. A stack of placards with everyone else's name was handed out and they settled into their accustomed seats, putting their placard in front of them on the table.

"So," said Garcia. "We're going to replay what happened at the board meeting one more time. Mr. Clark, will you play María? And Officer Gonzales will play Ana."

Alan Clark turned pale. He definitely didn't want to play María. The rest of the board looked sullen. No one wanted to be here.

"So, Mr. Clark, you're María. You're here at the head of the table with your back to the view. Correct, everyone?"

They nodded.

"Gonzales is Ana, here to the left."

They nodded again.

"Luis, you're at the other end of the table, back to the elevator. Stand up and point your finger at Clark."

Luis stood and stuck out a hand, pointing.

"Now, Alan, as María you've had it with Luis's crap. You need a smoke. You're going to turn and stomp out of the boardroom, passing the Judge in the hall, going to the stairs leading to the roof."

"María generally lasted an hour and then would have to call a break and leave for the roof to have her smoke," volunteered Pablo.

They nodded in agreement.

"I suppose it proves that nicotine kills," said Luis. They ignored his black humor.

"Go on, Alan," said Garcia. "Walk into the hall, go into the stairwell, and up to the roof. Gonzales is Ana and stays here. My other officer will escort you."

Alan looked sick. "I don't want to go to the roof." It was almost a whine.

Garcia folded his arms across his chest, signifying there would be no discussion. "This is not a dance, Señor Clark, do as you're told. Do it now."

Alan looked at the Judge for support but saw none. He reluctantly turned and followed the officer out into the hallway and then disappeared into the stairwell.

"Then what?" asked the Judge. "What did each of you do? You first, Rosa?"

"I got up, got my cell phone out of my bag behind me, and checked my messages," said Rosa.

"Do it," said Garcia. "Go through the motions."

Rosa stood up, produced a cell from her back pocket, pretended to take it out of an invisible bag behind her against the wall, plopped back down in her chair, stretching high heels and long legs sheathed in leather onto the granite table top, and thumbed her cell.

"Luis next," said Garcia.

"I was standing like this. I turned and started pacing back and forth across this glass wall that looks out to the elevators. Trying to work off some of the tension. María had gotten me stirred up."

"Angry?"

"Yes. Okay, yes, I was very angry."

"Do it," said Garcia.

Luis turned and paced.

"And what did you do, Pablo?" asked the Judge.

Rosa smiled. "Pablo's an old man. He mostly just sits. He just sat here."

"When you're old as I am," said Pablo, "each minute is to be experienced, enjoyed, savored… like a gift. I don't stress over small matters. I'm happy just to sit and breath."

"Is that correct?" Garcia asked. "Did Pablo just sit?"

They all nodded.

"And you Miguel?" asked the Judge.

"I made a call, then stood up and stretched, like this." Miguel put one arm above his head, palm stretched backward, parallel to the ground, and the other arm down at his side, palm stretched backward, parallel to the ground, and gave a good stretch. "Then I walked over here and got a water." He walked around the table, picked up a water from the marble counter that ran along the wall, and walked back to his chair, slumping into it. "These meetings are all so tedious, including this one."

"Is that what happened?" asked Garcia.

The others nodded. They were getting bored with the game. The Judge could tell.

"Who was the call to, Miguel?" asked Garcia

"Just a call to the company, responding to a text."

"We'll need to see your telephone records for that day, and verify the call."

"Sure."

"Who, exactly, was the call to?" asked the Judge.

"Oh, just a company technician. You know, a technical call."

"No, I don't know, which is why I'm asking. You called his cell, or the ASAM line at his office?"

"His cell."

"And his name, Miguel, specifically?"

Miguel sighed. "Pedro Mendoza."

"The technician at your Todos Santos plant."

Miguel, startled the Judge knew Mendoza's function at the plant, responded, "Yes," in a suddenly muffled voice.

"How about you, Roberto?" asked the Judge.

"I stayed put, right here. Got my cell phone out. Made a call as well."

"Who'd you call?" asked Garcia.

"My girlfriend, if that's any business of yours."

"What's her name?"

"Carmen."

Cabo

"You normally talk to your girlfriend with business partners standing around, eavesdropping?" asked the Judge.

"If she'd answered, I'd have stepped out. But she didn't. I left a message."

"I want to get your telephone records for that day and verify the call," said Garcia.

"Sure. Whatever."

"Is that what happened?" Garcia asked the assembled group.

They nodded, half-heartedly now.

"That leaves you, Mr. Moreno," said the Judge.

All eyes turned toward Moreno now, making him feel uncomfortable. His eyes darted around the group.

"I think I just sat here," he said. Uncertain. "I think I was on my laptop working on a contract for ASAM."

"Is that the way it went down?" asked Garcia.

There seemed general agreement in the group.

They all sat back in their chairs, except for Luis, still standing, relieved that the game was over. The elevator doors opened, and Gonzales stepped out, without Alan Clark, apparently still on the roof. Garcia made hand signals through the glass, conveying to Gonzales he should immediately retrieve Clark and return with him to the boardroom. Alan was probably having a heart attack up there, mused the Judge.

The Judge stood up, leaving his seat next to Garcia, and moved to the center of the table. All eyes turned in surprise.

"It's funny how our memories work," the Judge said. "What gets moved from our short-term memory to storage in our minds is often incomplete, or even inaccurate. Consider here and our replay of the events leading up to María's death. All but one of you has entirely forgotten something. There is something hiding in the shadows of your memory. What have you forgotten?"

They looked at each other, confused.

"When we did the replay of María's death last time under the Chief Inspector's direction, one of you got up and stepped away from the table. In fact, at one point they were out of sight for perhaps four or five minutes. Where did they go? Do you recall?" asked the Judge.

They looked blankly at the Judge.

"Rosa, you're observant. Think about it," said the Judge.

"Me?"

"What happened, twice? Who disappeared from sight here in the boardroom?"

Rosa's brow furrowed.

"Miguel," she said. "He's always going to the bathroom. He's like a leaky faucet. He used the washroom." She pointed to the opposite wall, and the small inset paneled door leading to the Executive Suite washroom.

"Very good," said the Judge. "Miguel, would you please step into the washroom, close the door, use the facilities and flush, like you did just before María fell?"

Miguel, still looking bored, got up, ambled into the washroom and closed the door. Two minutes went by, all ears on the sounds emitted from under the washroom door; there wasn't much else to do. There was sound of the toilet lid opening, Miguel's liquid stream, followed by a tight fart. Silence for a while, some rustling of toilet paper off a roller, then a long flush, punctuated by the rustle of more toilet paper, then a second flush. There was more running water, the clang of the paper towel dispenser, and the swing of the boardroom door as Alan Clark came back with his shadow from the roof and settled into a lean against the wall close to the Judge, for protection. Then Miguel opened the washroom door and stepped out, lingering there. "I was here, just stepped through the door, when I saw Maria fall."

"And in the Chief Inspector's morality play you reprised the same movements, as I recall," said the Judge.

"I did."

"Including your trip to the washroom?"

"Yes."

"So, of all the people in this room when María was about to fall, and later when Ana was about to fall, only one person was out of sight briefly from everybody else, on both occasions."

All eyes turned to Miguel.

Red in the face now, eyes blazing, he said, "That's crazy. I had nothing to do with their deaths. I was taking a leak for Christ sakes. They were my sisters. You're spinning crap out of thin air, Judge."

The Judge surveyed the rest of the room, then said, "Chief Inspector Garcia has determined that an insect-like, modified drone was the murder weapon, herding first María and then Ana off the roof."

"How in the hell could it do that?" asked Luis

Garcia said, "Señor, you run the high-tech division, under Miguel's supervision. Can it be you know nothing about drones?"

"What can I say?" Luis smiled, spreading his hands. "A good manager knows which details to leave to others."

The Judge said, "Drones can be programmed like a sheep dog to herd an animal in or out of an assigned space, equipped with long arms with sharp spinning blades capable of slicing your flesh to shreds on contact, and armed with a spray device laying a cloud of pepper spray and disorienting gas over its intended victim, blinding and confusing them."

They were all sitting up in their chairs now, Luis settling into his seat, processing this new information. Rosa and Alan Clark looked wide-eyed, Pablo was clenching and unclenching his hands. Garcia, standing beside the Judge as though the Judge were his new BFF, was all puffed out from the Judge's bestowing him credit for identifying the murder device.

"Of course," the Judge continued, "to use a drone, someone would have to have had in their possession a drone controller. So there remain three open questions. Who was controlling this drone? Where is the controller he or she used? And... what was their motive? I think Chief Inspector is prepared to answer each of those questions, here and now."

Garcia blinked.

"Let's go to the motive, first, shall we Chief Inspector?"

Garcia nodded, his eyes filled with questions as he looked at the Judge.

The Judge continued. "Interestingly, despite the statements of your company lawyer, Mr. Moreno here, who personally assured me there was no transfer of shares or voting rights associated with the ASAM stock, on checking myself with your transfer agent, it turns out an irrevocable proxy had been drafted, executed and filed by one of the ASAM shareholders, giving their right to vote their shares in ASAM irrevocably to someone else. So, Señor Moreno, you deliberately lied to me, and by extension, the Chief Inspector who had directed me to ask the question, stating you knew of no proxy arrangements shifting the voting rights of ASAM shareholders. Yet you knew full well such an agreement existed because you in fact drafted one, and at least nominally were the recipient of the voting rights so transferred."

"Client privilege," muttered Moreno.

"Do you admit you're the nominal holder of voting rights for ASAM shares for a client?"

"Yes."

"Who's the client?"

"Client privilege again, sir. As a professional, you know I can't ethically answer that question."

"Not unless you're questioned under oath in a murder trial," said the Judge. "Moreno, I'd say for you that's mistake 'one'."

Moreno glared at the Judge.

The Judge swung around to pin Roberto's eye. "Roberto, it's your shares whose voting rights you pledged, wasn't it?"

Roberto looked shocked, then defensive, then angry. "I had to do it! It was that or prison. You painted me into a corner, Miguel. You bastard!"

Miguel settled a little deeper in his chair and looked at the ceiling, making a blowing sound like a whale blowing off air.

"It was Miguel to whom you gave your irrevocable proxy to vote all your ASAM shares?" asked the Judge.

"Yes. Maria and Ana and Pablo were claiming I'd embezzled money from ASAM, committed bank fraud. They wanted to press charges, send me to jail. Luis and Rosa knew it was all bullshit. I'd just taken what I should have been paid in the first place. I proposed to the Board a settlement, creation of a loan outstanding with a payment schedule so I could pay the money back. I had Luis, Rosa, and my vote for the deal, but María, Ana and Pablo wouldn't budge. I needed Miguel's vote for my settlement or I'd be thrown in jail. He said he wouldn't vote for the settlement unless I gave him my proxy. The bastard. I had no choice."

"And the settlement was approved on a four to three yes vote by the board."

"Yes."

"Roberto, did your company lawyer, Mr. Moreno, discuss with you, or with all of the board for that matter, the corporate law principle that would preclude you from voting as a board member to approve your own settlement agreement with ASAM because of your conflict of interest?"

"No."

"Did he discuss the conflict of interest Miguel had in voting for the settlement when he had a self-interest in secretly obtaining your voting rights as part of the deal, even though they were nominally given to Moreno?"

"No."

"I think that may be mistake 'two' for you, Moreno."

All eyes turned back to look at Moreno, who pasted a silly smile on his face, but hunched down further in his seat too, spreading his hands in a gesture of 'I guess we all make mistakes sometimes.'

"Does the board generally meet in this boardroom for its meetings?" asked the Judge.

There was a group nod.

"Always?"

Another nod.

"Who has the key to the room?"

"Señor Moreno. He always shows up early and gets things set up," said Rosa.

"I think that may be mistake 'three' for you, Moreno. Let's explore what happened a little further and see. Now, when board members arrived for the board meeting, Moreno was already here, since he opened the room. But when Miguel arrived, did he have a briefcase, or package, or anything that might have contained perhaps a computer tablet?"

"I arrived next," said Rosa. "When Miguel arrived, he had no briefcase and no package."

"So, if a drone control tablet was used from this room to control a drone attack on the roof, Miguel wasn't the one who brought it into the room?"

"I guess not," said Rosa.

"You see," snarled Miguel. "I've told you and the inspector I had nothing to do with my sisters' deaths. I had no hand in this."

"But on the other hand, Miguel, we now know Moreno has been acting as your agent, in conflict with the duty of loyalty he owes as legal counsel to ASAM. Perhaps you two had a further understanding, and it was

Moreno who brought the drone control computer into the Boardroom for you, since he was the first to arrive."

"That's bullshit," hissed Moreno.

"Or it could be mistake number three, Moreno," said the Judge. "Pablo, are you're afraid of cats?" The Judge turned to look at the old man, slumped in his chair.

"Si, señor. Since I was a small boy. They are the creatures of the devil. They secretly hate us. They would pounce and eat us instantly if we were smaller. I fought with them when I was young, got rid of them, killed them when I could. Killed the kittens. I would exterminate them all. They are the arch-enemy of man."

"Did you know of this fear, Rosa?"

"No."

"Roberto? Luis?"

They shook their heads.

"Pablo, who knew of your Ailurophobia?"

"My what, señor?"

"Your dread of cats."

"María, Ana, Miguel. It was common knowledge among them."

"So, Miguel knew?"

"Si señor."

"And Miguel knew you had a weak heart?"

"Yes."

"What happened to you on the night you were attacked, Pablo?"

Pablo turned grey. His breathing accelerating into rapid little gasps.

"I saw death, señor. Death, he came for me."

"And in what form did death come?"

"In his form as a cat." Pablo was now whispering.

"And you collapsed?"

"Yes. My heart pounded so bad I thought he was taking me for sure."

"Thank you, Pablo."

"With all these odd facts, still a certain pattern does emerge. With the Chief Inspector's permission, let me summarize what he has determined and what he can posit:

Miguel originally held 11.1 percent of the voting rights for ASAM. With the death of María and Anna, their share voting rights were taken away for five years. Everyone else's share of voting rights increased proportionately. Miguel now has 14.3 percent of the outstanding voting rights.

Miguel secretly acquired all of Roberto's voting rights through an irrevocable proxy coupled with an interest. Since the shares weren't sold, it was a way to avoid sterilization of the shares, so the shares didn't lose their voting rights. As a result, Miguel now controls 28.5 percent of the ASAM voting rights.

Suppose Pablo had died. Died from fright at being attacked by a flying cat, or perhaps actually clawed to death by such a beast. The voting rights on Pablo's shares would have ceased, the shares sterilized. Everyone left would have proportionally more voting rights. In such an event, Miguel would have automatically increased his voting rights to 49.9 percent of the total outstanding voting rights of ASAM.

Did you know that Luis was attacked as well? Attacked while snorkeling in the lagoon in front of his house, a place he swims most every day. Attacked by a swarm of fish with apparently metal teeth."

The Judge pulled out a bottle containing a small, sharp, broken tooth. "This was pulled out of Luis' leg. It's white, but if you examine it, you'll find it's actually metal, with a porcelain coating."

"Suppose Luis had died as well in this attack. At that point, Miguel would hold sixty-six percent of the voting rights of ASAM. Miguel would have firm control. He'd have five years to issue himself substantially more stock as compensation or in a bonus, so that by the time the voting restrictions came off the sterilized shares, it wouldn't matter. He'd have so many additional shares he'd always control ASAM."

The room was stunned, considering the implication of what the Judge had said.

"And, the only person who was out of sight of everyone right before María fell, and again right before Ana fell, was Miguel. And consider Miguel is a person with supervisory rights over the plant where ASAM's only drones are developed and built. A person who was talking on his cell to Pedro Mendoza, the ASAM drone technician, as María left this boardroom and headed for the roof. The only person in the room, coincidentally, who is a pilot, likely capable of flying a drone with some precision."

Miguel's face twisted in anger. "Shut your mouth you Yankee bastard. You have no right to accuse me of anything. So, I stepped into the washroom to take a quick leak. That proves nothing."

Garcia looked at the Judge, more questions in his eyes, and now a touch of panic. No doubt wondering what would come of his career if the Judge couldn't prove these reckless accusations. Wishing now that the Judge had not given him so much credit for his steps in the investigation, brilliant though they had been. Thinking perhaps it was time to abandon the Judge and call this meeting to a halt; try to repair some of the damage done to his relationship with Miguel. The Judge watched these thoughts play across Garcia's face, then continued.

"If we could find the drone controller, we'd likely find the finger prints of those who handled it. If your fingerprints and those of Moreno's are on the controller, that would prove quite a lot.

"Our Chief Inspector here, with considerable foresight I might add, sealed the boardroom and the entire floor after Ana fell, did you not inspector?"

"Yes, I did."

"No one's been in or out until today, except for your officers?"

"That is as I ordered."

"And no one left with a fancy drone controller, a device about the size of a small tablet with knobs, because our Chief Inspector wisely insisted everyone, and their possessions be carefully searched by his thorough team before anyone left the building."

"It was my seasoned judgment that this precaution was required," said Garcia, switching loyalties again, subtly edging closer to the Judge, his gut telling him to put all his chips on the Judge.

"And although the Chief Inspector did a precursory search of the boardroom area, he craftily waited until today, now, to do a detailed search of the washroom."

Garcia had been standing on his tiptoes to look taller, basking in the Judge's praise of his actions; but now he grew shorter, collapsing on to flat feet, caught off-guard by this new line of inquiry. He simply muttered, "Right."

"In fact, the Chief Inspector is going to have his favorite man on his team, Officer Gonzales, thoroughly search the washroom now. This includes the under-sink cabinet, the towel cabinet, the ceiling well that holds the 'poop fan', the water reservoir behind the toilet, and any other opening or place where a small tablet might be hidden."

Garcia's eyes narrowed, giving him a slightly foxy look. "Yes. Officer Gonzales, proceed as we discussed. Go into the washroom and do a thorough search now."

Gonzales looked confused, a frequent expression for Gonzales.

"In fact, Gonzales, I'm going to personally help you with this search," said Garcia, marching into the washroom, shooing Gonzales ahead of him.

There was noise of banging as cupboards were opened and closed, the clink of a grate coming off the ceiling fan, a yelp as Gonzales stubbed his finger on a fan blade, the sliding of porcelain noise as the lid was slid off the toilet, and then a screech from Gonzales. "Mierda santa!"

"That means 'Holy Shit'," whispered Alan Clark.

Seconds later Garcia stepped out of the washroom, holding over his head, as though a proud father displaying his first born, a sealed plastic pouch, dripping, with a small computer tablet inside, its protruding control nobs and extra dials giving it an off-world look.

CHAPTER 36

"They deserved it. Both of them," snarled Miguel, rising from his seat at the conference table, giving up all pretense of innocence. "And Pablo too. My mother was a ballet dancer, the spirit of music in her soul. Unfortunately, she was born to a country that has no appreciation for ballet. She became an artistic dancer, taught music and folk dance, worked at cheap dance clubs to survive. Married my father, José, at twenty-one. She had me at twenty-two.

María, Ana, and you too, Pablo, you called my mother 'trash', often to her face; called me the same. When my dad died, we got nothing. Worse than nothing because you three continued to stamp us into the dirt. Discouraged people from renting to us. Discouraged companies from hiring my mother. Discouraged people from socializing with us.

My mother finally gave up, moved us to Mexico City, changed her name, and married an alcoholic truck driver with a taste for beating women and small children. I stood up to him one night over dinner when I was twelve and he was drunk. He launched into how my mother was a whore, useless, stupid, needed slapping around. I slammed a bowl of mashed potatoes into his face. He came at me. But he was drunk. I beat the shit out of him. He drank very little after that when he came home; didn't come home so much either.

My real dad made this company. ASAM should be mine. Pablo, you and Antonio were just barnacles clamped on to his success, and you know it. As were my idiot half-sisters, contributing nothing, swanning around, sucking up capital that should have gone to building the business. My selfish half-sisters deserved to die, as do you Pablo. Mean, belligerent, trying to quash me at every turn... ruined my mother's life, ruined my boyhood."

Pablo listened quietly to this tirade with his head down, slowly shaking it, trying to fathom where all this hate came from, how his entire family could just blow up like this. He wouldn't look at Miguel. He was too wounded.

"And you, Luis. An upstart with more money than sense. All you care about is money. You take no pride in what's been built, or what might be built. You want to dump ASAM down the sewer of marijuana and drugs. You'll ruin this company given the chance. I hate your silly airs, I hate your attitude that your somehow smarter than the rest of us. You're a pure asshole and deserve no role in ASAM."

Luis didn't take his eyes off Miguel. He was seething. It showed in his face, naked hate.

"What about me?" whispered Rosa.

"I'd never hurt you, Rosa. I've always loved you, despite our age difference. This was never about you."

Rosa nodded, one small tear sliding down a cheek.

Miguel sagged back into his chair, exhausted.

"So, you are confessing to the murder of María Cervantes and Ana Cervantes?" asked Garcia.

"I want my abogado," muttered Miguel through hands covering his face.

"That means lawyer," Alan whispered to the Judge, the pleased look on his face suggesting he was the one who'd just solved María and Ana's murder.

"I know, Alan," said the Judge politely.

"How did you get the iPad into the conference room?" the Judge asked Miguel.

"It was as you said, Judge, it was brought…"

"Don't answer that question, Miguel," shouted Moreno from down-table. "Not until you've talked with your lawyer."

"You acknowledge you acquired the irrevocable proxy to vote Roberto's shares?" asked the Judge.

Miguel nodded.

"Did you consult an attorney before entering into the transaction?"

"Don't answer any more questions, Miguel," said Moreno, in his best attorney's command voice now. "You're just digging yourself a hole you'll never climb out of. I object to this entire interrogation of my client without allowing him to first consult with a criminal defense attorney."

The Judge pressed on. "I assume you utilized the services of Pedro Mendoza, ASAM's drone technician at the Todos Santos plant?

Miguel nodded. "He lent me the bird and the controller, programmed them for perimeter duty, and showed me how to use the controls."

"Did he initially fly the bird over to this tower, then later to some remote location to collect it?"

Miguel nodded.

"And he delivered it to you to fly it again, on the beach, against my wife and I."

Miguel nodded. "You were nosing around too much, Judge. Too close. We were all scared. But the bird never came back. Something went wrong with its rotors. It ended up crashing into the sea. We shit rocks searching the ocean for debris, hoping no one else would find it first, but in the end, there was nothing to find."

"And Mendoza lent you a second drone, didn't he? The one on which you mounted a stuffed cat, its glass eyes bulging out, red and flashing, claws outstretched, mouth open to show its fangs?"

Miguel nodded again.

Pablo gasped. "Death," he muttered.

"And a set of six swarming fish drones with steel jaws, which Mendoza programmed to guard a perimeter?"

"Yes."

"You son of a bitch," muttered Luis, raising in his seat at the table, considering a lunge for Miguel, but Garcia's two officers were immediately to either side of him, easing him back down in his chair.

"How was it you could leave the programming tablet and walk back into the boardroom before anything happened on the roof?"

"I was here the day before, programing the actions of the bird. Instructing it on what actions to take when its territory was invaded. I gave it a three-minute wait from the point I pushed the control button, then stepped out into the boardroom to watch the show. These drones are quite smart."

"Yes, and it was some show. Two old helpless women, sprayed with pepper spray and disorienting gas, chased with unrelenting cruelty by sharp turning blades, cutting at their hands, arms, trying for their faces, forced in a panic over the edge of the parapet to a screaming fall down the side of the building, smashing to death on the concrete below."

"They deserved it."

Miguel turned in his chair to look out at the view, all streaming sunlight and blue water under a China blue sky, folding his arms across his chest, signifying he was through answering questions.

Things broke up quickly from there. The Chief Inspector strutted around, directing his two officers to handcuff Miguel and Moreno. He was already holding Pedro Mendoza, the drone technician, as a material witness. Moreno didn't go quietly. His vocal protests that he knew nothing about Miguel's planned murders echoed down the hall and into the elevator. Garcia's Chief of Police would have to sort Moreno's story out with the state's prosecutor, decide who to charge and for what, and determine the relative culpability of Pedro Mendoza and Juan Moreno.

The other members of the board pressed themselves out the door in a crush, scattering for the elevator, wanting no further contact with the Judge or the Chief Inspector.

CHAPTER 37

"So, explain how the shares of ASAM would have worked, Judge."

He and Katy were sitting under the palapa again in the morning sun, watching a gaggle of water exercisers, mostly women with huge thighs, two men with overlapping bellies, standing chest high in the pool, trying to keep up with an exercise coach who had them at a disadvantage, standing on terra firma at the edge of the pool shouting at them over the noisy racket of rap that pretended to be music.

The males were having trouble keeping up.

"It's pretty simple, Katy. Think of it this way. Suppose there were 999,000 shares of ASAM outstanding. To start, each shareholder owned 111,000 shares, or 11.1 percent, except for Pablo, who owned 333,000 shares, or 33.3 percent. When María and Ana died, their share voting rights were sterilized, so although their heirs owned the economic interest represented by the shares, the shares couldn't be voted. If Luis and Pablo had died, their shares would also be sterilized and wouldn't have been entitled to vote."

"Okay, I think I understand so far. But how did that change voting control?"

"So, with María, Ana, Luis and Pablo gone, the only shares outstanding that would still have voting rights attached to them would have been the 111,000 share blocks owed by Miguel, Rosa and Roberto. Each block would have represented one-third of the total shares with voting rights, the total of such outstanding voting shares being 333,333 shares."

"So, the siblings, Rosa and Roberto, would control ASAM?"

"Normally, yes. But in exchange for not being charged with embezzlement and going to jail, Roberto was forced to make a deal with Miguel. He signed away all his voting rights to Miguel on an irrevocable proxy coupled with an interest."

"So, Miguel would get to vote both his one-third of the voting shares, and also Roberto's one-third of the voting shares," said Katy.

"Right. Miguel would vote two-thirds of the outstanding voting shares, and thereby control ASAM for a period of five years, until the voting rights on the other shares were reinstated."

"So, Miguel could do anything he wanted with ASAM during the five years, like issue himself three million shares as a bonus, assuring him perpetual control, even after the five years."

"Yep."

"Wow. Tricky, Judge."

"Yes, well, I'm glad it's all over and we can now relax for the rest of what's left of our vacation. We've only got two days left." The Judge took a long pull on his margarita. He was acclimating to the heat and settling into Cabo.

His cell phone went off with a whistle. A wolf-whistle. The phone bounced around his pocket a lot. He was convinced it got even by deliberately resetting its sound alarm for calls periodically.

Alan Clark said hello at the other end of the line, jovial and excited. "Have I got news for you and Katy, Judge. The Lieutenant Governor's office called me this morning. He was so appreciative of your exposing the human trafficking at ASAM, he's invited us to go out on his private schooner this afternoon for a sunset sail. You, Katy, me and my date."

Katy, eavesdropping, mouthed at the Judge, 'Barbara', then shook her head vigorously.

"Are you bringing Barbara, Alan?"

"Sadly no. She had to go back to work, left this morning. I'm bringing that cute little gal from the ASAM timeshare resort, Mary... ah...Whittaker."

The Judge looked at Katy, who nodded okay. Katy had bonded with Mary Whittaker on their timeshare tour. It seemed ages ago now after all they'd been through.

They met Alan Clark and Mary Whittaker for drinks at 5:30 at a small bar called The Giggling Marlin. The bar was known for its large plank sign, showing a marlin standing upright on its tail, measuring the size of the fisherman it had caught; the fisherman hanging upside down beside the marlin from a scale. Katy would have nightmares about the sign later, but they laughed at it now, and at The Giggling Marlin's motto etched there: 'If our food, drinks and service aren't up to your standard... please... lower your standard...!'"

They entered under a second sign, a huge neon-lit affair mounted over the roof of a giggling marlin in sunglasses and hat, holding a beer, and showing a long row of smiling teeth. Inside was all primary colors, red, white and blue, with an expansive bar holding a prodigious stack of tequila bottles and other savory fluids, and a lusty crowd of Americans consuming them.

Alan and Mary waved from the bar, having saved them two seats, and they settled in, Katy experimenting with a shot of supposedly ancient tequila, the Judge sticking with his Dos Equis. The chips and guacamole were sensational, fueling an almost immediate need for another beer, as they were supposed to. They had to shout over the crowd to be heard, but it was all fun.

At 6:30 p.m. they wandered across the main street, and down a short-cobbled street to the marina. The Lieutenant Governor's office had called and said the big man himself was unexpectedly tied up, but the crew would meet them with the boat to take them for a sunset cruise in front of gate 26 on the dock.

They watched a beautiful schooner pull up to the guest side of dock 26. She was older but beautifully maintained, perhaps fifty feet long, white hull and twin tall masts, the aft one taller as befitting a schooner. The woodwork was polished to silk. Bright blue and white striped upholstered cushions gave a plush look to its wide cockpit, the Mexican flag hung over her stern, and an imperial flag was halfway up the mast, yellow stars and emblems on a purple field, perhaps the flag of the Lieutenant Governor.

She had a crew of two, a captain and a young lady deckhand. The deckhand was short and wide, late twenties, dressed in white shorts a tad too short and a tad too tight, and a soft red bandeau top of gauzy material which supported medium-size breasts and allowed her nipples to peek through. When she bent over to tie off the dock line, her rounded buns left little to the imagination. But she had a great smile, all teeth, which she turned on and off like a flashlight, using it to punctuate her statements in accented English.

The captain was scruffier. Cutoff shorts a bit too distressed to be in style covered powerful legs and waist, a blue polo shirt faded some from the sun rippled over muscular arms and shoulders, and his oily black hair was tucked under a disreputable-looking captain's hat that had seen better days. His narrow eyes were on alert all the time, scanning their party waiting at the gate, scanning the other boats, scanning the bulkhead cobblestone path which circled the marina. There was something disquieting about him, but the Judge couldn't put his finger on it.

The girl bounded up the gangplank to the dock gate and let them in, flashing her teeth-smile, introducing herself as Carla, and explaining they were waiting for a third crew member who'd show up shortly. She escorted them down onto the dock, and then into the cockpit of the yacht, introduced them to Captain Muñoz, and disappeared below to rustle up cocktails. Captain Muñoz looked older and wearier up close, mid-forties, ancient lines etched around his eyes, an old scar down one side of his face standing out white against his brown skin. He looked to have led a hard life, but there was no doubt he could pull sail and control the boat. The way he bounced on his toes as other boats slipped by, tracking small waves in the harbor and rocking the schooner, gave him away as a sea-going man.

They sprawled in the cockpit under an awning hastily rigged for them, and had delicious drinks poured from two iced pitchers, rum-punch, strong and laced with sugar, tropical fruit and Grand Marnier, and heavy hors d'oeuvres, guacamole, chips, chicken and beef quesadillas fried on a skillet below, and cut papaya soaked in lime juice.

The Judge watched Katy relax back in her seat, some of the tension of the last few days finally leaving her face, chatting animatedly with Mary Whittaker about Ralphie, the intricacies of raising young children, and secrets of getting your figure back and keeping it. Contrary to the Judge's cynical suspicions during their timeshare presentation, it turned out Mary did indeed have a young daughter, Lisa, who was four and just starting an American-run preschool in Cabo. Lisa's dad had slipped into a drug habit and disappeared up the Northern California coast, pursuing the perfect wave and the perfect joint. Mary hadn't heard from him in months. Pictures of children were shared all around, Alan Clark dutifully making encouraging clucking noises, although he had no kids and little clue on what the fuss was about.

Alan Clark bent the Judge's ear, expounding on the opportunities for mass profits in the U.S. marijuana market. "It's this way Judge. Because of a glut of growers entering the business, prices are dropping, and savvy growers are moving to grow their weed outside, under sunlight, using organic methods, and packaging their products as organic and natural. It's the opportunity of the century."

The Judge nodded, listening with one ear, wondering why Carla and the captain looked so tense as they scanned the dock for their third hand from the bow. Finally, a third man came to the dock gate, and Carla bounded up again to let him in. Younger than the captain, late thirties, and equally fit, he wore faded shorts and a white t-shirt, and waved to them as he approached with a friendly smile that didn't quite reach his eyes.

"Hola, my friends. Sorry I'm late. Are you ready for your cruise? I'm Eduardo." He undid the bow line and swung himself aboard, settling in there to watch for other boats as they piloted out of the harbor.

The captain jumped into the cockpit and started the engines, Carla expertly threw off the stern dock lines, and they were off, sliding by the docked boats in the harbor and out into the bay, steaming for The Arch at Land's End as the sun settled into the sea. The captain raised the main sail and the jib. Both filled immediately, sending the boat forward with a leap. He turned off the engine, leaving only the sound of the wind in the rigging and the taste of salt on their lips. It was as though they were on the back of some giant swan with its wings raised, as the schooner picked up way, tilted some, and began to skim the water.

The wind wafted across the boat, cooling them down, and the beautiful towering rocks leered up at them on the starboard side as the captain brought the boat in close to The Arch, and then out again, into nearby deep water. The sky was a vivid blue, tiny clouds in the distance picking up streaks of orange and pink on their undersides, as the last of the sun settled below the horizon and night fell, dropping the temperature some to the Judge's relief. In the deepening twilight, the excursion boats out on the bay turned back for the harbor, leaving their solitary swan spinning close to the Arch and then back to their deep-water patch in graceful circles.

Eduardo came forward from his perch in the bow into the cockpit, smiling at them, then disappeared below for a moment. He returned quickly but now seemed tense.

The Judge glanced up at him and realized Eduardo had a very large revolver pointed at the Judge's chest. It was amazing how much bigger a gun looked when you were staring down its barrel.

CHAPTER 38

The Judge turned to look for the captain at the wheel. And he was there, looking grim, pointing a small Beretta at Alan. Carla was beside him, showing all her teeth again in a smile that had lopsided into malice.

While two guns were trained on the four, Carla took zip lock ties and tied the Judge's wrists together, tightening them with mean pleasure, making the Judge wince. Then she tied Alan's wrists together, then Katy's, and finally Mary's. They sat there, passive, wide-eyed, too much in shock to speak.

Finally, the Judge muttered, "What's going on here? Why are you doing this? What do you want?"

The three of them just looked at the Judge.

"We can pay you," said Alan. "We have lots of money. Just take us back to the dock and we can make you wealthy."

"You've made some important people very unhappy with your no-trafficking campaign," said Eduardo, looking at the Judge. "Stirring up a lot of trouble for everybody, bringing the piss-ant Mexico City bureaucrats out to nose around and ask a lot of silly questions."

Eduardo pointed with his gun, separating the two couples. Carla snickered as the captain handed her his gun and directed her to take the wheel with her other hand and keep the boat on its tack. Eduardo marched Alan and Mary forward to the bow, the captain following behind. Mary started to whimper, stumbling on the deck block as she was pushed forward. Katy and the Judge were left together in the cockpit under the watchful eye of Carla, her gun unwavering in its bead on the Judge's chest.

The zip locks were cutting painfully into the Judge's wrists. He brought his wrists to his head, using his teeth to center the zip-lock between his wrists, trying to relieve some of the pressure from the bands cutting into his flesh. He nodded at Katy to do the same and she did. It didn't help much.

The Judge watched in horror as, on the bow, Eduardo gave his gun to the captain, then took a line and wrapped it around Alan and Mary, tying them together as they stood. Mary was sobbing now. As Eduardo stepped behind Alan, bringing the line around Alan's back, Alan lashed out backward with his foot in a rear kick, catching Eduardo in the groin and knocking him backward. Alan, off balance, toppled forward, bringing Mary with him, landing on top of Mary on the deck. Mary yelped in pain as her back smashed down on a deck cleat.

Eduardo cursed, bending over in pain for a moment, then grabbed Alan and Mary by the back of their hair and brutally hauled them to their feet, Mary screaming now, partly from her ripping hair and partly in fear. Eduardo completed the job of tying them together, then reached down and picked up a second line on the deck, tying it securely to the bands of line around their joined midriffs.

The Judge looked in disbelief at the second line, which was loosely coiled on the deck, then ran aft a few feet to a 50-pound anchor leaning loosely against a stanchion supporting the deck safety lines. Alan was screaming curses at Eduardo now, struggling to get out of the lines tying them together, but with no success. Eduardo looked amused. Mary's screaming reverted to a high-pitched keening that was painful to hear.

Eduardo moved swiftly, unhooking the forward lifeline to leave a gap in its protection, then turning and shoving the distraught pair off the bow into the sea. Their screams were lost as they fell paired into the water with a huge splash. Eduardo tossed the anchor into the water behind them.

Their heads bobbed up briefly, level with the cockpit as the hull careened past, mouths open gasping for air. Then their heads were yanked below the surface as the anchor line tightened, starting them on one last journey. The sea turned smooth and calm where they'd been seconds before, as though they'd never been.

The captain was laughing hysterically now, mad with excitement, dancing around the bow like an Indian, his gun dropped on a coil of line. Eduardo turned and started to make his way back the 40 or so feet to the cockpit, looking grimly at the Judge.

In the cockpit, Carla's gun had drooped, her eyes focused with fascination on the spot in the water where Alan and Mary had grabbed their last breath. Fascination, but no remorse.

"Oh, oh!" the Judge cried. "I think I'm having a heart attack."

The Judge brought his hands, bound tightly with the zip lock, up above his head, his face painted with the look of someone who couldn't breathe. Carla smirked at his discomfort.

"Probably an easier way to go, Judgy."

The Judge brought his arms down sharply in a V shape, smashing them into the sides of his hips. As if by magic, the ratchet on the zip-lock came apart, freeing his hands.

Carla gaped at him, very late starting to think about her drooping gun, as the Judge's fist, swung with all the torque his 225 pounds could muster, crashed into the side of her nose, pulverizing cartilage and bone, sending a spray of blood along with the gun across the cockpit as she collapsed in a heap at his feet.

"Katy, quick, do what I did, with your arms."

Katy tried it once to no avail, yelping as the band cut into her wrists, but a second try with desperate force succeeded in stripping the ratchets on her ties as well, freeing her hands.

"Now, Katy. Jump for it. Here, take my hand."

The Judge grabbed a life preserver from the cockpit, and they jumped together off the back of the transom.

CHAPTER 39

The water was warm, nourishing, like a bathtub. They sank, still holding hands, then bobbed up, the yacht twenty yards past them already, all turmoil and angst as Eduardo, still maneuvering to reach the cockpit, screamed at Carla for screwing up. The captain lumbered behind him, gun in hand. Carla was down on her knees in the cockpit holding her nose, her head held back, trying to stem the flow of blood choking her throat, all thought of the boat and its wheel forgotten.

With no one at the helm, the sailboat spun hopelessly around, propelled by the wind, the chop and the tide, bringing herself broadside to the rising whitecap, heeling way over to port, heading for the towering rocks by the Arch.

The Judge saw Eduardo make a final mad dash for the cockpit and the wheel. But he wasn't in time. The hull slammed across underwater rocks, jerking to a stop, throwing Eduardo to his knees, and heeling over to its side, exposing its beam to oncoming waves which crashed over it without mercy. Eduardo and the captain were carried off the boat by the force of the waves, their heads smashed into the towering rocks at the schooner's far side, their limp bodies sliding down into the churning water and disappearing.

The Judge's last view of Carla was her plunking her large bottom down into a tiny yellow emergency raft, shoving away from the broken yacht, and paddling like mad out to sea, away from the sinking schooner and yawning rocks.

The Judge and Katy kicked off their shoes and swam slowly, tired, stopping now and then to tread water or float on their backs, sharing their single life-preserver. The sun's departure left the surface of the sea dark, murky, almost black, matching his mood.

He showed her the resting technique of letting your entire body go, floating naturally on your stomach without effort, one arm stretched out and one on the preserver, head several inches below the surface of the water, eyes closed, slowly releasing bubbles. Totally relaxed. As you exhaled the last breath of air, you made a single low energy paddling stroke downward with your outstretched hand, using minimum effort, sending your head above the surface briefly for air intake. Then sinking back again to your natural buoyancy, just below the surface, softly blowing out more air bubbles.

It helped. It rested her. And as importantly, it rested her mind, focusing her energies on relaxing, letting go of the panic.

They were making headway toward The Arch he thought, and Lover's Beach beside it, slowly, but with persistence. Then suddenly a wave lifted them up high and slid them down onto the beach, grinding their tummies along the sand, then trying to pull them back again with the receding water. He grabbed her with one hand and grasped sand with the other, digging his feet in, trying to impede the backward undertow. The water finally let its clutch go for a moment and he half dragged half crawled them higher up the wet sand, collapsing over its top onto dry crusty sand which still held the departed afternoon's heat. They lay there for a time, sprawled, exhausted, almost in shock. The Judge finally sat up, pulling Katy up beside him. She looked at him then, eyes wide, frightened. He wrapped his arms around her. She buried her head into his chest and began to softly cry.

He waited perhaps ten minutes, letting her weep away the raw emotion bottled up inside. Then he released her and got unsteadily to his feet.

"We'd better move, Katy. We can't stay here."

"Where, Judge, where? We're surrounded by water on three sides and high cliffs at our back."

"There's supposed to be a path, Katy. Part path, part climb. Steep but passable, over to the other side, to our favorite Pacific beach where we almost drowned. We can walk from there back to our hotel."

"I don't see it Judge."

"I don't either. But it's here. Others have taken it. We just have to find it."

He pulled her up and they drew close to the cliff, feeling along its base for an opening. The moon had come up, still at a small angle to the horizon, casting weak yellow light onto the beach, deepening the shadows at the base of the cliff.

The Judge missed it, would have walked by, but Katy spotted it.

"Here, Judge. Look, there are even footprints in the sand. Leading in and up. This has to be it."

They stumbled into a narrow cleft that widened at its back. The rocks were arranged like steps there, leading higher, up into the night. It was the beginning of a twenty-minute climb, more rock wall than path, that took them to the top of the cliff, and then over, down the other side, to the beach where the drone had attacked them.

They rested briefly at the top, and again on the beach on the other side, but high up on the sand, giving the huge Pacific rollers licking up the beach no chance to reach them. They started a slow walk north along the Pacific beach toward their hotel, arms wrapped around each other for mutual support, like surviving remnants of some lost foreign legion. Exhausted. Emotionally distraught.

They reached their hotel and walked around the pool on its far side opposite the large palapa dining room where couples lingered over their dinner and margaritas, enjoying the moonlight and the ambiance of Cabo. They slipped into the elevator, avoiding the lobby, and rode to the third floor where the Judge persuaded a housekeeping lady to use her master key card to open their door.

Their room was the same as they'd left it several hours before, yet somehow different. There was no safety for them in Cabo any longer. Perhaps there never had been. The room hadn't changed. But they had.

They collapsed on the bed for a while, the Judge wrapping his arms around Katy, holding her very close.

"I kint bree," Katy muttered.

"What?" He pulled his arms away to look at her, worried.

"I can't breathe, Judge. You're holding my chest too tight."

"Oh. Sorry."

They smiled at each other then, her unsinkable Molly Brown attitude infectious.

"You've got to leave now, Katy."

"I know. I need you to come with me."

"I can't. I have to finish it here. Otherwise the next we know they'll be on our doorstep in Los Angeles. But you must go. Go back and stay with your parents, protect our Ralphie."

She looked at him, putting her hand to the side of his face, caressing it. Trying to imprint his image in her mind for eternity.

"You have to come back, Judge. I can't live without you. We have a life planned and everything. Ralphie needs you too."

"I'll follow as soon as I can. But come, let's get you out of here."

She quickly showered, changed, took just what she could fit in her purse, passport, driver's license, credit cards, cash, cell phone, leaving the roll-aboard suitcase in the closet under her hanging clothes.

They walked out the back of their hotel, past the pool, down to the rugged beach and its yawning surf, and along to the next hotel over, the Playa Grande Resort. Then up, past the Playa's lower pool and chaise lounges, circling the crowded tables around the second pool enjoying a show of fire dancers over their dinner, and up and through its lobby, to the taxi stand outside.

They grabbed a no-name taxi on a no-name basis and sped off to the airport, the Judge paying cash as they alighted, no credit cards. The Judge switched Katy's ticket for an immediate flight on Alaska Air leaving in thirty minutes, and walked as far as the security line with her. He gave her a long hug and kiss worthy of the end of World War II.

He stood to the side, watching as she went through the security check. There were no customs. Her

Mexican visa card would be collected by the airline at the gate. He lingered awhile outside the terminal over a stiff vodka-tonic, listening for the final boarding call for her flight, then watched outside against the security fence. A sizable weight lifted from his shoulders as Katy's plane raced down the runway with a roar, lifted, and soared up into the night.

He trudged back toward the taxi pickup area, stopping short as a voice rang out to his left.

"Judge. Wait up. I want to talk to you."

It was Chief Inspector Garcia, leaning against a roof support, folding a newspaper he'd been reading, positioned so he could scan both the flow of people in and out of the terminal and the taxi pickup line that had been the Judge's destination.

Garcia motioned toward a nearby table, and the Judge reluctantly changed his course.

"I heard of course that your wife had a change of plans and was flying out tonight. I was surprised you weren't accompanying her."

"Can I trust you, Garcia? Really trust you? Whose side are you really on?"

Garcia spread his hands, palms open, feigning innocence.

"I suppose in the end we are each only on our own side, señor. But I take my duties as a policeman seriously. We've caught the perpetrator who killed the Cervantes sisters. In no small part due to your help. I'd like to think we are friends."

"Trusted friends?"

"Yes. Which brings me to the small matter of a sailing yacht that ended up on the rocks off The Arch just after sunset tonight, and sank."

"Yes. That was unfortunate."

"More than unfortunate. It was the Lieutenant Governor's pride and joy. Someone stole his schooner this afternoon and took it for a joyride, ultimately smashing it on the rocks. There's a rumor in the harbor that two portly men in their fifties and two younger women in their early thirties took the yacht, but didn't know how to sail it. One of the women had long blond hair and startling blue eyes, or so I'm told."

"A pity," said the Judge. "I used to race sailboats like that. Too bad I wasn't aboard. Perhaps I could've helped."

"Let's not be coy, Judge. You and your lovely wife, Katy, and your friend Alan Clark, and another woman, the timeshare woman I believe, were seen boarding the boat before it set sail."

The Judge sighed, took a big breath, then launched into the sordid story of his ill-fated sail. It was as though he needed to tell the story to someone, anyone, to get it out, give it a life of its own in words, just so he could step back from it, gain distance and perspective, get it out of his head.

He could still hear the awful keening of Mary; the rage of Alan, and the plopping noise as they hit the water. His voice cracked when he told of his last glimpse of Alan Clark, face twisted, gasping for breath, tied back to back to his sobbing date, their struggling heads yanked below the surface by the sinking anchor.

They sat silent for a while after he finished, each digesting the tragedy that had been the sunset cruise. Finally, Garcia spoke, his voice subdued.

"You and Katy disturbed a profitable and expanding industry for the cartels here in Mexico, Judge.

Your commotion over human trafficking for sex and as work slaves upended their 'live and let live' environment where officials have been encouraged to look the other way. The cartels don't take such interference lightly, particularly from a Yankee judge.

You have a parable in your country, I believe. About an emperor who has no clothes. If no one acknowledged that the emperor had no clothes, there was no problem. But you, and even more your wife, by calling out the Mexico City Congressional authorities, your State Department, the United Nations, and various do-gooder organizations around the world, have got everybody talking about our lack of clothes. It has made things very uncomfortable for the cartels.

They can't afford to let this pass, lest people get the idea the cartels are not invulnerable. Somebody's head must roll to satisfy their sense of pride and balance."

"Yes," the Judge agreed. "Well, apparently they've decided it's to be mine."

Garcia nodded. "Let me give you a lift into Cabo and we can talk some more, unless you've decided to catch another flight out?

"No, Garcia. I don't think fleeing to Los Angeles will solve my problem."

"Unfortunately, in this, I concur."

They rode back to Cabo and to the Judge's hotel, mostly in silence, the Judge considering alternate courses of action, feeling like a rat trapped in a maze where each of its exits had been slammed shut.

As they approached the Judge's hotel, and coming up short of viable options in his own mind, the

Judge finally turned to Garcia. "What do you think I should do, Garcia?"

"There will be a primary overseer for human trafficking in Baja, Judge. Someone who coordinates the harvesting of people and their placement within clubs, organizations, factories, cooperatives and so on. Placed where they can't escape and where they can be used to best advantage for profit. You need to find that person. Take him out; put him in jail. Let him be the scapegoat for the cartels' unhappiness, and deflect attention from you and Katy."

"Do you know who he is?"

"No. He, likely not a woman, has been very careful to stay in the shadows. My guess is it's because he's someone of position, well known, recognizable in Baja society. Not just an average thug."

"How do we find that person?"

"Perhaps we can use the Lieutenant Governor's boat sinking to our advantage. You could talk to the press, call the henchmen who tried to drown you reprehensible. Challenge whoever is behind the human trafficking in Baja California to come forward and face you, face the community, admit the sickening business they are in. Use your flowery judge language to condemn them and their trafficking. Stir the pot some more just as your wife did."

"Wave the red flag at the bull."

"I'm afraid so. The cartels don't like heat. They could decide the person in charge in Baja should deal with you directly. Should 'solve the problem or become the problem', so to speak. The cartels often think that way."

"I would be the target."

"I think you already are. I can assign one of my men to shadow you, and to close in at the right time."

"Would it work? Would the big cheese in Baja come after me?"

"I don't know. It's all I can think of."

"Are there some civic-minded people or organizations that would stand up with me, speak against human trafficking in Baha?"

Garcia grew silent, considering.

"There might be a couple, foolish enough or hotheaded enough to stand up with you at that podium. Let me think about it. I'll develop a tentative list. I'm afraid it will be a very short list. And for God sakes don't mention my name."

CHAPTER 40

The Judge moved through the Finisterra lobby at a quick walk, swerving around clusters of Americans in loud shirts and shifts, like a full-back for the Miami Dolphins. He was desperate to reach his air-conditioned room and cool down.

He didn't notice the shape that lifted itself from the bowels of an overstuffed lobby chair and flitted after him, through the lobby, up the stairs and down the corridor to where he fumbled with the door key. As he opened the door, he felt a small tug at the tail of his shirt, which had been hanging out apparently some while. He whirled, ready to defend himself, scanning the hallway from his height and almost mowing down the small creature behind him.

He took a closer look. It was Cristina Reyes, the stowaway from the plant. She was dressed in a flimsy white sack dress that had seen better days, threadbare in spots, faint stains in others. Her hair was pulled back in a tight bun, severe on the sides, but she wore scarlet lipstick and full eye makeup, making her look older, and sadly wiser then her fourteen years.

"Remember me, señor?"

"I do. Cristina, from Téguz, right?"

"Yes. You remember. Is your wife here? She said she'd try to get me home. I've run away again. I've no other place to turn."

The Judge looked suspiciously up and down the corridor, finding himself staring into another pair of dark eyes leveled at him from twenty feet further along.

Shit, it was Officer Gonzales, assigned by Garcia to watch him, sitting in a chair tipped against the wall, a newspaper sliding off his lap as he assessed the situation. Officer Gonzales's face broke into a broad smile as he drew all the wrong conclusions, then he put his finger to his lips, signaling the Judge's secret was safe with him. Son of a bitch!

The Judge opened his door wider and invited the girl in. There seemed to be no other option. Cristina marched into the room, turned to look at the Judge with a faint smile, and launched herself backward on to the bed, landing on her back, spreading her arms and legs like a snow angel, her sack dress all askew, displaying scrawny legs with bruised knees, and a swath of once white underwear, now grey with age. She lay there for a moment and then bounced herself up and down on his mattress, testing the springs. Having fun.

This was all wrong and the Judge knew it. A stirring at the drapes and a blitz of light was the final straw. He made a mad-bull charge for the drapes and the balcony behind, almost catching the spry young man with the cell phone taking pictures, coming up short by only inches as the kid leaped over to the adjacent balcony and then disappeared through the adjacent empty room.

Where the hell was Gonzalez when you needed him?

Cristina's eyes had gotten big and round. She was in shock. The Judge could see she'd not been a party to the photographer. She leaped off the bed and began to sob, making a blind run for the bathroom, slamming the door behind her, scared she'd blown her only chance to go home.

The Judge left her alone for a while, calling the desk downstairs and inquiring about the unit next door, which indeed was vacant. He booked the second room, and five minutes later the bellhop was up to unlock the interconnecting doors between the two rooms.

As the bellhop left, Cristina finally poked her nose out the bathroom door, having heard voices.

"You're not going to call the police, señor?" It was a pleading question.

"Did you know about the photographer?"

"Oh no, señor."

"How'd you know I was here?"

"One of the technicians at the plant told me he'd seen your wife in town. He heard your wife get a cab and ask to be taken to the Finisterra. I came and waited in the lobby. When I saw you, I followed."

"I think we've both been played, Cristina."

"I'm so sorry."

"Nothing to be done about it now. My wife Katy isn't here, but perhaps I can help. I've booked the room next door, there, through those adjoining doors, for you."

"Oh, oh."

"You will sleep in your room, I will sleep in mine, and we'll close the adjoining doors."

"Si, señor"

"Now let's first have you go into your room and take a long hot shower, scrub all the dirt and grime off, and all the makeup. Let's see what you look like under that war paint."

A half hour later Cristina was standing before him again in her smock, now with a scrubbed face and no makeup, her shiny black hair freshly combed and spun in two braids, framing her small face.

"Much better, Cristina. Now come with me. We're going to the gift shop downstairs."

Gonzales looked startled when the Judge stepped out of his room with what was now clearly a very young girl, but put on a pantomime of acting discreet. His acting wasn't any better than his police work.

The gift shop was loaded with vacation gear American tourists found attractive. Together Cristina and the Judge picked out white shorts and aqua t-shirt with glitter and a palm tree, and a matching aqua baseball cap with 'Cabo' smeared across its brim. There was discussion about the shorts, the Judge insisting they had to be larger and looser then Cristina preferred. The Judge picked out Ray-Ban style sunglasses and deposited them over her nose, and Cristina picked out local sandals to replace her scruffy heels, lowering herself two inches in the process. The Judge left her to sort through underwear options and went to the front desk, hoping for some message from Garcia. But there was none. He recalled a Tijuana non-profit that had been involved in a case when he'd been on the bench. It had helped young girls from the Mexican streets. He went to the business center and online to find it: Casa del Jardín. It seemed to fit the purpose he had in mind. He emailed its Director, a Señora Vargas, and took down her direct telephone number.

Returning to the shop, the Judge paid the bill and sent Cristina back to her room to change while he sought a cold margarita at the lobby bar and assistance in dialing the Mexican number for Señora Vargas. It was very late, but he figured he could leave a message. Surprisingly, she picked up on the second ring. He had a twenty-minute conversation with her.

The Judge returned to his room to find Cristina on his side of the connected rooms, posing in one mirror, admiring her backside in her trim white shorts and aqua top. There was so much of her that was still a child, despite what she'd been through. They ordered room service, Cristina eating like there was no tomorrow. The Judge had ordered three desserts; all three were quickly consumed by his new friend.

"Cristina, do you want to go back to Guatemala, to Téguz, and your family?"

"Si, Judge. But of course."

"I can put you on a plane in the morning, and let them sort out your missing papers at their end. But there is an alternative."

"An alternative?"

"Yes, another option."

"I don't understand."

"There's an organization in Tijuana called the International Network of Hearts. They run a facility called Casa del Jardín. They help girls get back on their feet after they've had experiences and trauma like yours."

"You mean abused by men. Beaten, raped, savaged." Bitterness crept into Cristina voice, hardening it.

"Yes. You might be able to go there. Spend a few months there and perhaps recover from your experiences, put the past in perspective. Are you addicted to drugs? Or to alcohol?"

"I'm no addict."

"They'd give you a complete medical checkup. Treat any sexual diseases. Help you through withdrawal if there's any drug or alcohol dependency. They'd have counselors, experts, who could help you deal with the trauma and isolation you've suffered, perhaps help you put it behind you so it doesn't derail your future.

They would assess where you are in your education, what things you have a natural aptitude for, and help you chart a plan for on-going education which would give you skills to get a job in your country. There would be exercise, good nutrition, study classes, and counseling. You'd meet other girls who've had similar mistreatment, ahead of you in the healing process. You'd be assigned a job there, be expected to work, and to help with later arrivals, girls like you who start the program after you and could benefit from your attention."

"It sounds scary. I don't want to go back to a jail."

"It's not a jail. You could leave and return to Guatemala whenever you wished. You wouldn't be a prisoner. I'm concerned for what happens if you just return tomorrow to your home. Does your family have money to provide for medical treatment? For counseling? For education?"

Cristina shook her head. Tears forming around her eyes.

"Look Cristina, I'll do whatever you want. Don't make any decision now. I'm not even sure there's a spot there for you yet. But think about it. Sleep on it. If I can have the lady that runs Casa del Jardín come down here tomorrow, will you meet with her for a few minutes? Hear about what this opportunity might provide? No one is going to snatch you away again. What is going to happen is only what you decide you want to happen. But I need you to be very grown up now and think seriously about your options. The decision you make here will have a lasting impact on your life."

Cristina nodded dumbly, her face frozen with fear.

"Okay. Now I think we both need some rest. Let's walk you into your new digs for the night, and I'm going to lock the door between our rooms, but if you need me, just knock on the door, or call me through it. I'll hear you."

The Judge escorted her into her room, turned up the air-conditioning, made sure the door and balcony sliders were locked, then retired to his room, collapsing on his bed like a suddenly deflated sail.

CHAPTER 41

The Judge awoke the next morning to find his limbs stiff from his exertions from the night before. His wrists were sore from unsnapping the electrical ties, his feet bruised from the climb over the cliffs, and his head hurt from the strong vodka tonics at the airport. On top of it all his sleep had been fitful, filled with dreams of Alan Clark reaching up a seaweed-clad hand to grab at his face, all the while pleading to be saved.

The Judge shuddered.

An envelope had been slipped under his door sometime earlier in the morning, his name printed on the outside, no return address. He tore it open to find a small piece of paper with the names of three organizations, and contact information for each, neatly typed. No signature. There was also a date entered and circled at the bottom, under the words, 'press conference'. Today, this afternoon, three-thirty, in the hotel lobby.

It was already ten a.m. He'd have to get moving. He brewed stiff coffee, the kind that could hold a spoon upright, and slurped it too hot into his mouth, muttering under his breath and scalding his tongue. Damn he missed Katy. She usually made the coffee.

Then he reached for the hotel phone and dialed. What did they call it in politics, 'dialing for dollars'? This was far more desperate. He was dialing for support.

At three-fifteen p.m. the lobby had a small gaggle of representatives from various news outlets, assembling camera stands, producing flip-top notebooks, chatting like ducks among themselves, and busy with the mundane things to be done before a live news conference. It was a festive and colorful clutch, hot to hear what the controversial Yankee judge would say.

A small knot of people detached themselves from the back of the crowd, walking around to introduce themselves to the Judge. He was easy to spot he supposed, bigger and taller than anyone else (or was it just over-fed?), and obviously American. They were the people he'd spoken to on the phone. People who'd bravely agreed to join him in this press opportunity.

There was no one there to serve as chairman of the press conference. No Chief Inspector Garcia, no Chief of Police, no Mayor, no Governor or Lieutenant Governor. The gutless wonders were all hiding under rocks somewhere far from ground zero in front of the press. The Judge would have to run the meeting himself.

The Judge stepped to a small podium near the wall, centered in the half circle of press and lookee-loos, two and sometimes three people deep, and adjusted the mic, rattling static around the lobby and bringing the assemblage to attention.

"Thank you for coming this afternoon. As you know, they call me the Judge. I'm an American, a tourist to your festive city, and unfortunately the victim of an assassination effort yesterday that resulted in the sinking of your Lieutenant Governor's yacht just outside the harbor. Two of my close friends died in that sinking, as did two of the three thugs who stole the boat and tried to assassinate my wife and me. It was a cowardly plot perpetrated by an unknown person in your community; a person who supervises the trafficking of human beings for profit throughout Baja California for the Mexican cartels."

It had gotten so silent the Judge could hear his own breathing. At least he had their attention.

"The reason we were targeted was my wife's and my unflinching condemnation of the illegal network here in Baja California which conducts a criminal enterprise in human trafficking and misery. We saw the results of this enterprise first hand, meeting a fourteen-year-old girl, Cristina Reyes, from Guatemala, a victim of forced labor and forced prostitution, held at a high-tech manufacturing plant near Todos Sandos, a plant owned by ASAM.

We tried to help her escape, only to be stopped by your own Mexican military, who took her away from us and returned her to her enslaved condition. I also met a man from Guatemala, lured from his home and family to this same Todos Sandos plant on false promises of a better job and better pay, only to find himself trapped in a forced labor camp. These are just two examples, but there are many, many more. Your country is categorized a 'Tier 2' country by the U.S. State Department because it does such a poor job of protecting the human rights of its indigenous peoples and those who flee from the south into your country seeking a better life.

I call the attempt yesterday on our lives cowardly, because the effort to kill us was carried out by three hired thugs, while the person who hired the thugs hides in the shadows and runs the lucrative trafficking network in Baja California, never exposing his identity. Yet I believe him to be a socially prominent person located right here in Cabo. Someone you all know and respect."

Heads ratcheted up around the half circle, pens scribbling furiously now.

"I call upon this manager of the cartel's trafficking network in Cabo to step into the light, identify himself, and pledge to cease this godless trafficking in human misery that is a blight upon us all.

With that, let me turn the podium over to some additional guests I've asked to speak today."

The Judge vacated the podium, motioning the first of his guests to take his place.

Señora Vargas was a large woman, perhaps five feet eight, big boned and big bulked, black shiny hair pulled back in a bun, outfitted in a loose sack dress sporting a pattern of fuchsia flowers, all purple, magenta, and lavender. The Judge flashed on the falling María, fuchsias, purples and pinks of fabric twisting in the wind, the start of this nightmare in which he now found himself.

"Hello all. My name is Leticia Vargas. I'm happy to be here this afternoon on behalf of International Network of Hearts and the Casa del Jardín, to raise public awareness of the ugliness going on around us here in Cabo, and elsewhere in Baja and the rest of Mexico.

Human trafficking is the illegal trade of human beings, essentially modern-day slavery. We most often think of prostitution, or other illicit professions, such as exotic dancing, pornography, massage parlors, webcam sites and so on. But trafficking includes people forced to work in trades and factories, forced into housekeeping and restaurant work, and to participate for the cartel as kidnappers, as lookouts, couriers, and mules. These are all circumstances where people are forced to work under less than free conditions. When they are no longer useful, the victims are sometimes killed, and their organs harvested for sale on the black market.

Human trafficking is the fastest growing illegal trade in the world, second only to the illegal drug industry and tied with arms-running. It is estimated that six hundred thousand to eight hundred thousand people are trafficked world-wide annually. There are more than twenty-one million modern-day slaves in this thirty-two billion dollars a year industry. Many are children between twelve and fourteen, and even younger.

The International Network of Hearts is a bi-national U.S. Mexico organization chartered to counter the trafficking of human beings, and we're here today to support the Judge in his call for an end to this institutionalized trafficking in Baha.

The first step, as the Judge says, is to shine a bright light on those at the top who manage the trafficking network in Cabo and throughout Baja.

Thank you."

A small bird-like man stepped up next, identifying himself as Alejandro Torres. Perhaps 60, he wore a dark green polyester suit despite the heat, and a narrow black tie that was fashionable 30 years ago, perspiration showing around his short grey mustache and on his forehead under the rim of this thinning hair.

"I'm the Vice Chair for the Coalition against Trafficking in Latin American and Caribbean Women, based in Mexico City. We've been rescuing Venezuelans, Colombians, Argentines and Mexicans for many years.

Some history is relevant here. When the Mexican government increased its battle against drug trafficking, the cartels responded by diversifying their illicit activities, into extortion, kidnapping, arms trafficking, trafficking of migrants for forced labor, and sex trafficking.

They quickly realized that human trafficking was a lucrative business, providing them huge returns for little investment. If I took a dose of cocaine into the United States, I could sell it for between forty and sixty dollars. But that's it. The transaction is done; the income is over. A teenager or woman can be sold ten, twenty, thirty times a day, making thousands of dollars a day for the cartel.

This year has been especially difficult for our organization because we've had threats from politicians in the ruling party. They've come to the office to threaten us, left messages on staff cell phones with rape threats, and have been chopping away at our funding, no doubt to silence us.

Señora Vargas has outlined the breadth of this problem. We've seen the most cases in the age range of twelve to eighteen years old. Victims are recruited by force, by deceit and by seduction. Victims are also enticed to fall in love over social networks. They may never meet their intended love, finding themselves caught instead in a net from which they cannot escape.

The God-fearing citizens of Cabo San Lucas must band together and declare, 'Not here, not in our community.' Send a clear message to those who would perpetuate this travesty on humanity in Baja, in Cabo.

Thank you."

A slender young Mexican lady stepped to the podium next, well proportioned, dressed in fitted grey skirt and ivory blouse, long black hair flowing like a vine down both sides of her head and across her shoulders. She was beautiful.

"I'm Josefina Ruiz, one of the authors of Migrantes en Movimiento en México, better known as the Víctimas Invisibles. We have documented the violence used by the cartels to populate their human trafficking networks. They use kidnapping. When a victim's family cannot pay the ransom, he or she can be trafficked, used as forced labor, raped, or even forced to participate in kidnappings and the network's other activities.

Other methods of violence include use of confinement, extortion, blackmail, assault, robbery, physical and sexual violence, torture, amputation, and even individual and collective executions calculated to intimidate others.

Our only way to stop this plague is to band together in our local communities, such as Cabo, and say, 'No'."

Finally, a frail older woman tottered up to the podium, her iron-grey hair swept back and pinned, her face lined with age, heavy toil, and sadness. She wore the simple clothes of a peasant, a traditional cotton spun blouse with faint embroidery, and a black skirt.

"I am Juana Pena. I represent the Caravans of Mothers. We travel all over Mexico looking for clues to finding our lost loved ones. Ours is a heroic, tireless and sad struggle, journeying thousands of miles from Mexico's southern border along the migration routes looking for the lost, or their remains. We are supported in each place by local organizations, church personnel, and their migrant houses. We look for evidence of our missing children through interviews with local inhabitants, and search along train lines and caravan routes. We try to expose the violence that befalls the poor migrants who enter your country.

Tens of thousands of migrants have disappeared across Mexico, some buried in the mass graves we've discovered. Many migrants have simply fallen off the overcrowded train heading north, known as La Bestia, The Beast, and have their body parts strewn over the desert. Others are buried as unknown indigents in potter's field graves throughout Mexico."

Stepping to the podium again, the Judge opened the meeting to questions. Surprisingly, no one seemed interested in the sinking of the sloop; all the questions were directed to his compadres who had spoken. He wondered if he'd just stepped from the pan into the fire. Time would tell.

After the press conference was concluded, the Judge walked Christina across the lobby from her perch in a chair on its far side, and introduced her to Leticia Vargas. The two settled into a quiet corner of the lobby to talk. Cristina was defensive and nervous, but watching them from across the lobby, the Judge could see her begin to relax, gradually easing back in her leather seat as they chatted. Leticia did more listening than talking, building trust by listening to Christina's story, rather than trying to fill up with the importance of Casa del Jardín. He left them like that, satisfied he'd done the best he could for Cristina.

He was in his room again, settling atop his maid-made bed, air-conditioning going full tilt, hoping for a short nap, when the phone rang.

"Hi, Judge. This is Luis Cervantes. Nice press conference. The directors all watched it. ASAM is going to do its part. We'll get to the bottom of the forced labor issues you discovered at our Todos Sandos plant. We'll stomp it out. The individuals involved will be fired and prosecuted. Any forced labor workers will be fairly compensated for their past work, and given options to return to their home or continue under new, freely negotiated employment terms which will be fully honored. And I'm personally donating money to each of the organizations that presented at your news conference. We're going to put an end to trafficking in Baja once and for all."

"I'm glad to hear that, Luis. It's the right thing to do."

"It is. But there's another matter I wanted to discuss."

"Oh?"

"Yes. We've entered into negotiations to acquire a large San Diego fruit packer and have executed a non-binding letter of intent. It will fit nicely with our agricultural businesses. But we need U.S. legal help to assist us in negotiating the definitive terms for purchase. Would you be available to represent us in this matter? Come aboard as our U.S. lawyer?"

The Judge perked up. Clients were always hard to find. ASAM was a big company with solid cash flow. They could afford his rates and could pay. If they were expanding into U.S. operations, they could be a great client. Plus, representation might lead to other Mexican businesses needing similar U.S. work.

"I'd be most interested to discuss the possibility," said the Judge.

"Great. I've called a special dinner meeting of the board of directors for this evening, at eight p.m.

Might you be available to join us and discuss such a representation further?"

The Judge was staring at the likelihood of eating alone, which he detested. It was an easy decision.

"Sure, Luis. Tell me where."

"We're meeting at my favorite Chinese restaurant. I'm thinking rice and beans may be wearing a little thin with you in any event. Here, let me give you the address."

The Judge scribbled down the address of Mr. Wu's Golden Dragon Cuisine.

"I'll see you at eight, Luis, and thanks for thinking of me." Perhaps this vacation wouldn't be a total loss after all.

CHAPTER 42

Luis met the Judge at the door of the restaurant, ushering him, the little bell tinkling away at the top of the door as it closed. The place was empty, but still smelled of cooking oil, fish, and garlic, reminiscent of Chinese restaurants over the world. Luis led the Judge to a smaller dining area at the back of the restaurant, partially cordoned off at its entrance by thick curtains swagged to either side, and to a small table where they settled, facing each other across an opened wine bottle.

"Where's everyone else, Luis. I thought this was a board meeting?"

Luis spread his hand depreciatingly, smiling, relaxed. "María and Ana are dead, as is poor Alan Clark. Miguel is in custody for the murders of María and Ana. Old Pablo isn't feeling well. And Rosa couldn't be bothered. She had a date. So, I guess you just get me, Judge. Would you like some wine? It's Mexican, but quite good."

The Judge nodded. "Great. Tell me about your planned expansion into U.S. operations. It sounds exciting. Is there an urgent issue in the negotiations which needs to be addressed?"

"Yes."

"What's the issue about, Luis?"

"It's about you, Judge."

"Me?" The Judge looked up at Luis, then focused on Luis's left hand, which had been settled in his lap, but was now up and out, pointing a Beretta 360 semi-automatic at the Judge's chest.

"I don't understand."

"Sure, you do, Judge. Once you start thinking about it, isn't it obvious? My partners in my enterprise were very specific. Your head or mine."

"The cartel!"

"Yes. See, I knew you'd get it. I'm the one who instituted the 'forced' labor in our plants. Set things up so we could lower our cost per hour. When you don't pay half your work force, except for a little rice and beans daily, you'd be surprised how easy it is to compete with China and Southeast Asia. Miguel couldn't understand how my costs could be so low. He has no imagination. Once a bean counter, always a bean counter."

"It was your people on the boat, trying to throw us overboard."

"Yes. You're a quick study once someone takes you by the nose and turns you in the right direction."

"But why now, Luis? I'm about to leave Mexico. Katy is long gone, back in the States. We can't do you any harm now."

"You've stirred up a hornet's nest, Judge. Mexico prosecutors flying in. The U.S. State Department all over my partners' collective ass. Outcry from the press, and the United Nations. And now the unions are out in force, proclaiming illegal workplace pay and unfair work rules. You've created a regular shit-storm here."

"The damage is done, Luis. Disposing of me won't change any of that. You just dig your hole deeper."

"That's a rational argument, Judge. I respect it. And I might even buy into it, as I pride myself on not holding a grudge. But my partners….” Luis shook his head. “My partners are more primitive. Everything is emotional for them. Your actions are seen as an assault on their pride. They say there must be consequences for you. It's necessary to keep everyone in line.

So you see, Judge, there's no free pass. You must disappear in a semi-public sort of way. So everyone kind of knows what happened. Hears about it; knows how dangerous it is to disrespect our organization. I'm sure you understand. We must keep up the appearance of consequences, and invincibility. Regrettably, I've now been personally tasked with this unpleasant duty, because I allowed Alan Clark and inadvertently you into one of our plants. They hold me accountable for starting the whole chain of unfortunate events.”

The Judge had allowed his hands to settle in his lap as Luis talked. He turned them palms up under the table. It was the only thing he could think of.

“This is a public place. You can't just shoot someone here.”

“Foremost, this is Mexico, Judge. And I can. In fact, a cartel owns this joint. And the staff was quite happy to go home early. Closed for a private meeting. I must admit, I'm enjoying watching you squirm more than I thought I would. You've been such a pain in my ass since you arrived.”

The Judge moved then, shoving his hands up against the underside of the table on his side with all his might., tilting the table up and over, slamming it down on top of Luis. The gun went off, and a slug buried itself in the ceiling above the Judge's head. The table crashed over on Luis, sending him backward in his chair and over onto his back, the table crashing down on top of him, propelled with all the Judge's bulk crashing down on top of the table's now exposed underside. The chair splintered into kindling, flattening Luis under the table as the gun went flying from his grasp.

The Judge grabbed the wine bottle where it had fallen to the side on the floor, and, throwing himself further out on top of the upended table, pinning Luis underneath as he struggled to free himself, swung the bottle with all his might in a roundhouse blow, smacking the side of Luis's head. The bottle broke with a satisfying crunch, showering shards of glass everywhere. Luis's eyes went blank.

The Judge picked himself up from the table, snatched up the gun from where it had fallen, and dragged Luis out from under the wreckage of the table and chair.

The Judge turned to the curtains separating their smaller dining area from the rest of the restaurant, and grabbing the cord swagging one curtain to the side wall, twisted it away. He rolled Luis onto his stomach and used the cord to tie Luis's hands behind him, and then his feet, hogtie style. He felt for a pulse. It was there, but Luis was still out, dazed, quiet.

The Judge moved to the front door of the restaurant, peeking out its front window. There was a car across the street, two men in it, just sitting, waiting. They didn't feel right. Luis's help no doubt. The Judge locked the front door, then found his way to the back, through the kitchen, and checked a rear door. It was already locked.

CHAPTER 43

The Judge fished out his cell phone and called Chief Inspector Garcia, hoping Garcia was the right person to call. It was hard to know in this crazy town.

Garcia's gruff voice answered on the first ring. The Judge explained his situation.

"Where's Gonzales?" asked Garcia.

"I wish I knew. You said he'd have my back, but I've seen no sign of him."

"Shit. Lazy bastard."

"And there's a car parked across the street with two unsavory looking guys in it."

"Okay, I'm coming over. Just sit tight until I get there."

"What if these guys across the street come charging in before you get here?"

"Then... how do your American comrades say? You're toast! I'm leaving now."

Garcia hung up before the Judge could respond.

The Judge turned, hearing commotion behind him. It turned out to be Luis, conscious now, struggling to slip from his bindings. But the Judge was a sailor, or had been. He'd tied the knots in seaman fashion. Luis had a small abrasion on his forehead where the table had hit him. And a bruise on the side of his head, wine bottle size. A little blood was trickling down the side of his face, but he looked like he'd live.

The Judge pulled up a chair next to Luis's prone body and sat down. Luis glared hatred at the Judge from the floor. They sat like that for about twenty minutes, the Judge tired, looking at Luis. Luis mad and damaged, glaring at the Judge. Finally, there was a knock at the front door of the restaurant. The Judge peeked around through the blinds and saw Garcia standing outside, looking impatient, Gonzales in tow behind. The car with the thugs across the street was gone.

The Judge opened the front door and the two policemen stepped in.

"Where is he?" asked Garcia.

"In the back, on the floor. Tied up."

"Let me have a peek."

"Sure. He's all yours."

Garcia stepped around the corner, bent down, and spoke in Spanish to Luis on the floor. Luis responded in kind, a flood of vindictive-sounding Spanish spilling out. Garcia shook his head, and waved a pointed finger under Luis's nose. Then he hauled Luis to his feet, undid the knots with some difficulty, took him by the arm so he couldn't run, and walked him over to Gonzales.

"Take him out and lock him in the back seat, Gonzales. Give me a few minutes here, then we'll take him to a hospital for a checkup."

The Judge handed Luis's pistol over to Garcia, as though washing his hands of the whole mess.

"Sit down, Judge. Let's talk this over a bit."

"Sure."

"I'll take Luis to the hospital, and then back to the station. But the Chief will release him."

"What? He tried to kill me. He admitted he's the head of human trafficking in Baja California for the cartels. He's the one who gave the order to kidnap Katy. He's the one that arranged for Katy and me to drown on the sunset cruise. He needs to be charged, convicted, and put away for a long time."

"Yes, I know, Judge, but this is Mexico."

"So?"

"So, Luis' mother is married to my Chief's uncle. The Chief will let him go."

"But… but… but there must be something that can be done."

"Let me whisper a suggestion in your ear, Judge, but again you didn't get this from me."

"Alright."

"As soon as I pull out of here, call these numbers." Garcia scribbled three phone numbers on a scrap of paper, and handed it to the Judge. "The Cabo San Lucas Daily News, the Los Cabos News, and the Gringo Gazette, our primary papers here. Tell each them of this arrest and how Luis is the kingpin for the cartel-led human trafficking in Baja California. And this is very important. Have them send their photographers to the police station to take pictures of Luis as we arrive, bringing him in. We'll time it to get out of the car in front of the station in an hour from now."

"I can do all that. But how does it help?"

"Luis is a high-profile person in Cabo. Well known, if a bit flashy, throws money around, contributes to charities and schools. He runs with community leaders and high society."

"So?"

"The paper will print your complete story, your charges against Luis, your suspicions. There will be unflattering pictures of Luis hauled up the steps into the police station in cuffs, with his bandaged head. Gossip will spread like wildfire. Luis will be dropped from all the parties and social goings on in Cabo as an unwelcome guest."

"And that helps us?"

"It may well serve justice, Judge. Without his social credentials, isolated from the cartels, the myth of cartel protection vanished, Luis will be vulnerable. Then his enemies, and he likely has many, may come to call without fear of reprisal."

"That's all? That's all you can suggest? No trial? No due process? No marshalling and presenting of evidence, no clear conviction of guilt, no prison sentence, no nothing?"

"It's the best we can do under the circumstances, Judge. Hardly anyone gets prosecuted under our human trafficking laws right now. Particularly if they have influence. Besides, we have no proof he was behind your ill-fated sailing cruise, or responsible for your wife's kidnapping. Look at his condition when I walked in here. Your discussion with him and any admissions he made tonight would be considered admissions made under duress. They'd be thrown out by a Mexican court as not presentable evidence. I believe it's the same in your country... no?"

The Judge nodded, shaking his head in frustration as he spread his hands to protest. "But in an investigation, a thorough investigation, it'd all come out. Unexplained cash, bank records, offshore funds, questioning and flipping of subordinates, rolling up the whole network, you could put the entire cartel out of business."

Garcia gave a sad smile.

"If Luis were a nobody, Judge, he might well be prosecuted. But he's not. As I've said, my best guess is it will not happen. As to the cartel he works with, if the Mexican cartels were actually within our reach, what do you think would happen? They'd no longer exist, right? But unfortunately, they're not.

They exist because there is so much money in what they do, money provided by you Americans consuming their products, and because they liberally grease the wheels of justice in this country to look the other way, and because they operate ruthlessly to stamp out all perceived threats, and because everyone is afraid."

"But isn't the war on the cartels by the army slowly driving them underground?"

"No, señor. I only wish it was so simple. The cartels are organized like a well-established business. It is not just a bunch of crazy men with guns who sell drugs and kill their competitors. It is more a para-military organization with similarities to a multinational company. There is a well-defined structure, rules and policies, a finance department, an HR department, a supplies department, operations, legal, security, and executive officers.

The cartel hires young men to sell drugs, and to clean up after violence. These people are the lowest rank in their organizations. Or they may use trafficked slaves caught up in their network and forced to work for the cartel. They also hire violent gangs to enforce their will within their territory.

In a middle level, they have people who distribute or sell in bigger quantities, and the hit-men, available to kill someone when needed, or to kidnap a politician or important figure, or a member of his family. These middle level people supervise the drug labs and the violent gangs.

At the top, there will be a family or group that runs the cartel. They negotiate the prices and the territories with other cartels. If they do not produce the drug directly, they negotiate the wholesale purchase of the drugs for distribution within the markets they control. They are also responsible for opening new 'legal' businesses for money laundering, and new illegal enterprises which have potential.

And the drug cartels have already diversified into other illegal activities: kidnapping, extortion, illegal mining, petroleum theft, and, as you have seen, human trafficking. There are reports some cartels have moved into human organ trafficking.

The cartel must comply with local government rules, pay their taxes and follow all the local regulations. Of course, 'being compliant' isn't about filing tax returns and paying licenses fees and payroll taxes like a legal company. Being compliant is about the fees and bribes you must pay to government officials, politicians, attorneys, police officers, medics, entrepreneurs, and military officers, among others. Each cartel has a similar cadre of these people on their payroll. It is an expense of doing business."

"So, the entire society is compromised."

"Yes, I'm afraid so. Drug cartels have infiltrated the Mexican government at all levels. Acting politically against them is like trying to bring the entire government

Cabo

down. Our government will praise the courage and intentions of an anti-cartel politician. But off the record they will find any dirt in his past and use it to blackmail him to stop. If they can't find blemish in his past, undercover federal agents will 'discover' contraband or incriminating evidence planted in his car or his home. If all else fails, he'll be assassinated."

"So, it's pointless then. I leave. They follow me back up to California and try to extract their revenge there. I'm a target still. We've accomplished nothing here."

"I don't believe that's the way it will play out, Judge. Not if you take my advice.

Anyway, your thug friends across the street in their car have gone. I've got to take Luis to the hospital and then to the police station, and report to the Chief. I'll order you a cab now and we'll send you back to the hotel to pack. I'll pick you up at nine a.m. tomorrow morning and give you a ride to the airport. I think it's time you rejoined your wife in Los Angeles."

Garcia gave the Judge another soft smile.

"Besides, I think you've done enough damage in my town for one vacation."

CHAPTER 44

At noon the next day the Judge trudged through the customs hall at LAX and up the long curving ramp into the cavernous reception hall of the Bradley International Terminal, past the countless heads leaning over ramparts to peer down at him, waiting for loved ones and friends to arrive from somewhere else. He was tired and he was despondent.

He'd accomplished some few things, he supposed. Miguel was under arrest for the murder of María and Ana. Cristina was ensconced in Casa del Jardín, would begin the process of healing, and would pick up new skills. He'd never been able to locate Felipe Martínez, the enslaved workman at the ASAM plant, but he'd dutifully sent the man's requested message back to the small village in Guatemala, letting his family know he was alive.

But he'd mostly failed in Cabo. Failed to bring Luis Cervantes to justice. Failed to find the subordinates who'd kidnapped Katy. Failed to find Carla, the third crew member who'd participated in the brutal drowning of Alan Clark and Mary Whittaker. Failed to make any dent in the human trafficking misery inflicted by the Mexican cartels on their own people and the migrants from the south. Failed, failed, failed.

He glanced up again at the eyes peering down at him from the top rail of the ramp.

Cabo

But then there she was. Katy. All excited. Jumping up and down like the young girl she was, waving one hand in the air and yelling, the other clutching a small bundle bewildered by all the people, lights, noise and hubbub of the entry hall... Ralphie!

Her wide smile, showing perfect teeth, reached up into her aqua eyes. Her pale skin in a soft white cotton dress, her blonde hair trailing out from beneath a large-brimmed white hat. He loved her fancy hats. God, he loved them so.

And then they were together, clinched into a three-way hug, Ralphie recognizing his dad immediately, offering to share a half-soggy cookie clutched with a death grip in his tiny hand, pressing it to the Judge's lips.

It was so good to be home.

EPILOG

Two weeks later, as the Judge sat at his breakfast table in Palos Verdes, enjoying the view and his morning coffee, Katy came into the breakfast nook, handing the Judge a small envelope with a foreign stamp, Mexican, addressed to the Judge. Curious, she lingered as the Judge used his fingers to tear open the letter.

The Judge pulled out the enclosed card, an old fashioned personal card with initials at the top, the message written in Indian ink in a long flowing hand. A newspaper clipping fell out beneath the card along with two photos. The Judge looked at the photos.

The first was of a small freezer, its door open to display its contents, the backs of two severed and very frosty looking human heads jammed into it for preservation.

In the second photo, the heads had been turned around and then placed back into the freezer. The Judge stared at the frozen face, open eyes and frosty-white eyebrows of Luis Cervantes, his mouth locked in an awful grimace. The other head belonged to Castillo, the ASAM Plant Manager, bearing an equally unhappy expression.

The Judge picked up the card, read it, then looked up grimly at Katy, handing her the card. It read:

Hope all is well with you, Judge.

Our justice in Mexico is not like California. Often very slow, but sometimes moving with lightning speed.

I wasn't sure you'd heard about this, so I've sent the clipping along and two pictures. We found the two severed heads in a freezer last week, just two blocks from the Tourist Zone in Cabo San Lucas.

I hope the unfortunate events of your vacation here won't deter you from coming back to enjoy the sights, the sounds, and the gaiety that is Cabo. I guarantee you a better time on your return.

Your compadre,

Chief Inspector Garcia.

Davis MacDonald

A Note from the Author

If you'd like to know more about the topics raised in this book, here are some sources:

US Department of State, Trafficking in Persons Report 2017:
https://www.state.gov/j/tip/rls/tiprpt/2017/.

Human Trafficking Survivor:
http://www.cnn.com/2015/11/10/americas/freedom-project-mexico-trafficking-survivor/index.html.

The Pentagon's new drone swarm heralds a future of autonomous war machines, by Kelsey D. Atherton January 10, 2017:
https://www.popsci.com/pentagon-drone-swarm-autonomous-war-machines.

Police in India Will Use Drones to Spray Protesters with Pepper Spray:
https://gizmodo.com/police-in-india-will-use-weaponized-pepper-spray-drones-1696511132.

Cat Drone:
https://www.dronethusiast.com/dead-cat-drone/

How to Escape from Zip-Ties:
http://www.itstactical.com/intellicom/tradecraft/how-to-escape-from-zip-ties/.

Man Sentenced to Death for Throwing Couple of Yacht. *https://www.nbclosangeles.com/news/local/Death-Sentence-Delivered-in-Plot-to-Kll-Couple-on-Yacht.html*

In Mexico, 'It's Easy to Kill a Journalist': *https://www.nytimes.com/2017/04/29/world/americas/veracruz-mexico-reporters-killed.html?mcubz=0*

Two Severed Heads Found Near Cabo Tourist Center: http://www.foxnews.com/world/2017/06/13/2-severed-heads-found-near-tourist-zone-in-cabo-san-lucas.html.

I hope you enjoyed reading "CABO" as much as I enjoyed writing it, and perhaps here and there it made you smile a little…. Please leave a REVIEW for me on Amazon if it was a positive read.

Davis MacDonald

ACKNOWLEDGEMENTS

A grateful thanks to those good friends who helped me to write and edit CABO. Dr. Alexandra Davis, who was the first to see every word; my amazing Editor, Jason Myers, who did yeoman work on the edits and kept me on the straight and narrow; the multiple good friends that agreed to read and comment on the early draft, and Dane Low, (www.ebooklaunch.com), who helped me design the distinctive cover.

Thank You All.

Davis MacDonald

This is a Work of Fiction

CABO is a work of fiction. Names, characters, businesses organizations, clubs, places, events and incidents depicted in this book are either products of the Author's imagination or are used fictitiously. Any resemblance or similarity to actual persons, living or dead, or events, locales, business organizations, clubs, or incidents, is unintended and entirely incidental. Names have been chosen at random and are not intended to suggest any person. The facts, plot, circumstances and characters in this book were created for dramatic effect, and bear no relationship to actual businesses, organizations, communities or their denizens.

About Davis MacDonald

Davis MacDonald grew up in Southern California and writes of places about which he has intimate knowledge. Davis uses the mystery novel genre to write stories of mystery, suspense, love, and commitment, entwined with relevant social issues and moral dilemmas facing 21st Century America. A member of the National Association of Independent Writers and Editors (NATWE), his career has spanned Law Professor, Bar Association Chair, Investment Banker, and Lawyer. Many of the colorful characters in his novels are drawn in part from his personal experiences and relationships (although they are all officially fictional characters).

Davis began this series in 2013, with the publishing of THE HILL, in which he introduces his new character, the Judge. THE HILL, Book 1, is a murder mystery and a love story which also explores the sexual awakening of a young girl, how sexual manipulation can change lives forever, and the moral dilemmas love sometimes creates.

THE ISLAND, Book 2, is set in Avalon, Catalina, and continues the saga of the Judge and his love, Katy, as the Judge finds himself in another murder mystery, and forced to make key decisions about his relationship with Katy. The story explores the dysfunctional attitudes of a small town forced to drop old ways of thinking or face extinction.

SILICON BEACH, Book 3, is set in Venice, Santa Monica, Playa Vista and Marina del Rey, and opens with a sundown attack on the Judge on the Santa Monica Beach. It carries the reader through the swank and not so swank joints on the Los Angeles West Side, as the Judge tries to bring down killers before they bring him down, dealing along the way with the plight of the homeless.

THE BAY, Book 4, is set in Newport Beach, Balboa, and the Orange County Coastal communities, and finds the Judge pressed into service by the FBI to solve a murder of one of their own, as he stumbles into a terrorist plot that could devastate Orange County. The story takes a close look at Islam in its many strains as it exists in our country.

CABO, Book 5, is set in Mexico, and finds the Judge and Katy on holiday in Cabo San Lucas; a holiday which turns deadly as they unravel a stealthy double murder, and go head to head with human traffickers in Baha California.

THE STRAND, Book 6, is set in Manhattan Beach, Hermosa Beach, and Redondo Beach, and tells the tale of a pre-School seeming perfect for the Judge's young son, until a body is discovered in the locked maintenance room, followed by allegations of 'sexual child-abuse' at the school which causes a frenzy in the newspapers and local community. When the DA decides to grandstand on child abuse allegations with press conferences to buttress his re-election campaign the Judge finds himself pressed into service to help defend an old friend, rallying against a corrupt American justice system on a rush to judgment which emphasizes livid press vignettes of false news over accuracy, permits political self-promotion to trample the rights of the accused, and encourages prosecutor misconduct in the name of winning at all cost

The first Chapter of THE STRAND is included at the end of this book. THE STRAND will be published in the Fall of 2018.

All books are available on Amazon on Kindle, in paperback, on Audio-book, and available in other fine bookstores and outlets.

HOW TO CONNECT WITH
Davis MacDonald

Email: Don@securities-attys.com

Website: http://davismacdonald-author.com/

Twitter: https://twitter.com/Davis_MacDonald

Facebook: Davis MacDonald, Author

Blog: http://davis-macdonald.tumblr.com/

LinkedIn: Davis MacDonald

Amazon Author's Page: Davis Macdonald-Author

THE STRAND

Look for THE STRAND from Davis MacDonald, book six in the Judge series, to be published in the Fall of 2018.

What follows is the first chapter of THE STRAND

THE STRAND

A MYSTERY NOVEL SET IN MANHATTAN BEACH, HERMOSA BEACH & REDONDO BEACH

"'tis much more Prudence to acquit two Persons, tho' actually guilty, than to pass Sentence of Condemnation on one that is virtuous and innocent.'"
Voltaire

"Ethics is knowing the difference between what you have a right to do and what is right to do."
Justice Potter Stewart

CHAPTER 1

The Judge tried not to grind his teeth, preferring to pulverize the brake-pedal with his foot, grinding back and forth across its surface, occasionally releasing it to move forward an inch or three before pushing it hard again. The line of cars slowly crawled forward now and then, with all the speed of a geriatric snail.

Little Ralphie, snared in his raised car seat behind the Judge, pitched so he could see out the front window and both sides like some Oriental Potentate, didn't mind. He grasped a brown paper bag in one hand with a death grip, his snack bag, and was all big eyes on a tiny swiveling head, watching the people and the bright colored cars and SUVs finally reaching the head of the line and dumping their small passengers.

This was a new system. And a foul system it was. The pre-school had decided that rather than having parents walk their kids onto the premises and into their designated classrooms, it would put a stop to such aimless and generally uncontrollable swarms of adults invading their sacred grounds twice a day, once in the morning and once in the early afternoon. This new system had teachers and assorted staff meeting the little buggers at the designated car drop-off point, helping them out of their car-seats and cars, and escorting them hand in hand into the school.

The plan sounded fine in theory, but was quickly wrecked on the shoals of the reality. Most of the drop-off parents were moms and most of the pre-school staff were female. The resulting adult female interaction was a golden opportunity to use female words, chit-chatting with each other at length, leaving a line of stranded cars and females behind, waiting their turn to use their female words. It was a female thing.

The line of cars seemed hardly to move. It was the last time Katy would sucker him into drop-off duty, he swore to God.

"Daddy."

"Yes, Ralphie"

"I like Mr. Campbell."

"That's nice."

"He can fly."

"Oh. Well that's pretty cool. Have you seen him do it?"

"No. But he told us."

"I see."

"He's teaching us to play 'Naked Movie Star'."

"What?" The Judge swung his head around in his seat to look at his small son, eye to eye, suddenly focused.

"Yep. 'What you say, is what you are,… You're a naked movie star'."

Ralphie giggled. "Maybe you'll play with me."

"Yes, Ralphie. You'll have to show me how you play when I get home tonight. Your mother can play too. I'm sure she'll want to hear all about it."

Ralphie nodded in satisfaction.

The Judge shook his head. You never knew what his young four-and-a-half-year-old would come up with next. It was all very… disconcerting.

Cabo

The Campbell Preschool had been a South Bay institution for over 20 years, the oldest and most prestigious preschool school servicing Redondo Beach, Hermosa Beach and Manhattan Beach, the small cities that checkered the beach from Palos Verdes to Play Del Rey along what was called "The Strand". Many of the sons and daughters of the beach cities' elite had attended the school. Old Mary Campbell had founded the school but was recently retired. The School was now run by Mary's daughter, Laura Campbell, and Mary's son, Harvey or Harry or something…Campbell. The son did the back-office work and taught a few classes, but was rarely seen by the parents. Demand was so great it was difficult to get a child into the preschool. There was a long waiting list. It was rumored the list could be circumvented if you knew the right people.

And the Judge did. He'd known the old lady, Mary Campbell, since his youth when his mother and Mary had been close friends. He'd made a discrete call, and magically Ralphie had gotten an invitation to attend three days later, making the Judge a hero at home. That had been a month ago. And Ralphie seemed to be enjoying himself at the school.

The Judge finally pulled his car up to the assigned speed bump and unlocked the passenger doors. The right-rear door was opened by Miss Johnsen, a lady of long years and loving girth who'd never had any kids of her own, but seemed to love all kids, everywhere, all at once. With difficulty, she squeezed her bulk across the rear seat and child seat to reach the belt releases for Ralphie, and he immediately propelled himself out like some jet pilot hitting the sheets, using the old rubber man, sliding to the floor beneath her and squeezing out onto the pavement before she could regain her balance. He hopped up and down on one leg and then on the other, testing to be sure they still worked. They seemed okay.

"Hello and goodbye, Miss Johnsen." Said the Judge, beating her to the draw, precluding some lame comment about the weather, giving her his best boyish smile.

"Goodbye, Judge. Here, grab my hand, Ralphie."

It was then the front-seat passenger side door opened and a pretty redhead in a white silk blouse and pleated skirt squatted down beside the car so she could see the Judge. It was Miss Laura Campbell, the daughter and now Head Mistress, mid-thirties, recently divorced, a workaholic. She looked around carefully to make sure no one would overhear her. Then said in a tense whisper.

"Judge. I've got a big problem."

"What?"

"Someone's dead."

"What?"

"Someone's dead."

"Who?"

"Jeffery Simpson, our maintenance man."

"Where?"

"In the maintenance room. I don't know what to do. You must come."

The Judge sighed. Why was it always him?

"Okay. Let me pull over there and park. Have you called 911?"

"It's too late for that."

"Are you sure?'

Cabo

"Yes. Jeffery's very dead. I can't have my children upset by a fire engine and a rescue truck and an ambulance roaring into the school."

And the parents, thought the Judge cynically. The parents who paid the freight. The children would love to see a fire engine roll in.

"Give me a minute."

She slammed his passenger door with a vengeance, taking her anxiety out on his car, then stood back from the car-line, arms folded defensively, waiting for him to park, chewing her lower lip.

He parked and walked back to the drop off bump, past the congregating cars, to the side wall of the school where she leaned. She was shorter than he'd thought, perhaps only 5'4". He towered over her as she pushed off the wall and stood straight. The Judge was a tall man, broad shouldered and big boned with just a bit of a paunch around the middle. Big hands, big feet, big ears and a big nose set in the middle of his squared Welsh face, ruddy now with concern. With his short-cut dark hair, faded blue Polo shirt and ragtag jeans, he might have been a roustabout, or a teamster. Except for the eyes, large piercing blue eyes restlessly sweeping the people and space around him, missing nothing. Except that he thought like a judge.

He rarely used his given name anymore. When he had ascended to the bench some years back, people began calling him just "Judge". Even old friends he'd known for years affectionately adopted the nickname. Back then it had seemed to fit. And somehow it had stuck even though he was no longer a Judge. Now just another L.A. lawyer, scrambling for business in an over-crowded profession in an over-crowded city.

"Ok, Miss Campbell, let's have a look."

"It's Laura, Judge. This way."

She marched him though the line of disembarking toddlers, each with a keeper's large hand wrapped around one paw, and a snack bag or lunch box clutched in the other. They walked through the iron gate entrance and across a red-tiled inner patio into the school building, then down a long hall to the left that ended in a door. She produced a key and unlocked the door, opening it just enough for the Judge to squeeze through, which turned out to be considerably open given his paunch, then partially closed it again, allowing just enough room for her to slip her narrow frame through. She quickly closed the door again and flipped the lock to secure it.

Gauzy light peered in from a high window set in the opposite wall that didn't look like it'd been cleaned since the structure was built sometime in the late thirties. The room was musty, smelling of old floor polish, paint, turpentine and something else. The something else wasn't good.

A wooden work bench ran down the right side, anchored by a vise at the front corner, and pinned by a table saw of ancient vintage at the other. Boxes of nails, screws, electrical parts, and hand tools were scattered across its surface, along with two small cans of touch up paint and a box of rags. More tools hung on plyboard nailed on the wall above the workbench, each tool bracketed in a cutout drawing of its inner self. It looked like a man-cave, but without the refrigerator, the beer and the big-screen TV.

Four feet out from the wall on the left side of the room was a rack of metal shelving, running the length of the room, extending almost to the window wall, placed so one could walk behind it and access its contents from either side. It was laden with dusty looking cardboard boxes, perhaps old school records, boxes of old light fixtures, a box of plumbing parts, several electrical tools neatly stowed in their green plastic cases, and an assortment of other dusty looking junk.

"This way, Judge." Said Laura, standing on tip toes to reach a string to an overhead light, giving it an anxious jerk to shed neon white on the floor and walls around them.

She marched him down to the window wall and then stopped, turning her head away, pointing him around the corner of the shelving. The Judge stepped around her into the narrow space between wall and shelving rack. The light didn't penetrate much into the gloom here. But he immediately ran into someone's shoe floating three feet off the floor.

Springing back, he looked up. A pipe was anchored cross the ceiling, perhaps for water, or a sprinkler system. A large shape dangled from it,… a body! It swung partly around from his collision with the shoe, displaying dusty jeans and a kaki shirt with large pockets, the beltless pants starting to slip down over narrow hips on one side. The missing belt was wrapped around the pipe and around the body's neck. It was a man, or had been.

The man's head slumped to the left, his face fixed in the contorted agony as he'd asphyxiated. He looked to have been early thirties, lean and short, perhaps five and half feet tall, with long blond hair and a surfer's good looks. But now his face was mottled and splotched. His pants were wet with the release of fluids, and a small pool had formed on the floor under his hanging feet, scenting the air. A wooden step-stool lay turned on its side on the floor behind him.

"This is Jeffery?"

"Yes." Said Laura Campbell in a small voice, her face still turned away.

The Judge reached over and took hold of one of the Jeffery's hands. It was ice cold. Laura sounded like she was having a dry-retch behind him. He turned and moved back to her, catching her from behind as she started to fall, leaning her against the wall under the window, holding her there as she fought to recover. He took her hand after a minute and led her back past the workbench and out of the room, closing the door securely behind them, taking the key from her and locking it.

"Oh, sweet Jesus, what are we going to do?" She asked.

"We need to call 911."

"But the school, the kids?"

"I don't' suppose we can just send them home." Said the Judge.

"No. This is preschool. Working parents and all. There's likely no one at home, and no one available to pick up the kids at this hour.

"Let's put everyone in the auditorium." Said the Judge. Close the doors. Your staff can entertain them there. Let 911 and the police do their work without an audience."

"Yes. That's exactly what we should do. You're right Judge. Can you call 911 and talk to the police? I'll organize the kids and the staff into the auditorium."

"They'll want to talk to you too."

"Yes, I guess they will."

"Jeffery is your maintenance man?

"Yes. He's been here for over three years."

"How did you find him?"

"I saw him come in this morning. Then he disappeared. We've a hall light out. It needs the big ladder to replace the bulb. I couldn't find him, so I went looking. I finally tried the maintenance room. Oh God. I can't believe this is happening."

"You found him like that?"

"Yes. I touched him. He was ice cold. So I knew."

"Was the door to the room locked?"

"Yes. I unlocked it when I came in, and locked it again after... after I found him and walked out. I didn't want any of the kids to see."

"Did he seem depressed or despondent when you saw him earlier?"

"Not that I noticed."

"Okay. You go organize your staff. I'm going to call right now."

"Can you give me a five-minute head start, Judge."

"I suppose. He's not going anywhere."

The Judge wondered back to the maintenance room and entered, this time taking a very curious look at what was there. The body was as he'd seen it before. On the shelf beside the body were pruning shears. He leaned over to look without touching. There were tiny strands of twine on one blade, twine had been cut at some time. Looking closely at the floor, there was a bit of fluff of similar color. Had twine been recently cut and used here? Had Jeffery's hands been tied with twine? There was no note. No sign that said, 'This is suicide, I'm taking my own life.' Only the position of the body and the kicked over stool suggested he'd snuffed himself. Puzzling.

The Judge returned to the hall and called 911. He requested that the police be informed, and that sirens not be used when approaching the school.   Then he wondered out to the front of the school, out again to the speed   bump,   and   waited   for   people   to   arrive. Fortunately, all the kids had been dropped off and the parents had all roared away in their silly cars.   He wondered how much wasted gas got burned sitting in the damn drop off line. Next time it'd damn well be Katy's gas and Katy's time.

The fire rescue truck arrived, along with a fire engine, an ambulance, and not one but two Hermosa black and whites. And they were all blaring their sirens. Boys would be boys, mused the Judge. It was a little odd there were two police cars rather than one, but the Judge brushed the thought aside. He was required to explain the situation first to the 911 truck crew, then again to the fire engine crew, then again to the police officers, and finally to the ambulance team. They each took a trot into the school and down the hall to the maintenance room with him to have a look, taking turns like relay teams in a cross-country walk-a-thon, but in some pre-determined pecking order only they knew.

The sergeant from the second car returned, identified himself as Sergeant Oliver, and told the Judge they were sealing off the entire end of the hallway in front of the Maintenance room, and there'd be a full investigation. He brought out his flip-top notebook and took down the Judge's statement, then asked him to retrieve the Head Mistress from the auditorium so he could take down hers.

The Judge stuck his head into in to Auditorium and waved for Laura Campbell. The kids were busy on the floor of the gym, organized in four groups approximately by age and size, and were painting on cardboard boxes, or throwing blocks at each other, or playing in solitary mode with a truck or a doll, depending on their age and sex.

"Judge, can you come with me to talk to the police?"

"I've got business to take care of Miss Campbell,… Laura. I really can't stay."

"Oh please, please, Judge I'm so nervous. Just ten minutes more Judge, I beg of you. The police are so… intimidating. And after that awful letter that went out, I just need you there for support. Please."

"What letter?"

"You haven't seen the letter?"

"No."

"Well, I'm sure you will. Please Judge. Just ten minutes more."

"Okay, Laura. Let's go do this quickly and get it over with."

The sergeant listened to Laura's story with an expressionless face, taking down careful notes. Was there a hint of underlying animosity in the sergeant's attitude? The Judge couldn't be sure.

"So you just walked into the maintenance room and found the body of Mr…" The sergeant consulted his notes. "Simpson?"

"Yes."

"I understand there's another entrance to the maintenance room, through an old tunnel. Is that right?"

"Not that I know of."

"So, you came in through the door from the hall here?"

"Yes."

"Was the door locked? Did you use your key?"

"Yes"

"So, you do have a key?"

"Yes."

"So, when you stepped into the room, you couldn't see the body?"

"No."

"So, what made you go to the window in the back and peek around the shelves?"

"I don't know."

"Was it because you already knew he was hanging there?'

"No."

"Then why?"

"I don't know."

"That's not good enough."

"Officer, Miss Campbell has answered the question. You're not allowed to badger her." Said the Judge.

The sergeant glared at the Judge. "You her lawyer?"

"For the moment I guess I am."

"So, she needs a lawyer?"

"Everyone's entitled to have a lawyer if they wish, and Miss Campbell is entitled to be free from badgering by local police."

"I'd got your full name and address, Judge. I'm putting you on the list."

"What list?"

"The list our department is developing of those potentially connected to the child pornography ring operated here."

"The what?"

"You heard me. I'm done here. But our detectives will be contacting you both for an 'at the police station' interrogation of what's gone on here this morning."

The sergeant snapped his flip-book closed, spun on his heel, and stalked off to his cruiser to call the county morgue, leaving a totally baffled Judge turning to Laura Campbell for an explanation. She covered her face with her hands and softly began to cry.

Look for THE STRAND to be published in the Fall of 2018

21972606R00193

Made in the USA
San Bernardino, CA
07 January 2019